CASTLE OF HORROR
ANTHOLOGY
VOLUME 6

CASTLE BRIDGE MEDIA
DENVER, COLORADO, USA

CASTLE BRIDGE MEDIA
Denver, Colorado
Edited by P.J. Hoover
Edited by Jason Henderson, Edited & Designed by In Churl Yo
Cover Photo Eugene Partyzan/Shutterstock

© 2021 Castle Bridge Media and Individual Authors
All rights reserved.
ISBN: 978-1-7364726-8-2

Listen to the Castle of Horror Podcast
www.spreaker.com/show/castle-of-horror-podcast

Or find us online at:
www.facebook.com/castleofhorrorpodcast

TABLE OF CONTENTS

INTRODUCTION

By P.J. Hoover

I REMEMBER SO WELL WHEN Glenn Close boiled the bunny rabbit in *Fatal Attraction.* Talk about making the wrong choice when it comes to a one-night stand. One minute you're getting a little fast action on the kitchen sink. The next, your daughter's childhood pet is turned into stew (sadly with no potatoes or onions to go along with it). What was it about Glenn Close's character, a book editor named Alex, that made her absolutely flip out and seek retribution? She was spurned. She was angry. She was also a bit unhinged. Femme fatale? Oh yes. But this is just touching the surface of the territory of the femme fatale.

In the sad fate of household pets at the hands of femme fatales, *Single White Female* must be mentioned. If you think having a one-night stand with the wrong person is a big mistake, try living with one. This movie is about the ultimate wrong choice in roommates. It's unforgettable murder-by-stiletto when Jennifer Jason Leigh tries to keep her roommate from getting back together with her fiancé. Also, yes, the puppy dies at the hands of this psychotic femme fatale.*

When I was asked by the folks at Castle Bridge Media if I was interested in editing their next anthology, I jumped at the chance. Finally a horror anthology from women, about women, edited by a woman. We were going to get this right. Historically, women have gotten some crappy cards dealt them when it comes to horror. They freeze in the face of terror, only being able to emit ear-piercing screams. They catch their foot on a tree root at the most inopportune of times, their only hope thus being getting saved by a man. They go into dark basements alone. They forget to lock their doors. They open closed glass cases with creepy dolls inside.

When the publishers asked me about the theme I wanted to go with for the anthology, I knew that age-old stereotype of weak women had to go. But I wanted the anthology to be something more than just "strong women." Even now, in horror movies and books, things are looking up for our girls. Our female leads in horror movies arm themselves with weapons. They control and contain random whimpers while hiding. They manage to not needlessly knock cutlery to the tile floor. They are strong and powerful. Women have had enough. They are officially leveling up. No longer does Princess Peach need to be rescued. She's doing the rescuing. Three cheers for the self-reliant, powerful female. But again, I wanted something more.

Enter the Femme Fatale. Strong. Powerful. Self-reliant. And dangerous.

Right, so what is a femme fatale? In the strictest of definitions it's an often beautiful and often seductive temptress whose actions are likely going to cause disaster or destruction to a man. In a way she's the exact opposite of the females that horror movies portrayed, which is, in and of itself, empowering to the woman. That said, the femme fatale is often portrayed as the villain. Like with Glenn Close in *Fatal Attraction* or Sharon Stone in *Basic Instinct* (wait a moment . . . what is it with Michael Douglas and the femme fatale? Let's not forget Demi Moore in *Disclosure*.), these were not the characters we were rooting for. We were looking for the nice family man to make everything right. To escape from the evil femme fatale. But in this anthology, I wanted to turn that on its head.

Our femme fatales can now be our heroes. And that's exactly what I am so thrilled to present to you here. Sixteen stories from women about woman who have had enough of being cast in the weak-female role. They are changing the face of horror. They are rewriting the script. Coming from some of the most brilliant female minds are sixteen tales of ghosts and aliens, of vampires and demons, of taxidermy and mythology, of snakes and strip poker, of Shakespeare and royalty, of hunting and woodworking, of revenge and retribution and a bachelor party gone horribly wrong. And if, as you read, you see something of yourself in these stories, feel reassured. These are the stories of all women. ♜

For your peace of mind, no household pets were hurt in the making of any of these stories. But on that note, I had a bad roommate once. It was back in college. The first year we lived together things were great. The second year, she decided she couldn't stand me anymore. But you know what she didn't do? Start killing off my friends. We just ignored each other until the lease was up. And just for full disclosure, there was one unfortunate mishap with a pet. She had a bird. I couldn't stand the bird. One weekend when I was away, she left the screen door open, and the bird flew away. I wasn't sad. And I had nothing to do with its untimely demise.

THE HUNT

By P.J. Hoover

SWEAT COVERS ME, DRIPS DOWN my forehead. I try to lift my hand to wipe it, but something's tied around my wrist. I open my eyes . . . to darkness. I yank on my wrists, but the bonds bite into my skin. Sticky wetness runs between my legs, and I'm overcome by the desperate need to piss. I scoot until my back—my naked back—presses against a cold wall, and I try to bend my legs, to bring them in close to me. But like my wrists, they're bound. And then I do piss. The warm liquid pools between my thighs, mixing with . . .

My heart pounds as I fight to remember what happened. How I got here. Bits of memory flash around my brain but don't solidify. Drinks. A game of pool. Then . . . I let the memories slip away.

I pull on the ropes again, trying to yank my wrists free, but the harder I pull, the tighter they get. Grunting and straining, I yank again. I have to get them off.

Then I hear the voices. Laughter. Low conversation. And I know that if I don't get out of here, they'll come back. Think. I have to think. The wall behind me feels like it's made of old wood. Splinters dig into my bare skin. The floor underneath me, wood also. I lean my head forward so my right hand can reach it. My hair is a mass of tangles. A spot on the upper left side throbs with my heartbeat. It's sticky and wet.

My head slams against the floor. Something wet drips through my hair. My vision blurs.

"Bitch."

I push away the memory. If I focus on what happened, I'll never get out of here. They'll come back. I search my hair for a barrette, a ponytail holder, anything. My fingers tangle in the mats, and a large clump pulls free.

A hand grabs my hair, twists it around his fist, yanks hard.

I let the memory of the pain course through me. The voices aren't far away. I need to get out of this room. My head is swimming, but I focus on what I know. I'm twenty-eight years old. My name is . . .

I bite my lip as I try to remember my name. It's like a script that's been erased from my brain. My name is . . .

I can't remember. But I do know that I will not die here in this room. That's definitely not part of the script.

I let the ropes that hold my wrists go slack, and I feel around. The floor is made of wooden slats, and like the wall behind me, they're filled with splinters.

My back is filled with splinters.

My fingernails just catch the end of one of the boards, and I try to pry it up. But my muscles are aching from fighting. It won't budge. I try another. And another, feeling all around, until my fingertips brush against something cold. Metal. Sharp. Just out of my reach.

I scoot an inch. Two. Just barely my wrist can reach it. And even though I know I could slice a vein open doing it, I rub the rope holding my right hand against it, over and over. The voices outside make me speed up. They're saying something about going back in. About another round. The metal slips and cuts into the back of my hand. I keep rubbing, ignoring the flash of pain that flares out even with the collection of scrapes and cuts I already have. I need to hurry, because I'm not altogether sure I can survive another round.

The rope is getting hot, burning the skin on my wrist. And then it snaps free. Blood rushes into my hand, and with it, memories hurry back to me. Three of them. No, four.

Laughter. A slap across my cheek.

I try to grab the piece of metal, but whatever it is, it's bolted to the floor, so instead, I reach over and start picking at the rope on my opposite hand with my fingernails. Every second feels like an excruciating eternity where my future ticks away. The rope holding my left wrist is tight, but now that my right hand is free, I'm able to bend down and use my teeth also. My mouth tastes like blood, and my head throbs. I grab the thick rope and pull, looking for just the slightest give. And then I find it and it unravels. I can't get the knot out, but I manage to loosen it enough to slip my hand free. There is no time for celebrating. I fumble with the knot holding the rope around my ankle.

There's a sound from off to my left. Like a doorknob turning. The scrape of wood against a frame. But the door never opens. There's cussing. "How the fuck is it locked?"

How the fuck is it locked? It can't be locked. It must just be stuck, which means I only have a few moments.

I focus again on the knots around my ankles, and amid the cussing and laughing and pressing against the door that separates me from them, the bonds loosen, and I'm able to pull my legs free.

I stand, and the moisture between my thighs runs down my legs, dripping until it reaches my feet and the wooden floor. I press my hands against me. I have no clothes. No shoes. I'm covered in sweat and piss and remnants of memories that fill me with rage.

My eyes have become accustomed enough to the dark that I can make out the outline of the door separating me from them. My freedom is not that way. They'll gain control. Tie me up. It will repeat itself, and I am not willing to let that happen.

Slowly I look around as best I can in the dark. I run my fingers over the wooden wall behind me. Cool air comes through the cracks between the slats of wood. I move to the right, pressing and searching with my fingers. There are two metal rings with ropes attached. These are what they'd used to secure me. Quickly I untie one. A piece of rope may not be much, but it's a start.

On down the wall, the cool breeze picks up, and then there's a knothole that's come free, exposing nighttime outside. I wrap my fingers through the hole and try to pull the wood, but it's still too secure, almost like something is holding it in place.

I run my hands downward. A wooden board runs horizontal to the floor. It's been lowered into some metal braces, but with a little effort, along with a godawful squeal by the wood, the board comes free. The makeshift door swings open, falling downward. It's two feet wide by about three feet high, almost like it's for dumping grain or feathers. Like I'm in an empty storage building previously used for animals. I scramble over the wooden lip. Splinters cut into my knees and palms. The pain is bliss. The pain means I am free.

But I'm not as free as I'd like. From behind me, inside the building, there's an enormous squeak of wood scraping on wood, and then light bursts into the room. They've gotten the door open.

"She's gone," one of them says, nearly spitting out the words.

"She's there," another says.

THE HUNT

They've spotted me. I do the only thing I can. I run.

#   #   #

There is a rush of cussing and yelling and heavy feet on wooden floors, but I don't look back. I run hard. There's a field in front of me and across the field, a building. My bare feet cut into stones and sticks, but the pain will be worse if I'm caught. The building is my best shot.

Actually it's my only shot. And even though it's going to be obvious to the ones pursuing me, I don't see any other immediate options. It's this building or . . .

Fingers press down on me. Hands hold me against the wooden floor. I open my mouth to scream, but a hand covers my mouth. I can barely breathe, but they don't care. It excites them. Plays into their fantasy.

I run to the door and shove it open, then dash inside. One second later, I slam the door closed and look for some way to barricade it. A wooden table sits off to the side. It scrapes on the floor as I drag it in front of the door. Outside, they shout and call, whistling, hooting. My head still throbs from where it was slammed on the ground. The blood has since crusted into my hair.

In the center of the room a string hangs from the ceiling. I pull it, clicking on a dim, yellow bulb that barely lights up the area around me. I'm in a shed. Metal tools hang from pegs in the wall. Sheets of scrap wood are stacked at random. Dried animal hides are tacked to the wall. There's a single window on the back wall, but it's been boarded up. Nailed in place.

"Come on out," one of them shouts from outside.

"Let's have some fun," another says.

To the right side of the door is another window, also boarded up like the first. But the slats are imperfect, leaving me enough room to see out.

I come around from the side and dare to peek, only letting one eye be exposed. There are four of them out there. Four silhouettes in the dark. One short and stocky. A second thin like a scarecrow. The third is average height and build. Longer hair grazes his shoulder. Like someone I would see at a bar and want to strike up a conversation with. The fourth is tall. Bulky. Muscle and strength fill out his massive frame.

His hands hold me down, squeezing my nipples until I cry out in pain. He uses his knees to spread my legs apart. He's rough, like it's a game. He waits for the others to finish before he pushes himself inside me. My head slams into the wall with each thrust. And he calls me names. Bitch. Whore. He tells me to beg for it.

The memories rush into me, but instead of trying to get them out of my head, I let them come. They mix around and fill my brain. They stir the fury that has been hiding below the surface. And with that fury, I formulate a plan. But having that plan doesn't help my current situation. I am locked in a shed, completely naked, and I have four creatures hunting me.

THE HUNT

I spin around and grab one of the tanned animal hides from the wall and wrap it around myself, cinching it at the waist with the rope that had tied me up and securing it with the spike that held it to the wall. I need to cover up, not because I care if they see me, but because if I leave this shed—when I leave this shed—I'll need something to protect me from further injury. I'd love a pair of shoes. Given enough time, I could make something from more of the hides. But time is not a luxury I have right now. I need to hurry, and I need to be smart.

Once covered, I survey my surroundings. The walls and workbenches are covered with saws as tall as I am, hammers larger than my arm, pliers, nails, screws. Aside from the dim bulb in the center of the room, there is nothing electric. What I wouldn't give for a chainsaw in my hands. They would never mess with me again. But I need my hands free. I have no idea how far it is to safety. No idea how far I'll have to run.

"Come out," one of them calls. I'm pretty sure it's the short stocky guy, but I'm not going back to the window to check.

Instead, I being work on my escape plan.

#   #   #

They have been outside for the better part of ten minutes, drinking, throwing beer bottles against the outside of the shed, calling for me. They don't use my name. Bitch, they call me. Slut. They tell me what they're going to do to me. They grab their crotches, getting hard as they think about it. They're going to tie me to a tree in the forest. They're going to piss on me. Shit on me. They're going to slap me. Smash my head against the tree trunk. They're going to make me suck their cocks. They're going to film everything. They brag about how they already did. Then they're going to make me beg to fuck them.

Fuck them.

Really. Fuck them.

I scoot the table away from in front of the door and step back.

"I'm in here," I call through the window. "Which one of you is brave enough to come get me first?"

I know which one it's going to be. The short one with the stocky build. He has his shoulders permanently back, chest out. His hair is cropped short, like he's military. But no way is he military. He may have entered boot camp and then dropped out. He'd never make it through. His ego is much bigger than his actual abilities.

"I'm coming for you, cunt," he says, and he runs up to the door.

I step back until I'm right under the dim yellow bulb. I want to bite my lip, but I force myself not to. I steady my heart.

Then he pushes open the door and steps inside.

"There you are, cu—" he starts, but his words are cut off as the giant ax swings down and embeds itself in his scalp.

"Fuck!" one of the guys from outside shouts.

The ax is enormous and has enough momentum that it picks Shorty up as it continues on its upward swing. When it reaches its full height, it tosses him off. He falls to the ground and slumps against the wall.

The ax swings back the other way, back and forth, its height lower with each upward path, until it finally comes to a stop in the center of the open doorway.

I step up so I'm directly behind it. "Who's next?" I shout to the remaining three.

They're floundering around, stumbled on their own feet, unable to process what they've just seen, trying to puzzle out how the ax could have accidentally killed their friend.

I run my finger over the bloody blade of the ax until it slices through and blood beads to the surface of my skin.

"You killed him, bitch," the skinny guy shouts.

"My name isn't bitch," I say, shifting my stance so my legs are slightly apart. The script has come back. I remember it now. "It's Amy, not that you ever bothered to ask."

"This was never part of the deal," the guy with the medium build says.

I take my bloody finger and trace it between my legs, leaving a trail of red on the animal hide. "This was always part of the deal," I say. "What? You thought you could just show up here, rape me, and go on with your lives? That's not how it works."

The big guy steps forward. "You're dead, bitch."

"Amy," I say. "And I'll give you five minutes."

"Five minutes for what?" he asks, taking my bait.

The right side of my mouth curls up. "Five minutes head start. Then I'll kill you."

I'm not sure if it's the tone in my voice or the psychotic look I'm sure covers my face, but it works. The skinny guy is the first to run. He glances back at the storage house where they raped me, but maybe thinks better of it, because then he takes off toward the trees. The guy with the medium build is next, running off after his friend. But the big guy stands there, his eyes locked onto mine.

I step in front of the ax, lessening the distance between us. Then I say, "I'll save you for last. I know you like that."

He actually laughs. Then he says, "Bitch, you are crazy," and runs off.

"Amy," I say. "My name is Amy."

#   #   #

Five minutes. I step back into the shed and stare at the short guy's body. Each second I wait is excruciating. This is the worst part. I want to run after them. Slit their throats. But I force myself to count out the promised time.

"Did you expect it at all?" I ask the dead guy.

He doesn't answer. He's slumped in a heap with his head gashed open and a pool of blood coating the wooden floor of the shed. The wall behind him is splattered with blood and bits of brain. It's fucking gross . . . and glorious. He'd been the first to shove himself inside me. The first to high five his friends when he was done, like I was some kind of carnival ride that he'd dared to go on first. Like bungee jumping. First one to reach the bottom, but in this case, the reward was deadly.

His fault.

First to play. First to die.

Four minutes have gone by. I'm tempted to look out the door to see if I can catch sight of them, but I would never do that. It can't be too easy. This guy—this fucking loser—he'd been too easy. Somebody always is. It's so predictable.

When my brain hits the five minute mark, I look away from the dead guy. Then I count out thirty more seconds, step around the ax, and outside, into the fresh night air.

The moon is high in the sky. It's got to be close to midnight. Perfect hunting time.

They won't be back in the storage building. They'll be in the woods. With my bare feet, I make my way across the field until I reach the edge of the woods. I don't step in. I'm not stupid. I wait for it. One. Two. Three.

I roll to the side, ducking under the cover of the trees, right as something propels toward the spot where I was. A quick glance and I see that it is a spear, quickly carved from a tree branch. This tells me two things. One, at least one of them is close enough that he just threw this, and two, he has some kind of knife that he used to carve the point. A pocket knife. A hunting knife.

They grab lengths of rope and one of them pulls a large hunting knife from a sheath at his waist. He uses it to slice off a piece of rope which he ties first around my wrist then to the loop on the wall. I struggle as it pulls tight. I scream, but he puts his hand on my throat. "Shut up, bitch, or I'll tie it around your neck instead."

He has a hunting knife.

I'm on my belly in the forest, the trees blanketing my form. I slowly lift my head and look for him. He's nowhere to be seen, but something is running away, deeper into the forest. I grab the makeshift spear and take off after him. He knows I'm here, so I don't need to cover the sound of my approach. Not yet. Only when his footsteps stop, do I go silent. My bare feet are a blessing. I feel every twig that might snap, every leaf that will crunch. I sink my toes into the soft pine needles and earth.

He's so close. I can hear him breathing. I slip behind a tree trunk, an evergreen so big my slight form is easily hidden behind it. Then I wait. He'll come to me. I resist looking. I listen. There is nothing for the longest time, and then finally a twig snaps. So quiet he may not even realize it. It's close. He's close. I do not move.

Then he can't help himself. He says, "Where are you, cunt?"

I turn to my left, coming out from around the tree, and I thrust the spear forward. It strikes his chest and goes clean through.

"Nice spear," I say.

He gurgles something in reply. Blood bubbles at the corners of his mouth. Then he falls to the ground and doesn't get up.

I leave the spear but grab his hunting knife, not bothering with the sheath. It's got a nice heft to it. Two down. Two to go. I can hardly wait.

I step forward, deeper into the forest. There is no sign of the field behind me, through the trees. I turn back, toward the woods. Toward my prey. The hunting knife balances perfectly in my hand. I may have to keep it. Of course, this asshole brought a hunting knife. Probably thought he was going to cut me up, have some fun. What he should have done was try to attack me with it directly, not carve some spear. But these guys have ego. I can use it to my advantage.

I'm sure the last two are together. I stand still, letting the breeze blow against my face. I sniff the air for a scent. Nothing. They're hiding. I've never been here before, so I'm not sure what else is out here. Based on the shed and storage building, this is some kind of farm. The trees are normally planted to keep wind from eroding the crops. I walk forward. If I'm right, there will be one of two things ahead: another field or a river.

I turn my head and listen and am just barely able to make out the sound of the running water. Blood in water is glorious. I can almost see it now cascading down over rocks on its way downstream, nourishing fish as it goes. But I'm getting head of myself. I'm good, but I'm still capable of making mistakes. But I do know that they'll be at the water waiting, most likely on the other side. They'll think that makes them safe.

I'm like a phantom as I make my way through the woods, in my element.

As I near the water, I crouch down to go under a branch. My hair catches, but I pull it free, yanking a bit of the tangled hair from my scalp, which screams in blissful pain. But in doing so, I let out a small sound, just a yelp. And the world seems to go silent aside from the rushing water.

"I can hear you," one of them calls.

I was wrong. He's on this side of the water. They've set up a staging area, one on this side of the bubbling brook and the other on the opposite side. Clever. The groups are not always clever.

I've got the knife. They've got . . . I try to remember if either of them has any kind of weapon, when something rushes toward me. It's the guy with the medium build, longish hair. The one I'd have a drink with at a bar were circumstances different. He wraps his arms around me, making it impossible for me to grab the knife. My arms are pinned to my side. Then he drags me to the water and shoves my head under.

"Bitch!" he screams over and over again. I hear it each time he pulls my head out of the water and shoves it back under. My skull slams into a rock, and I'm sure it's my blood that's pooling downstream, feeding the fish. "I got her!" he shouts. "Bitch!"

The world is a frenzy of activity. He's drunk and high on adrenaline. He wants revenge for . . . what? Raping me and then having to pay the price? It's the most twisted logic in the world.

I try to shout at him to stop. I struggle against his grip. But he's on top of me and holding me so tightly that I can't move. The lack of oxygen is making the world go black. Water fills my mouth and lungs. I'm blinded by the struggle. The knife is still in my hand. If I can just get him to loosen his grip.

"Come on, I got her," he shouts.

Then I knee him in the crotch, so hard I imagine my knee coming up between his shoulders and out of his neck.

He lets go of me, and instantly I pull my arm up enough to stab him in the neck. Over. And over. Again. I stab him.

"You got me," I say as his dead body slumps on top of mine, pushing me under. But the water helps lift him, and I shove him aside. It's too dark to see the pool of blood, but I imagine it there, so thick it's nearly black in the bubbling water. I bend down and let it wash over me, drinking it in. Then I say, "We should get a drink sometime."

He doesn't answer.

The current carries his body downstream, and I let it take both him and the knife. Then I stand tall and continue through the water clear to the other side. My prey is waiting. And I don't want to disappoint him.

I wait until I'm clear of the water, far enough away that the sound won't interfere. "Are you scared?" I call.

I'm answered by scurrying through the woods. He's running, not trying to cover his tracks. He's sure he can outrun me. But I'm fast and I'm steady. I can wear him down, even if it takes until the sun rises.

He must realize this because right as we reach the edge of the woods, he stops. A field lays beyond the last trees, blanketed in corn waving in the darkness. And at the very edge of those trees is his silhouette. He's so tall, he dwarfs some of the nearby trees. The span of his shoulders makes it look like he could crush me with sheer strength.

"What the fuck is going on?" he shouts.

I slow down and then stop altogether. But I don't answer.

"Why are you doing this?" he yells.

I have no fucking idea what his name is. I never do. He's like all the others. Sick. Twisted. Sure that money will let him get away with whatever he wants.

I step forward, holding up my empty hands.

"You ready for more, bitch?"

"Amy," I say.

"Fuck you," he says.

I'm pretty sure he already did that. I doubt I need to remind him.

"How was the bachelor party?" I ask.

"You are fucking sick, you know that?"

Sick? I don't think so. Sick would imply that I wasn't aware why I was doing what I was doing. Sick would imply that there was something wrong with me.

"I like to think of it a kink," I say. "Turns me on."

"You're fucking crazy."

I shrug. "So what are you going to do now? Your friends are dead. You gonna go back home? Go back to your bride-to-be? Oh, maybe you could report this to the police. Tell them how you were looking for one last good time before you married some poor girl you planned to fuck around on every chance you got? Tell them how you and your friends paid to rape me? Is that what you're going to tell them? What do you think your future wife would say about that? How do you think that would look for your dad's company? I can almost see the headlines now. 'Rich groom pays to gang rape girl before wedding.'" I laugh. "That's gonna go over really well. Just wait until they interview me."

"They'll never have the chance," he says, and he lunges forward. Then I'm up against a tree. The wood presses into my back. I scrape against it, feeling it rip into my skin. I spread my legs, letting the full glory of his rage come to me.

"Fuck me, please," I beg. "This is what it's all been about. Just fuck me."

Reason leaves him in that moment—that brief moment. His eyes fill will illogical hope.

"Please," I say. "I was saving you for last."

Then I grab the spike that holds the rope belt closed at my waist and plunge it into the side of his head.

#   #   #

I stumble across the corn field to the house in the distance. Blood pumps through me, but with each step, the adrenaline lets up. What a night. The rush is going to fill me for a week. A quick glance at the full moon tells me it's got to be maybe three in the morning. I'm going to sleep the entire day.

The front door is unlocked, but the hinges need oiled. It lets out a horrible squeak as it swings open.

"Couldn't you at least oil that while you were waiting?" I ask as I walk toward the only room with a light on. It's some kind of old fashioned sitting room with a piano in one corner and wallpaper covering every exposed surface.

Casey is sprawled out on a purple velvet sofa that looks like it's maybe early twentieth century. I've never been great at identifying antiques.

"I was busy," Casey drawls, taking a long pull on a cigarette.

She's in a silk robe and not much else, so I'm pretty sure I can guess what she's been busy with.

I walk to the sidebar and pour myself a Scotch. Two fingers. I finish it in a few swallows. Then I pour another and sit in an armchair opposite her.

"How was it?" she asks.

"Assholes," I say. "It was perfect. The setup was—"

"Incredible?"

I laugh. "Yeah. Incredible. It's been months since we've been to a farm. You did good."

Truly, she did amazing. It hasn't been this good in nearly a year.

She reaches for her drink and takes a solid look at me. "You look like shit. You okay?"

"Perfect." I take a sip of my drink. "Four down. Blissful." And I fill her in on every detail.

When I'm done, she gets up and refills my drink. "Lindsey, you are a fucking badass."

That's right. The script is over. My name isn't Amy anymore.

"I know." A badass with a badass kink, so long as you're not some guy looking to fuck a whore the night before his wedding. If that does happen to describe you, well . . . I can't be responsible for what happens.

Fine. I can be. But that's not really my fault, now is it?

Casey says, "I thought we might change the ad up a bit. Make it a little more exciting."

I have no idea what she has in mind, but I've found it's better that way. The less I know, the more real it is.

"I trust you," I say. "Make whatever changes you want. I'm game for the hunt." ♜

THE THING THAT HAPPENED TO ANDI GOLD

By Joy Preble

IT WAS BITTER OUT, THE kind of February in Chicago cold that seizes your lungs with every breath. Andi Gold squinted at the slate grey sky. The clouds were low and full. Not even her ugly but functional Gortex coat was doing its job.

Andi wasn't doing her job, either. Oh, she wanted to. But an hour ago, she'd been unceremoniously handed that pink slip and told to hang up her Rosie's Biscuits and More apron.

"It's not you," Rosie told her. She meant the reason for the pink slip, not the apron, which actually fit quite nicely.

Rosie was flipping pancakes at the griddle, pencil tucked behind her ear, hair pulled into a sloppy tail, her own grease-spotted apron tied over jeans and a mustard-colored T-shirt—all of which somehow managed to look chic.

Rosie's Biscuits and More was that kind of place—overpriced all-day breakfast with biscuits and pancakes the size of hub caps, artisanal, single-sourced coffee, and house music humming softly in the background.

Rosie dotted a pancake with a handful of over-sized blueberries. "Actually," she said. "It *is* you."

"But—" said Andi.

"You've been late every shift," said Rosie, ear-pencil bobbing. She flipped the blueberry cake. "Yesterday you told Dashiell McElroy he could get cheaper coffee at Costco."

"Actually—" said Andi.

Rosie shook her head. Attended briefly to the applewood bacon and the chicken sausage patties. "It's clear you don't want to be here. I'll pay you through the end of the month. But I need you to leave now."

The end of the month was tomorrow, so gee thanks for that.

But Rosie was right. Andi was not cut out for extoling the virtues of chicken sausage and cherry jam sourced from some Michigan cherry farm outside Traverse City.

Andi Gold had many failings, but self-awareness was not one of them. She huffed a vaguely self-righteous huff and hoped she could get out the door with dignity. But not before stuffing some biscuits into a to-go bag. Because why the hell not.

It was ten below zero. She was wearing the same jersey dress and tights from last night with Noah, and the cute knee-high boots that really made the outfit but were miserable failures in the warming department. Her underwear was MIA, most likely tangled in Noah's sheets. The three bottles of wine they'd downed with dinner had been a mistake.

She would go home. Take a hot bath. Hydrate. Dive into her bed and regroup. Everything would look better once she was warm and fresh and tucked under her way-too expensive down comforter, wearing sweats and not-missing underwear and sipping hot tea.

She'd have a good cry once her eyeballs thawed.

At the bus stop, no bus in sight, she shivered. The wind picked up, so fast and hard that Andi found herself gripping the corner light pole to keep from being blown into the street. Traffic trudged by. Ice-coated snow was piled everywhere, and those low grey clouds promised more. Soon.

The icicles hanging from the roof of the lone Victorian house with a For Sale sign across the street were long daggers.

In the recesses of Andi's shoulder bag, her phone buzzed, long and insistent. She rummaged for it with a mittened hand.

Noah.

If her face wasn't frozen under her scarf, she would have smiled. Maybe given a little cheer.

She withdrew one hand from its mitten.

31

Sorry, said the text. *I don't think this is working out. It's been fun, tho.*

Had Noah just broken up with her over a text? She read the words again.

The juvenile "tho" stung as much as everything else.

She jammed her mitten back on her hand with enough force that her thumb popped a hole. At the same moment, the heel of the right boot of her fashionable but useless pair, gave an ominous crack.

And the other text that slid into view as she slapped at Noah's? From her landlord. Her rent was overdue. Two months, to be exact.

Across the street, one of the dagger-cicles cracked and fell in solidarity, taking a frozen piece of gutter with it, crashing into the snow.

Andi imagned Noah lying there, the icicle piercing his stony heart. The thought was briefly satisfying. She snatched a biscuit from the bag and bit a huge bite. It was mealy and heavy, but she chewed and swallowed anyway.

The bus still wasn't coming.

A rational person would have called a ride. But a rational person would haven't maxed out her credit card on the stupid, broken boots or promised money to her landlord that definitely was not in her account.

A rational person wouldn't have borrowed rent money from her friend Hannah that she hadn't paid back for so long that Hannah was currently ghosting her.

Andi ticked off her other options. Walk home and risk freezing to death because of the underwear situation. Call Noah and pretend she hadn't received the text. Call Hannah until she answered. Call her father and listen to him complain—mostly about her (some of it, she knew was well-deserved). He might even help her, although chances were solid that he wouldn't. Even if he did, what was she going to do? Slink home with her tail between her legs (so to speak) and take up residence in the guest room of his Sheridan Road condo? They had never agreed on much except that his view of the skyline and lake was damn nice, and that they both missed Andi's mother, who had died with shocking suddenness three years ago on Andi's birthday.

"You look cold."

The observation came from the woman standing by the bus stop sign. Had she been here all along?

"Your glove needs mending," the woman added. She was tall and thick-bodied, her head wrapped in a plaid babushka, her wool coat long and red. It tied in the front and caped in the back. Her boots were rubber-soled and sturdy. Her gloves were thick brown wool, and a matching scarf was wrapped around her mouth and nose.

Her eyes were a deep blue. No. Brown. No. Darker than that. Even with her own scarf muffling her nose, and the scent of cold and impending snow, Andi could smell her. She wreaked of cloves and garlic and tobacco. And something damp and decaying, too, like maybe she'd stepped in dog shit.

The strangeness pricked Andi's nerves, a quick adrenaline rush of

33

wariness, but whatever, right? Andi Gold had other things to worry about.

"What did you say?" the woman asked.

Andi blinked. She hadn't said anything, had she? The woman's weird eyes seemed briefly darker, like two pools of oil.

The snow started then, small hard flakes filling the air around them.

"You can tell me," said the woman. Her breath filtered through Andi's scarf, fogging the air with her fetid smells, and something worse now, like that time a rat died in Nana Gold's attic and fell down the wall.

Later, Andi would wonder where the words came from. But out they flew. "I want . . . ," she said, and didn't know how to finish. "Something," she managed, breath wheezing as the wind dipped down her throat.

The woman stared at her with those oil slick eyes. "Something it shall be," she said.

Somewhere behind them on Devon, a car backfired. Andi whipped around to look.

When she turned back, she was alone.

The snow was falling harder now, and Andi's heart was beating like a trapped animal.

Ridiculous, she told herself. *Just a crazy person.*

She ran anyway, jogging toward home, shoulder bag slapping her hip, right foot hobbled by the broken heel, chest heaving, body pressing into the wind, snow coating her face and lashes.

As for the forest, it simply appeared. One minute she was passing Levinson's Bakery with its scents of rye bread and pastries. The next, she was in the woods.

Andi stopped in her tracks, so abruptly her broken boot heel snapped off completely, sinking into a pile of dead leaves and twigs and soil. The bag of stolen biscuits dropped from her hand with a thud.

"What?" Her heart was attempting to flee through her throat. Inside her mittens, her fingers had gone numb.

Her breath was coming in short gasps that didn't seem to be reaching her lungs. She wrestled her scarf under her chin.

It'sokayit'sokayit'sokay, she told herself. "It's okay," she said aloud. The words echoed around her.

She closed her eyes. Tight. *When I open them,* she told herself, *I will be standing in front of Levinson's. I will walk inside and buy a sesame bagel and a cup of coffee with the last of my cash, and eat it right there in the store. The bus will pull up to the corner, and I will go home and figure things out.*

Andi counted to ten. She opened her eyes.

She was still in the forest.

Trees, tall and everywhere, blocking out all but a sliver of grey sky. Smells, gross and grosser. Dead leaves. Dead things. Earth and moss and dampness. The light filtered on an uneven angle through the branches, dim and foggy.

35

An eerie silence, thick, as though her ears were plugged. And then, a screech from some unseen overhead bird, a flapping of wings, and more disturbingly, a scuttling sound just out of sight. Something heavy was moving across the ground, rustling leaves and detritus and making Andi's pulse leap.

The words, "I'm not in Kansas anymore," slid through her brain. A giggle bubbled in her throat but didn't quite escape. Andi Gold hated *Wizard of Oz*. Those flying monkeys. That ugly, green-faced witch. Judy Garland singing about a place where there isn't any trouble.

As if.

And something else: It wasn't snowing. The air was cold, but no longer freezing.

Impossible, she thought as a yowl split the air, long and high-pitched.

Two eyes appeared from the thatch of bushes to her right. The cat itself—yes it was a normal-looking feline—slipped into view. Sleek grey fur and golden eyes. And a dead bird in its mouth, which it dropped unceremoniously at Andi's feet.

Bile rose in her throat.

But dead was dead. Nothing to harm her, right?

The cat circled her. Once. Twice. Three times.

Then it trotted off at a brisk clip through a narrow path Andi hadn't noticed until now, leaving Andi and the dead bird.

"Hey, cat," Andi said.

Almost out of sight, it paused. Fixed her with those strange gold eyes. And although they were nothing the same, the image of the old woman at the bus stop with those oil slick eyes came to her.

As with everything else in her life, Andi Gold was out of workable options.

Except for one.

When the cat trotted off again, she broke off the heel of her other boot, and followed.

It's a bad dream, she told herself as she narrowly avoided a thin branch scratching her cheek. *Maybe I'm still drunk from all that wine. Maybe Noah drugged me. Maybe it was the damn, over-priced stolen biscuit.*

None of this seemed true. The cat wound its way around a fallen tree. Andi careened along in its wake, and this time a thin branch did whip hard across her forehead.

She touched the spot with her thumb, felt moisture. Saw it was blood. She wiped her forehead with one mitten, then stuffed both mittens in her pockets.

The Gortex coat was heavy now and way too warm. She unwound her scarf and let it hang from her neck. When it slipped to the ground, she left it behind her.

"Slow down, damn it," she called to the cat. Her wrecked boots were wearing thin, the forest floor stabbing through her tights.

Her forehead was bleeding freely now, dripping onto her lashes and into her eyes. Her stomach ached from fear.

How long ago was she waiting for the bus? Since Rosie had handed her that pink slip? Was she really chasing blindly through the woods after a cat?

She'd been making mistakes and pushing people away, and she had hated working the breakfast rush. All those pancakes. All those biscuits. All that applewood-smoked bacon from hand-fed pigs on someone's organic farm just past Winnetka.

Noah had been as huge a mistake as those three bottles of wine. She was twenty-seven years old, and my God wasn't she supposed to have more to show for herself by now?

The cat dashed through a thinning stand of trees. Andi followed. When she saw the house in the distance, she felt a rush of relief. There were lights along the fence. Someone must be home. Someone would help her.

Only when she ran closer, swiping at her bloody forehead, did she see that the lights along the fence were each inside a bleached out human skull.

The house shuddered. It seemed to be breathing. Also, it was propped on what looked like chicken legs. They scratched the ground as though getting ready to flee, fence and skulls and all.

But it was the pair of disembodied hands that did it—giant and gnarled, scurrying toward her as the door creaked open.

Andi Gold was a mannerly sort. She was not one to scream and puke herself. But she bent anyway, heaving undigested biscuit bits onto the ground by the skull fence, splattering her ruined boots.

"Well," said the woman who now stood in the doorway of the chicken leg house as it huffed and puffed and pawed the ground. "That simply won't do, will it?"

With effort, Andi's heart skipping a beat or maybe three—cutting her oxygen enough that she felt like maybe (more than maybe) she was about to pass out, Andi straightened. She'd have held on to the fence but ewww, the skulls.

The woman smiled. Her teeth were grey. Iron-grey to be exact. As in made of actual iron—at least as far as Andi could tell in her poorly oxygenated, puke at the toes of her ruined boots, about to pass out state.

Also? The arms of the woman's bright red wool coat were flapping emptily.

The same red wool coat the lady at the bus stop had been wearing.

Because it was the same woman. Here. In the creepy forest that had somehow appeared out of nowhere off Devon Avenue.

The giant hands scurried past Andi, up the steps, vaulting themselves into the empty, flapping sleeves of the red wool coat and, as far as Andi could tell, reattaching.

"Come inside," the woman said.

Andi hesitated. Partly because she was gagging from watching the hands.

39

"It really isn't a choice," said the woman. "It's my forest. I make the rules. I could slit your throat and put your head on my fence, or simply swallow you whole, but you look agitated and stringy, and besides, I'm in the mood for company. I'm betting you're quite the chatterbox once we get your warmed up."

Andi was not a chatterbox. But her feet began walking, through the fence, up the steps which were vibrating from the scratching of the chicken feet on the ground. Through the door. Into the cabin? Hut? Hard to say.

"Welcome," said the woman. "My name is Yaga. Baba Yaga, to be exact."

Andi's voice quavered, but she made herself ask. "Like the witch? Like in those Russian fairy tales?"

Baba Yaga smiled broadly. The glint from her iron teeth was so bright that Andi was momentarily blinded.

The witch cleared her throat. Coughed expansively and spit something into her giant left hand. Something that looked like a bone.

A human bone. A finger bone.

Baba Yaga spit again. The stench was powerful. Skin and sweat and piss and maybe the tiniest hint of bubble gum.

The finger bone was small. Like that of a child.

"Sometimes they stick in my teeth," Baba Yaga said. "Especially the skinny ones."

Andi did not usually upchuck on a stranger's floor. But when your hostess puts a spit-up child's finger bone back in her mouth and chews it up with her iron teeth, making audible crunching sounds, it's hard not to.

"My dear girl," said the witch. "You need to pull yourself together. Come. Sit at my table. It's been far too long since I had an interesting dinner companion. Tasty, yes. But interesting, not for longer than I can remember."

Yaga gestured to one of the two wooden arm chairs placed at the oak table that was angled from the fireplace. This time when Andi hesitated, the witch did not. She raised her arm and one of the hands shot out from her sleeve. It landed on Andi's arm, its thumbnail slicing neatly through Andi's Gortex coat and the sleeve of her jersey dress, digging into the tender flesh of the underside of Andi's arm, right near the armpit.

Andi screamed. Long and high-pitched.

It hurt like a mother-fucker.

"I am the Crone," said Baba Yaga. "The Bone Mother. The most powerful witch that has ever been. I am ancient. My power comes from the Old Ones. Do not disrespect me, girl."

The disembodied hand continued its progress down Andi's coat, thumbnail cutting into Andi as it went. She was bleeding freely even though she couldn't see it: Her arm, her side, a quick nip at her belly, her hip. She felt the nail ripping through her jersey dress and stupid tights. It scraped hard against the side of her leg, then took a quick dip to her inner thigh, then down, down, to her ankle.

Andi kept screaming.

The witch's thumb kept cutting. And then, just like that, it stopped, the hand pulled away, dropped to the wooden floor and skittered back to the witch climbing into her sleeve, thumb dripping Andi's blood.

Andi stopped screaming. Or rather, her mouth was open in an O, but she had no sounds left, just a sort of dry heave weeping. She could feel her blood sliding down her legs, feel the warmth of it dampening her still underwear-less crotch.

Or maybe she had peed herself. Mostly like it was both.

Baba Yaga lifted her once again reattached hand to her mouth. Sucked Andi's blood noisily from her huge thumb.

The witch licked her lips. Then she frowned, lines etching into her forehead deep as canyons amidst age spots and dots of blood like freckles, possibly not all of it Andi's.

She spat blood on the floor, hitting near the same spot where she'd spat that child's finger bone.

"Your name?" she said.

"What?" said Andi.

"Tell me your name."

Now Andi had read fairy tales. In point of fact, she had been an English major once upon a time before she changed to business which might have been more productive had she not dropped out. She'd meant to go back. She would someday. She had wanted to travel and have adventure, but her funds ran low during that trip to Italy and then there was the whatever variant of Covid that had laid her low, and she'd lost interest and then her mother died and she started up with Noah and there was that help wanted sign at Rosie's.

And so it had gone. Until today.

But the point was that she'd taken that folklore elective. And so she knew that in fairy tales, names had power. Had she fallen into a fairy tale? Impossible, right? But if she had, she should keep her name to herself.

Except she was bleeding in a witch's hut and probably about to die and so "Andi," she said, her voice croaking hoarsely.

"Now that's the spirit," said Baba Yaga. "And stop making that face. The cuts aren't deep. Just enough to get your attention. Pain is only what you make of it. A means to an end."

"I—" Andi began, voice shaking. Violently. The single syllable hung alone in the fetid air.

Baba Yaga gestured again to the other chair. "Now let's start again. Sit. Join me. We'll have some tea, and we'll have some talk and we'll see what that 'something' is that you want."

She gazed contemplatively down her long, bulbous nose. Flicked her tongue against her thumb, swirling it at the tip. "Although from the taste of you, I suspect it isn't something nice." Her dark pool eyes glittered. "Good on you girl. Ladies don't last long in this world. And nice is in the eye of the beholder."

Andi scrabbled to put the pieces of whatever was happening together, but her brain had gone numb, back to the primordial ooze.

So she sat. The witch went about making tea in two thick, white mugs. The cat that Andi had followed appeared like a grey wraith from some hidden corner of the hut and wound itself around Andi's ankles. Briefly, it nipped her skin with sharp teeth, jumping away when she sucked in a hard breath.

Tears slid silently down Andi's cheeks. Somehow, this let her find her voice.

"I want to go home," she said. "I don't know how I got here or why. I don't understand any of this. I appreciate the tea, but please. I need to get home. I... Please."

Andi heard the begging in her voice. Her tears fell faster. Her legs felt damp again under her ruined tights and dress and coat. This time she was sure she was dribbling pee. The sharp odor rose to her nostrils. The urine stung as it seeped into the line of cuts.

Baba Yaga set the mugs of steaming hot tea on the table. Heavily, she sat, her body filling the other arm chair. The cat leaped into her lap and curled up, purring. She patted its head, stroking the grey fur.

"Drink," she told Andi. "Hot tea with honey." She ran her tongue over those hideous iron teeth. "And don't worry about the smell. Yours, I mean. Bodies are frail. I frighten you. I hurt you. That's how it goes, girl. You'll see."

Now the last thing Andi Gold wanted to do was drink whatever was in that mug. But "Drink," the witch said again, and so Andi took a tentative sip.

She swallowed, the hot liquid warming but not burning her throat. The sweetness of the honey settled her, just the tiniest of bits.

Her mother had made her tea with honey when she was sick. The memory of that surfaced—of sitting wrapped in a soft blanket on the couch while her mother set the tea on a little folding tray, two small sugar cookies next to it on Andi's favorite melamine Little Mermaid plate.

Andi sipped again, a bigger swallow. She waited. It seemed to be… just tea. She sipped some more. Across from her, the witch drank, too, albeit noisier and slurpier, but still. Like two friends, having a little cuppa.

It all felt weirdly calming. But only if Andi didn't think about the bleeding and the terror and that finger bone and the fact that Andi had puked and peed herself (more than once), and how she was somehow in a forest in a witch's hut with chicken legs that even now were scratching the earth beneath them like maybe they were getting ready to run.

She warmed her hands on the mug as she drank. And suddenly another memory surfaced—of walking with her mother through this weird, tiny zoo in Indian Boundary Park.

It had closed long ago, the animals shipped off to Lincoln Park Zoo, but when she was a little girl, they'd gone there. Just a bear and some goats and chickens and a few other assorted animals. But there was this odd castle-like apartment building on the edge of the park and somehow the combination of zoo where no zoo should be and a building with turrets like it had dropped from Medieval days, felt heady and strange and wonderful. Every time they went, Andi never wanted to leave.

Her mother would take her to the Thorne Miniature Rooms at the Art Institute, too, these tiny little displays of period furniture in a darkened hall in the museum. Andi had to hop up on this little ledge step to see them. Her mother next to her, they'd peer carefully into each room, studying the tiny couches and chairs and curtains and rugs. Like dollhouse after dollhouse, and once her mother had whispered in her ear, "Who do you think lived in there?"

The question in its past tense had stayed with Andi always. Not just because it was fanciful, this idea of tiny people in those tiny spaces. But because childhood Andi—Andi at five and six and seven and eight—had always thought her mother had said it wrong. Not who *lived* there but who *lives* there. Surely when the museum closed and Andi and her mom and everyone else was gone, the people would filter back into their rooms and live their lives and sit on their furniture and look out their tiny windows.

Of this, Andi had been positive.

"So tell me," the witch said, leaning an elbow on the table, which creaked in response.

Andi did not ask what. Even in her currently distressed and wounded and majorly frightened as shit condition, she knew a general opening question when she heard it.

A word surfaced like those memories. *Lost.*

It was true on every possible level. The cut on her inner thigh itched now, and she assumed it was closing. Her body working overtime to heal itself even as she anticipated that this might not be the last terrible thing to happen here.

Wherever here was.

"Lost my job," Andi said. Might as well give the word a spin. "And Noah. Well. Noah was a mistake. But who breaks up over text?"

Did the witch know about texts? The question tickled her and she almost laughed, but thought better of it. She thought about those dagger-length icicles on the Victorian house near the bus stop. And how, if she did get out of this mess, she'd have to buy a new winter coat.

She thought about her father on the 37th floor of the Sheridan Road Condo, looking out over the lake.

She thought about Rosie, flipping organic flour pancakes.

She remembered how she used want to run away to the Indian Boundary Park zoo and live in the castle apartment building. Or shrink down tiny and live in one of those Thorne miniature rooms, specifically (although not limited to) the one called California Hallway with its tidy mid-century modern furniture, always making Andi feel as though if she could see out the little door, she would glimpse the Pacific Ocean, broad and deep and wild and endless.

She thought about Noah, but only briefly.

She had told the witch she wanted… something. But what? Andi Gold was filled with desires, but how to put them into words? That was another story. She wanted so much that felt impossible to name.

Except maybe for one other word. Andi Gold realized that honestly? She was angry. At Noah, for sure. At Rosie, a little. At her friend Hannah and at her landlord although probably neither of them deserved it. At her father, for lots of things. At her mother, for dying. At herself for, well, she'd have to ponder that.

"Tell me the rest," said Baba Yaga. They had both finished their mugs of tea now, with only the dregs of tea leaves left at the bottoms. "And then I will tell you."

Andi looked up from her empty mug. "Will you?" she said, her tone sharper than she had thought herself capable, given the circumstances. Despite appearance to the contrary, Andi Gold had no plans to go gentle into the night.

Andi looked the witch square in the eyes. It was easier than looking at those terrifying detachable hands. "And why would you tell me anything?"

Baba Yaga's laugh filled the hut, her breath foul but honey-scented from the tea, her pendulous breasts jiggling, her teeth glimmering. The skull hovering inside the fireplace, suspended by some invisible power just over the flames, glowed bright then brighter.

"Hang on," the witch said. Beneath them the floor shook. A loud scrabbling sound arose. The grey cat tumbled from Baba Yaga's lap, landing on all fours, looking highly insulted.

The hut moved, then moved again, and then they were racing through the forest on those impossible chicken legs, fast enough that Andi gripped the table, her pulse quickening as the pace picked up again.

Eventually, they came to a stop. How deep into the forest had they gone? Would it be possible to find her way out if the witch let her go? Clearly you could leave this place. The witch had been at the bus stop. Andi was certain she had not imagined that. She was also certain that it was a distinct possibility that she might never get out. At least not alive.

But Andi Gold's brain stopped on this: Baba Yaga had still not answered Andi's question.

"This whole thing is getting old. So I'll ask you again. Why on earth," said Andi, working to catch her breath from all the chicken leg running, "Would *you* tell *me* anything?"

No laughter this time. No chicken legs taking off like two poultry bats out of hell.

They stared each other down. Each with her own questions. Each waiting for answers.

A game of chicken, if you will. Chicken legs… okay the whole thing was not funny.

"Because you called me," Baba Yaga said. "Because you wanted, so loudly, that it drew me from the forest."

"Bullshit," said Andi, but the witch simply shrugged one giant shoulder. Her left hand popped out of her sleeve and hovered and then popped back in again. Then it slipped out a second time, quicker than a blink and sliced a cut across Andi's knuckles. Nail in. Slide. Nail out. Back to its sleeve, then thumb to witch's mouth and lickety lick, Andi's blood was swallowed.

With relish.

Again.

"For fuck's sake," said Andi. She tried to sound brave and pissed off. Mostly she sounded surprised.

"You're right," said the witch. "I am not obligated to tell you the truth. But you must not assume I will lie to you, either. Here is what I tell those who wander into my forest: You will not leave unchanged. Possibly you will never leave. Possibly, I will let you go. I may devour you whole and chew your bones. Or I may sit with you at this table, as we have, and share a pleasant cup of tea. I may promise you something and still pull it back. This is my nature. This is power the Old Ones place within me. Whether you are good or whether you are evil or something in between matters not one whit. Your destiny in my forest has only to do with chance and whim. Sacrifice and hope, bravery—none of it matters. You might even be a sniveling coward—although girl, I see you are not—and that alone will not force my actions. Time and geography work differently here. My forest can be anywhere, any place, any time that I choose. The chicken legs help protect me if I am otherwise occupied. Plus the optics are terrifying, as I'm sure you'll agree. That is how it works here. How it has been since the Old Ones pressed my powers into me. Turned me from a foolish, preening girl to a woman with power beyond measure. How it always shall be."

Andi considered all this. The witch pressed a giant palm to Andi's knuckles. When she lifted the hand away—or more precisely, when the hand lifted itself because, well, you know, the cuts were gone. Not just healed but vanished as though they had never been there.

Baba Yaga's hand drifted down Andi's wounded side, from shoulder to ankle. Nothing hurt anymore, although her tights were still damp from pissing herself.

"And so," said the witch. "I ask you again. Tell me the rest of what you want. And I will answer and you will decide if it is a truth worth hearing or if it is a truth at all. After that, we shall see what happens. How hungry I get. That tea was not particularly filling for a ravenous old crone. It is equally possible that you smelled delicious and so I opened up my forest simply to lure you in as a tasty snack."

Baba Yaga smacked her wrinkled lips. She made a yummy nummy

51

sound deep in the thick of her ancient throat.

Well, thought Andi in that desperate way one conjures up a narrative when choices seem limited or none. Damned if you do and damned if you don't, quite literally. And really, was it that much different from everything else in her life? Take help from her father and she would be in his debt. That whole "precious fruit of my loins" thing held no water with the man. Her best friend had dumped her in her hour of need, and weren't your true friends supposed to be the ones who stuck by you when you were acting like a shithead? The ones who slapped sense into you and refused to let go? And then there was Noah. What kind of man drank with you and fucked you (admittedly he wasn't bad at that, but certainly not the best) and possibly hid your underpants and then broke up with you when you were at your lowest?

As for Rosie, Andi held no grudge. Rosie needed someone who could cheerfully lie to the customers about the value of a $20 dollar plate of eggs.

As for Andi's mother, there was no point in being angry at the dead. Not even the dead who had refused to go for regular check-ups, believed vaccinations were a government plot to control the citizenry, and assumed that healthy eating and taking supplements would heal anything as long as she did her yoga and Pilates on the regular.

So no, Mom, rubbing CBD oil on a cancerous lesion was not a solid choice. But it was also not one that could be undone.

And so Andi told Baba Yaga all there was to tell. She talked until she was hoarse. Until the tears she thought weren't left were once again slipping down her cheeks and into her empty tea mug. Somewhere in the middle of all that telling, the dark pools of Baba Yaga's eyes had turned into two grinning skulls.

And the skull floating just over the flames in the fireplace, its eyes were glowing, too. Occasionally, Andi would see images in them. A young woman who she realized was Baba Yaga at some time in the past. Crying. Pressing her hands to her belly. Wading into a stream, transformed into the monster that now sat across from Andi at this wooden table.

It seemed there were lots of choices in this world. Lots of bargains. Lots of moments you couldn't come back from. And some you could.

As for what Andi wanted, that took a little longer. In the end, she kept thinking about the lethal icicle. And Noah. And, well. One's imagination can do the rest. She had essentially been kidnapped by a witch and terrorized. Andi Gold might be self-aware, she might be brave, she might even have sensed that Baba Yaga herself occasionally regretted whatever bargain she'd made with those Old Ones.

But Andi was really pissed at Noah. It changes a girl. Sometimes not for the best.

Back on Devon Avenue, a woman snacking on a sesame bagel from Levinson's and waiting for the bus, noticed a man lying in the snow in front of the empty Victorian house across the street. He'd been dead for about an hour, stabbed through the heart with an icicle the length of a dagger. Freak accident, the news anchors said. Poor bastard. It was all anyone in frigid Chicago could talk about for at least two days.

As for Andi Gold? Well, if this was a traditional fairy tale, the Disney-ized ones that stream to good little boys and girls, this was the place where she would learn a lesson. Where she would get her happily ever after. Where everything would be okay in the end.

But Russian fairy tales weren't like that. Sometimes you wander in the forest with unspoken desires and you don't find your way out. At least not the same as when you lost your way and wandered in.

In Russian fairy tales, you found the source of your misery. That was basically it.

Andi got a little more than that. Freak icicle revenge and all that.

Baba Yaga did let her leave the forest.

Andi did go home and take a hot bath and change into fluffy pjs and curl up under all three of her comforters and sleep like the dead, pun fully intended. She remembered that she had once upon a time memorized her father's Amex number, and she used it now to order Thai food and a new winter coat and thick, sturdy boots and a six pack of Fruit of the Loom granny panties. Also to pay three months of her rent, giving her some room to get caught up.

She applied to Roosevelt to finish her business degree.

She found a new job waiting tables at a 24-hour diner in Lakeview, one that had an early bird breakfast special favored by its elderly clientele—eggs and bacon and toast and fruit for $5.99, which was barely breaking even for the diner but brought a lot of good will from people like Mrs. Markowitz who loved when Andi saved her the little mixed fruit jelly packets to take home in her handbag.

She found an extra two-day-a-week gig at Levinson's slinging bagels and coffee and getting all the free day-old bagels she wanted.

She apologized to Hannah, who apologized back, and promised that she and Andi would go out and celebrate their renewed friendship once this crazy yeast infection Hannah had mysteriously developed finally cleared up and she stopped itching and scratching and crying when she peed. The doctors were currently stumped. One had even recommended acupuncture. Another had suggested supplements.

It was all going stunningly well.

The whole Baba Yaga thing seemed like maybe she had imagined it.

Well, it did until a random Tuesday morning in late March, just as the temperature had finally began to work its way out of death wish cold into normal cold, which is what passes as Spring in Chicago, and the lake was bright blue, the sun shining through Andi's window as she woke up.

She felt strange, her body heavy, her hands stiff, and what was up with her nose? Totally congested. Ugh.

Her boobs, too. Still under the covers, she lifted her hands to feel what the situation was. Since when did she have nipples the size of mushrooms?

Shrieking, she leaped from bed. Almost smacked her head on the low ceiling of her bedroom.

Even then she might have thought she was hallucinating, had her right hand not headed off on its own and scuttled back to her with a glass of water.

The mirror confirmed the truth.

Seemed that Baba Yaga was about to claim her price.

As for the witch herself, currently transformed to look a lot like Andi Gold—original version, that is—she was about to step on a plane to Paris. Do a little sight-seeing. Eat a few hundred croissants. Maybe check out the wine country.

Not forever, mind you. Baba Yaga loved her power too much to give it up.

But for now.

Turned out the witch was telling the truth. The rules of the forest worked differently.

Just ask Andi Gold. But you'll have to enter the forest to find her. ♛

DO YOU WANT TO LIVE FOREVER?

By Christina Berry

"DO YOU WANT TO LIVE forever?"

It's the standard question I ask all my clients. The answer is always the same. But I never take that for granted, never assume. People should have a choice, especially about something as important as this.

Judith takes her time answering. Her hands tremble, and the china cup rattles almost imperceptibly against her teeth as she sips her tea. She's nervous and far weaker than she was when I last saw her, paler and thinner too. She's fading fast. This is the time to decide, but I don't rush her. If there is one thing my clients do not have enough of, it's time.

I glance around as I sip my tea. The room is cozy, cluttered with sentimental knick-knacks and dozens of photos of Judith and her family. One photo in particular catches my attention. It's Judith as a young woman, arm in arm with a handsome young man, both in their wedding wear, smiling wide for the camera.

"No," Judith says.

I turn my attention back to her; she's the same woman in the wedding photo but different now. Her blue eyes have clouded, her complexion wrinkled with time, her shoulders stooped with exhaustion. She's ready to rest.

"You wish to die?" I ask.

Judith nods, but I wait for verbal confirmation. Consent is key, and on this point, there can be no misunderstanding—a nod will not suffice. My use of the word "die" triggers anxiety in Judith, the acrid smell of fear peeking through the floral notes coming from the potpourri bowl beside me. She elaborates, "I wish to see my husband and my son again."

That will do. I set my teacup and saucer aside and move to my feet, crossing to the wedding photo on the mantle. "How long have you been widowed, Mrs. Clements?"

"Twelve years."

"And your son has died too?"

Judith grimaces. "He died in the war."

I don't ask which war. It's not important. "And you have no other family?"

"No, ma'am."

Ma'am. My lips twitch at the formality of her response. When people learn what I am, they assume I'm much older. Truth is, I'm young enough to be Judith's granddaughter. But she seems to find comfort in the formality, so I let it pass without comment.

I bring the photo over to Judith and set it in her lap as I ask, "What is your husband's name?"

"Stephen," she answers as she tenderly traces her finger across the glass over his face.

I move behind her, out of sight. "You were happy together."

"We were. I miss him terribly," she says with a sigh.

I ignore the stab of envy. I've never known the quiet contentment that comes with love, and I never will. Clearing the lump from my throat, I instruct: "Close your eyes and think of Stephen. Imagine what it will be like to see him again, to hear his voice…"

It's strange to witness my clients surrender. Judith faces the moment of her death with dignity, looking queenly as she shuts her eyes, lifts her chin, and relaxes the tension in her neck, welcoming her end.

My eyes narrow in on the flutter of her pulse in the blue-veined column of her neck, and my throat runs dry, desperate for a taste. I grip the back of her sofa with trembling hands, trying to quell my darker impulses. I don't want to harm Judith. But it's been two months since my last feed, two months in this tiny Texas town, sourcing clients, two months waiting for someone to get sick enough to invite death. I'm starving.

With a steadying breath, I calm myself, then, in an instant, I'm on her.

Judith lets out a meek yelp, and her shoulders stiffen with shock as my teeth prick her throat, penetrating her carotid artery. She doesn't struggle though, letting me drink deeply of the blood meant to supply her brain.

Judith only endures a few seconds of consciousness while I hang off her neck like a leech, gorging as each pump of her heart fills my mouth with what's left of her life. Her heart pumps faster, recognizing the blood loss and sending a panic of activity through her system. It won't be long now.

Just a few more flutters, and her heart stops. I pull away and wipe the smears of blood from her neck as I lick my lips. Like some snobby Oenophile, I swish the last of the blood over my tongue and consider the rusty notes and bitter tang of her sickness. Working exclusively with terminal patients as I do, it's a taste I've grown accustomed to. I wash the aftertaste away with cold chamomile tea.

I handle Judith's body with care, positioning her on the couch in comfortable repose. Then I move through her home, removing any trace that I was there. When I set the photo of Judith and Stephen back on the mantle, I wonder if she's with him now, together again. I hope so. I like to think happy endings exist in this world.

#   #   #

I call 911 on my way to church, effecting a debutant drawl as I request a wellness check on an elderly neighbor. It won't be long before Judith is discovered, a lonely woman succumbed to the ravages of age and late-stage pancreatic cancer. Should the medical examiner notice her exsanguination, it will be a curiosity but no concern of mine. I'll be gone by morning.

Thunder rumbles in the near distance. I hadn't sensed the coming storm, but it's nearly upon us now. I ditch the pay-as-you-go phone in a trash receptacle at the DQ and walk the remaining blocks.

Lightning flashes with a kaleidoscope of color through the cathedral's stained-glass windows as I step into the nave. Responding thunder rumbles moodily through the cavernous, neo-gothic space. I turn away from the light and color, away from the rows of pews and ornamental altar, and move toward the stairs in the corner.

My clammy palm squeaks as it slides along the metal railing, spiraling downward into the bowels beneath the building. Above, the sweet scents of perfume and the smoke of prayer candles linger. Down here, the walls seem to weep with moisture, the air earthy and thick as a grave. I follow the narrow hallway to the last room on the left, a community meeting room currently occupied by the Terminal Diagnosis Support Group.

I shouldn't be here; it's risky. But there's another hunger I need sated before I leave town.

Matthew stands at the podium, watching as the members of the group collect their kolaches and cups of coffee and take their seats. He smiles when he sees me, and I smile back. He's attractive in that lost sort of way—ruffled and tragic with such sadness in his eyes—exactly my type. We've been fucking for about a month.

"What's killing you?" he asked me after our first kiss.

"Breast cancer." I lied. Once upon a time, I hated lying, now it's all I do.

He said nothing, just kissed me again. We fucked that night, and then he told me about Cassie.

Cassie, his betrothed, was killed by breast cancer, and her diagnosis drew Matthew to this support group. He initially attended to hear terminal people talk about their mental and physical anguish so that he could better support her in her final days. Two years later, Matthew is the sole survivor of that original group, and, as the last man standing, has become the default leader.

"Evening everyone," he says in that low, rumbly voice that tickles the back of my neck. "Looks like a small group tonight. I suppose a few of us stayed in from the storm." Everyone nods, quietly praying it's the weather to blame for Carrol's, Anson's, and Judith's absences. "Who would like to speak?"

Henry clears his throat and ambles to his feet, barely balancing on his aluminum cane. We can always count on Henry to talk. The gristly old man has plenty of stories to tell.

When he reaches the front of the room, he leans heavily on the podium, breathing heavy from the lung disease, and leads with a joke, "Did y'all hear the one about the trees that can't be trusted?"

Matthew chuckles and asks, "Why can't they be trusted, Henry?"

"Well, I don't know, Matthew, but they seem kinda shady to me."

Everyone laughs. I do too. I like Henry. If it hadn't been Judith for me tonight, it would have been him. I'd given them both my card; only Judith called.

"The doctors tell me I could have six months left to live, and they smile when they say it—as if that leftover time is the most important thing. But what the hell am I supposed to do with those extra months? Everyone I love is dead."

Henry coughs, clears his throat. "I think about all those times my Imelda made me toast without butter. 'Better for your heart,' she'd say. But then she was the one taken too soon. And my heart…well it hurts, but it ain't cuz of the butter.

"I know that it's wrongheaded. I know that life is a gift. But I'm ready to give it back." With a wry grin, he finishes. "All's I know is, nowadays, I spread my butter on *extra* thick."

I smile though I want to cry. His words hit close to home. I know the loneliness he means. These past few weeks, I've considered staying here. I like this town. I like its people. I like Matthew.

It's been ten years since my transition, ten years of the same routine: prowl, hunt, devour, and move on. What would it be like, for once, to stay?

63

Maybe I will. As Henry comes back to his seat, I consider staying for him, too—give him the gift of death.

A few others speak, but I hardly listen, wrapped up in my thoughts, considering the possibilities of my future. Then the meeting winds down, the elders exit slowly, and I help Matthew stack the chairs.

When the others have left and we've tidied the room, I follow Matthew to the alley behind the church, to his truck parked in the shadows. It's still raining, and we run to get out of the downpour.

We don't speak when we're inside the truck. I think it's the shadow of death that looms over us from all the talk at the meetings. What more is there to say? So, we don't use words, but we have plenty to say with our bodies.

I push my wet hair out of my face as I move onto Matthew's lap. His hands grab the hem of my shirt, and he slides it over my head to toss it on the seat beside us. He's never said as much, but it's clear that this is his favorite part of me, my scars.

It's his kink.

He traces the lines of my tattoo, the petals and stems of the bramble of blood-red roses that cover my chest and mask the parts of me that are missing now. With a hungry sound in the back of his throat, he kisses me there, right on the tangle of thorns over my heart, then runs his tongue along the marks left by my double mastectomy.

Cassie didn't get one. Matthew had wanted her to. He'd wanted her to do anything she could to save herself, but by the time they knew about Cassie's cancer, it was too late for her. She died with her tits on.

I didn't. When the cancer first tried to kill me, I cut it out. But it came back and spread. And when the end came for me, I didn't face it like Judith. I fought. I begged. I made a bargain for my life, a bargain with the devil. When asked that all-important question—"Do you want to live forever?"—I answered yes.

"Hey, what's the rush?" Matthew whispers against my chest with a hint of humor.

I'm practically tearing the zipper out of his jeans, trying to get at him. Why am I so desperate for him tonight, so desperate to chase my orgasm and with it chase these thoughts from my mind? Maybe it's Judith. With her blood nourishing me, I can leave now. I *should* leave now. But...

"I want you," I whisper back, still wrestling with his jeans, but a little more gently. Since that first time with Matthew—a first kiss by the basement coffee pot that turned into our first fuck in his truck—I always wear skirts on group nights for easy access. So it's just a matter of moments before I free him from his pants and sink down onto him.

We both gasp at the connection. Matthew has a good dick. I like the way he uses it, clasping my hips in his fists as he pushes up into me, his hot breath trailing across what's left of my chest. I brace my arms against the roof of the truck and ride him with relief. No more thinking. For the next few minutes, all I have to do is feel. And it feels fucking amazing. I come too soon. Matthew does too.

When it's over, I huff out a tired breath and slide onto the seat beside him, twisting my shirt right side out and tugging it back on. Matthew's head lolls against his headrest, and he watches me with a satisfied grin on his handsome face. *That's a face I wouldn't tire of.*

Jesus, I really need to leave. My thoughts are all wrong. For the last three-and-a-half weeks, every Tuesday and Thursday night, Matthew and I have come together here in the shadow of the church. Without meaning to, I've grown fond of the man, and if I don't leave now…

I give him a forced grin, then reach for the door handle. He sets his hand on my knee, asking for the second time tonight, "What's the rush?"

"I figured you'd want to get home."

His lips quirk up on the side, a sad attempt at a smile. "Probably should."

I nod, moving again for the door handle—

"Why don't you come with me? We could go at it again, take our time, in an actual bed."

The rain dribbles down the grimy alley wall on the other side of his truck window as I try to understand what he said. Did he just invite me to his house? He's never done that before. It's a boundary we've never crossed, never even considered crossing.

His house is hallowed ground. It's Cassie's house. His bed is Cassie's bed. And, for all intents and purposes, Matthew is still Cassie's too. He's lost without her. I knew that the moment I met him. These little fucks of ours? That's all they are, just sex. At least here in the truck they're just sex. But in a bed, in *her* bed, that's different. That would change everything.

"Why would you want...? I mean..." Shit. I don't know what to say. I *should* say no; I have to leave, though a growing part of me wants to stay.

"I think about you sometimes," Matthew admits.

I think about you too. I don't admit that out loud.

"More and more, I catch myself wondering what you're doing." Matthew's little quirk of a smile is back. "But you never gave me your number, so I didn't have a way to find out."

Matthew turns his attention to the windshield; the rain splatters and runs down it in rivulets. A flicker of lightning illuminates his profile, and I see so much future in the lines of his face, so much life he's yet to live. He's stuck loving a dead woman and fucking a monster. I can help set him free... by leaving.

"But apparently I do have your number." Matthew gives me a smirk as he reaches into the front pocket of his shirt and pulls out a business card, *my* business card.

"How did you get that?" I try and fail to hide the panic in my voice.

"You handed it to Henry last week. He must have dropped it because I found it on the floor as we were cleaning up."

I reach for the card, but he's faster than me and switches hands. He's not playing keep-away per se, but he's effectively keeping it away from me unless I want to climb across him to snatch it from his fingers.

"Do you want to live forever?" He reads the text on the front of the simple, white rectangle, then flips it over. "I called this number last night, and it was your voice that answered."

That explains the hang-up call.

"What does it mean? What is it you do, exactly?"

It occurs to me that I could tell him. I could ask him the question he's just read aloud. But what if he said yes? Am I really ready to do *this* to a healthy person? I've always been intentional with my hunting. I pick my prey carefully, already knowing their answer before I ask the question, and their answer has always been no. With Matthew, nothing is certain.

So, I lie. "I offer religious counseling and bible study for those who are close to death." And to really sell this bullshit, I add, "I help them achieve eternal salvation through repentance, for the Kingdom of Heaven is near at hand."

I don't think a person could look more surprised than Matthew looks right now. It's as if he's really seeing me for the first time. *He's not.* And he doesn't like what he sees. *It's better than the real view.* I'd rather he think I'm a religious nut than a monster with a killer craving. How would he react to knowing that every time we fuck, I have to restrain myself from sucking the life out of him?

Matthew slowly hands my card to me. I tuck it into the pocket of my denim skirt as I open the passenger door.

"You should probably head home now, Matthew."

The sound of the rain nearly drowns out his voice when he asks, "Are you even sick, or do you come to the meetings looking for clients?"

The answer to both parts of his question is yes. But I don't answer that question; I answer the one he hasn't asked yet. "I won't be back."

#   #   #

Pete's is a dingy little bar with high, tin-tiled ceilings and weathered brick walls a couple blocks up from the church. I shiver at the door as the air conditioning chills my wet clothes and try not to curl my nose at the stench of stale beer. The place is mostly deserted, just a smattering of haggard regulars and a few young bucks at the back, shooting pool.

I eye the bartender as I settle atop one of the sticky stools. She could be anywhere from late twenties to early fifties; dim lighting and hard living make it difficult to gauge. She doesn't smile when she asks, "What'll it be, hon?"

I don't smile when I answer, "Two shots of Jack."

The woman pours my drinks then wanders off. Her years behind the bar have taught her to know which customers want to chat and which don't. It's a relief. Except, alone, I have only my thoughts for company.

Someone puts a Kansas song on the jukebox, and the singer croons something about peace and being done. My mood sinks to a new low. There will be no peace for me, and there will be no done for me either.

I shoot one of the whiskeys. It has no effect. I used to have the alcohol tolerance of a hummingbird. My new metabolism, however, makes it impossible to get drunk. I could drink every drop of alcohol in this godforsaken place, and it would run through me like water. Eternally sober—this is my hell.

"Haven't seen you here before," says a man as he slides onto the stool beside me. I give him a glance, recognizing him as one of the pool players come to sniff me out. He's handsome in that awful sort of way—well-built with thick hair that has a just-fucked tussle to it, but his probing gaze and wolfish grin scream *predator*.

I drink my second shot.

"What's your name?" he asks.

Bored, I answer him with the current lie. "Angela."

"Angela." His tongue tickles each syllable as he repeats it with an exaggerated drawl. "Like an angel sent down from heaven."

I chuff. "I fell."

Confused, he frowns.

"I *fell* from heaven."

"Did it hurt?"

"Oh Jesus." I laugh at him, and the sound bounces around the room. "You're terrible at this."

"At what?"

"Pickup lines."

His smile sinks, and I feel bad. Have I read him wrong? Have I been terribly rude to a sweet man? But he quells my guilt when he sneers at me, hissing, "What's your problem, lady?"

"At the moment, *guy*, my problem is you."

In an instant, his expression hardens, and his eyes turn cruel, exposing the ugliness beneath his handsome mask. He grabs my elbow, his fingers clawing me in a bruising grip as he wrenches my arm into an awkward angle. His words wet my cheek when he comes in close to whisper, "Who the hell do you think you are, comin' in here acting like a stuck-up bitch?"

I can tell by the way he handles me that he's done this before. He's a man who doesn't take no for an answer.

I go very still as I consider my options. It is not a good idea to draw attention to myself, especially so soon after a kill, but this guy has pissed me off. I could easily punch him in the—

"Billy Caulfield," the bartender shouts. "You take your goddamned hands off that girl, pay your tab, and get the hell out of my bar."

She stands before us now, a baseball bat in her hands. When Billy doesn't immediately release me, she cracks the wooden bat solidly against the bar top, making it clear that she has every intention of bunting him out the door if he's not quick to comply.

Muttering a few choice curses about "bitches" and "cunts" along the way, Billy releases my arm, throws a wad of cash at the woman behind the bar, and scrapes his stool across the floor as he leaves.

When he's gone, the bartender lowers the bat and turns her attention to me, asking quietly, "You all right, hon?"

"I'm fine. Thank you."

She pours me one more shot and winks when she says, "I'll put this one on Billy's tab. Least he can do."

I force a grin, nod my thanks, and gulp down the whiskey. The drink does nothing to improve my mood and only seems to compound my exhaustion. That's what this mood is, not heartbreak or anything so emotional as that, just plain old exhaustion. But, as tired as I am, I can't wallow at Pete's all night. It's past time for me to go.

I push a couple bills under the empty shot glasses and head for the exit. Outside, the storm has slowed, the rain a dribble not a downpour, easy to ignore as I move toward the cheap motel room I've called home for the past two months.

It's late now, the streets of this town deserted as families settle into sleep. The only sounds are the trickle of raindrops from the eaves of the old courthouse and the solitary set of footsteps behind me.

I could have predicted as much. Billy Caulfield doesn't strike me as the sort of man to willingly carry the weight of humiliation. All his kind knows are rage and retribution. So he waited outside Pete's, and now he stalks me through town, not bothering to hide the heavy clomping of his boot treads on asphalt.

"Well, if it isn't the fallen angel."

His tone is menacing. He wants to scare me, wants me to run. He's psyched himself up for the chase. Which is probably why he looks so surprised when I stop and turn to face him.

I'm in the dark, that black void that exists between the incandescent illumination of the streetlamps. He's in the light, the amber cone a spotlight shining in the strands of his hair. *The world is your stage, Billy. How are you going to act?* He stands there for a moment, dumbstruck, then comes into the darkness with me.

"You ready to continue our conversation?" he asks in a harsh whisper.

I don't answer. I don't move. I just stare, waiting.

My silence unsettles him. His whole body vibrates with anxiety, eyes darting around the darkness, nerves jumping at shadows, pulse fluttering like butterfly wings in his neck. For men like Billy, pleading is what they crave, fighting is what they know; silence just confuses them.

True to form, Billy hisses with rage when he asks, "What's your problem with men, bitch?"

Typical. He interprets an affront to him as an affront to all men.

I can predict, almost to the nanosecond, when his explosive temper will combust. He puffs up his chest like a gorilla and takes a heavy step forward, grabbing for me.

In the dark, my senses are honed, sharp. I see him coming before he makes his move. I step away, leaving him to grasp at air. We continue this—two steps forward, two steps back—and I lead him deeper into darkness, retreating inside the gaping maw of a pitch-black alleyway. Then I let him catch me.

Billy clasps his arms around me like a vise, pulls me tight against his hard chest, and chuckles in my ear. "Gotcha."

I can smell his excitement. Its rank stench seeps from his pores along with the cheap beer he's been chugging all night.

He walks me backward—I let him lead the dance this time—until I hit the wall. With me pinned, he gives a wicked grin, flashing those sharp teeth, the big bad wolf ready to devour a little girl. As if thinking the same thing, he reaches up and touches my hair, sweetly stroking it as he says, "I've always wanted to try a redhead."

He grabs a fistful of my red curls and wrenches my neck into a painful angle, exposing my throat like *he's* going to bite *me*. I laugh at the notion.

Billy frowns, confused by my reaction. He wrenches my head back harder and uses his free hand to reach for my chest, aiming to grope a breast. He's confused further to find nothing there, so he moves his hand down to the bottom of my miniskirt and gropes between my thighs.

That is his capital offense. I don't consciously decide to kill him; I simply react. My mind shuts off, and my body takes over, flush with violent energy, a base response to the desperate hunger gnawing within.

I use one hand to wrench Billy's probing fingers away with such force that a bone snaps in his arm. The man howls in agony, and the moment his grip loosens in my hair, the tables are turned. I fist my own hand in his lustrous fuck-tussled hair and wrench his head back, exposing his neck. I watch his pulse quiver, adrenaline pumping through him so fast, so warm, so delicious. I want to taste it. I *need* to taste him.

My teeth slice into the sinewy column of his throat, biting through flesh and muscle, severing veins and arteries, tearing at tendons and cartilage. I spit the chunk of his meat onto the ground and huff in the copper-tinged air. Blood arcs from his neck, bathing me in the warm spray.

I look at the mess I've made—pure carnage, shredded meat—then clamp my mouth over his gaping wound and feed. More than just feed, I *devour* him. Slurping and groaning with satisfaction, I drink him dry.

My God, he tastes exquisite—so young and virile. Despite my meal of Judith earlier, I'm ravenous, starved for the delicious elixir of his life's blood.

Billy tries to struggle against me, but his strength quickly wanes. His legs buckle beneath him, and we both fall to the hard ground at the mouth of that dark alley. I land on top, never releasing my hold, never stopping as I gorge myself.

He gurgles as he tries to breathe, tries to speak, but there are no last words for Billy; there is nothing more for him to say as silence takes him away. His eyes dart, panicked and wide, but he sees nothing as darkness closes in. With one last twitch, he goes out with a whimper, not a bang.

When Billy is empty, I wrench my mouth away, licking my lips and sucking on the tips of my fingers as I stare at the ravaged body beneath me. His pale skin is a stark contrast to the dark smears of blood that mar his once-pretty face. He still looks confused, even in death.

Well, shit. There's no debate about it now. I have to leave tonight. An exsanguinated old woman dying of cancer is one thing. But a young man found with this throat ripped out right off Main Street is another.

I stand, swaying a little, drunk on Billy's blood, then stumble out of the alley and flee. But in my post-binge delirium, I go the wrong way.

I should have gone back to my room, showered and changed, tossed all evidence of tonight—along with my remaining business cards and the SIM card from my phone—into a bag to burn later. Instead, I stand here in the shadows of an oak tree, across the street from Matthew's house.

This isn't the first time I've stood here watching, but it will be the last. One of the upstairs windows flickers blue; he's watching television. He can't sleep. He, like me, is a creature of the night. I wonder what he's watching. I wonder what it would be like to lay with him, curled against his side, watching television in bed together.

I stand there for a long time, waiting for something that will never happen, imagining a future that can never be. Then I cross the street and hurry into the shadows of the carport adjacent to his house. There I find Matthew's old pickup truck and jimmy the lock to let myself inside. It smells like him, smells like us.

I breathe in the scent as I pop off the panel under the steering column and pull out the wires I'll need. Unlike newer models with all their computer gadgets, these old trucks are a pinch to hotwire.

When the next flash of lightning signals thunder, I use the deep rumble to mask the sound as I engage the ignition, then leave the headlights off as I back out onto the road. I watch Matthew's window through the rearview mirror, but there is no flutter of the curtain. He won't know his truck is gone until morning. By then I will have cleared out. Just need to make a quick stop at the room to clean up and pack, then it's on to the interstate ten miles north of town.

I have until then to decide where I'm heading next, east or west, toward the rising sun or away. I click on Matthew's radio and fiddle with the knob until I come to a station playing George Strait. He sings about how all his exes live in Texas, so that's why he moved to Tennessee.

Hmm, I've never been to Tennessee. ♜

PRESERVATION

By Shelli Cornelison

THERE WAS A TIME WHEN I wouldn't have believed I could be comforted by the presence of blood in my closet. But traces still remain on his hunting boots, and every morning I stand and gaze at them for a while. I run my hands along his hangers, enjoy the hush of sleeves rustling as if a swift wind has blown through them. It's important to remember our departed loved ones. I will have to donate my husband's clothes soon, if for no other reason than to establish my sanity. My family is worried I am losing touch with reality, harboring a shrine in my closet. They have voiced their concerns.

"You could have a pillow made from one of his shirts," my sister said.

"There's a company that will make them into a Teddy bear," her daughter said. "They'll even insert a sound box to simulate a heartbeat. You can sleep with it so you won't miss him so much."

"You can get a blanket if you send in enough of them," my sister-in-law added.

All the women in my family had helpful ideas about how I should commission a memento. If you ask me, it's gotten out of hand, all this repurposing we do now. What need do I have for some silly plaid and denim bear? Things should be allowed to retain their original form.

The artist came highly recommended. I didn't even know you could find that kind of thing on the internet; but then again, I didn't know much about the internet at all. Apparently, there's an underside to it. The dark web, they call it.

All this technology can lead to such nefarious stuff: people looking to steal your identity, and scammers poised to swindle you out of your life savings. It's a shame the things people will resort to, the place some minds will go.

My husband always insisted hunting was not about the killing. We tell ourselves all sorts of things, our own personal brands of justification. It's not as if I begrudged him having a hobby. A life of nothing but responsibilities and routine would eventually bore even a simpleton, and my husband was smart, cunning even. He could always find a way to make things work. Our interests may have diverged over the years, but I never underestimated him. I stare into his eyes in the framed photograph in the hallway. His broad shoulders, long gun, death slumped at his feet. A god in blood-smeared boots, deciding who got to live and whose time had come.

Perhaps I should've given the artist the hunting boots when he inquired about the matter. But some things a wife just prefers to take care of herself. I've always taken joy in putting the finishing touches on projects.

The artist worked discreetly with the funeral director, a kind man, who said he could hardly fault the artist's work, not when he himself had desecrated many a corpse at the pleading of a family member. It seems the bereaved often make unorthodox requests. Skin removal to preserve a tattoo, for crying out loud! I can only imagine what one does with a piece of illustrated dead skin. To each his own. It's not for me to judge. I trace my husband's strong jawline through the glass.

I assume a portion of the hefty commission fee I submitted to the artist made its way to the congenial funeral director. Electronic transfer of funds still makes me a bit nervous. All that money floating around in space somehow. I didn't want too many details. Both men assured me everything was received and the project would be brought to fruition. I took them at their word. What more could I do? My husband always said I was too trusting. In retrospect, I suppose he knew better than anyone.

My husband was a man of many opinions. He maintained that taxidermy was a natural product of human nature. Man likes to commemorate his accomplishments, and that includes his kills, he insisted. I have a much better understanding of all that now. It's a pity, the way we often understand things after it's too late to matter. Empathy is such a puzzle, isn't it?

I am anxious to see my husband again. To gaze upon him as he must have envisioned himself: the mighty hunter and his adoring huntress. It's only fair. After of a lifetime of hard work, a man certainly deserves to have his fondest desires at his fingertips.

I adjust the thermostat down another degree. Installation of the separate cooling unit for the office was delayed until this morning. I'll have to keep the whole house a little chillier than I generally care for until it reaches the proper temperature. Fortunately, my husband left behind plenty of thick socks and cashmere cardigans. I was never one of those wives who schlepped around in her husband's oversized clothes like a child playing dress-up, but necessity begs a change sometimes. It's only temporary.

It hasn't escaped me to be thankful that the new unit arrived before the artist. Small mercies. I've encountered many since becoming a widow. Cosmic consolation prizes, small but useful.

Sasha's barking alerts me to the doorbell. It's hard to hear it back in this part of the house. Hell, it's getting harder for me to hear it at all, but I cut a quick path to the front door.

"Hello," he says. "It's me. I have your deliveries." I'm taken aback by the artist's small stature, but his long, slender fingers signify agility. I imagine certain aspects of his work do require a nimble touch.

"Welcome," I say. "Please, come in. Would you care for some coffee?

A slice of cake?"

"Thank you, but I try to make deliveries as expedient as possible. Due to the delicate nature of my art."

"Yes, yes, of course." I open the door wider and step aside.

The crates are large and, as one would expect, unmarked. How on Earth would they label such a thing, anyway?

My hands open and close involuntarily at my sides. I've never been present when an artist unveiled commissioned masterpieces before. I certainly never fancied myself becoming a patron of the arts. And of such an exclusive artistic medium, no less. Life is full of surprises.

The smell of fresh-cut wood is a sensation I didn't anticipate. It lends an unexpected nostalgia to the project. I'm not sure if it's the crates themselves I smell or if this scent has been incorporated in a way that will linger. If it fades, I think, I'll start to keep fresh shavings in the room to preserve the aesthetic wholeness of the pieces. Rugged. Woodsy. So perfectly him.

He is unpacked first. "Oh, my." I'm breathless as I take it in from various angles. The attention to detail is exquisite. "Will the stubble remain on his face?"

"You said he never shaved on a hunting trip."

"Yes. Yes, I did." It was the only thing I liked about his hunting. He always came home with a certain unkempt free-spiritedness that I found alarmingly appealing, though I never told him so because I didn't want him to take things too far and get lax in his personal hygiene. "I like it," I say. "I like it a lot."

The artist unpacks her next. "I hope you don't mind, but I employed a little artistic license with her. You didn't provide me with much in the way of direction for this piece, and I completely understand that you had no knowledge of her until the end, so I fashioned her as if she chose not to shave during their time away as well. I hope I haven't overstepped."

Oh, how I adore seeing her shapely legs all covered in coarse, dark hair. She was a beastly woman at heart and the artist has captured it beyond my wildest dreams. "You are truly a master."

My husband is positioned at his desk, seated in his high-back, leather chair, one hand curled around a crystal glass of his favorite whiskey, the other resting gently on the polished mahogany. His prized trophy elk looming overhead. As it should be. The perfection is positively staggering. And his most cherished trophy hasn't even been positioned yet.

She is seated across from him, leaning over the desk, her scrawny fingers brushing his hand, as if by accident. A recreation of how I imagine it was when they met, the day she became his client. Before she became his huntress. It's a scene to behold. The artist lifts her breasts until they are spilling from her lowcut dress and fully supported by the mahogany desktop. I experience a momentarily pang of humility on her behalf before reminding myself it's unlikely this is the first time a stranger has groped her.

In fact, this man has seen her fully, touched every inch of her. Both of these men have, actually.

I set the bloody hunting boots in the center of the desk, and persuade the artist to have a slice of the red velvet cake I baked this morning.

While the artist disposes of the packing materials, I plate the cake and turn the thermostat down another degree, just to be safe.

"The bucket from the funeral home has been kept frozen for you," he says. "I set it on your back patio. It should be fully thawed in a few hours."

"Thank you. You've handled everything beautifully."

After the artist departs, I return to the office and study the two of them on opposite sides of the desk in their eternally preserved states. I try to break down what he must have found so attractive about her. It's only then that I notice the artist has enhanced the bullet hole in the top of her head. The bloodied, matted hair around it has been cleaned and swirled into a classic design. Pin curls, I imagine. It's a flourish that warms my soul, I must say.

It had shocked me how much it had bled, but the only remaining blood seeps out a few scant inches from the entry point in her skull. It's almost pretty the way it fades to pink around the edges against her blonde hair, like a tiny, bloody rose placed with such precision. Artistic license and all that.

It was a murder-suicide, they say. Two officers came to the house to break the news to me after the gruesome discovery was made. The young one was a sensitive guy, but the older one was grizzled and jaded.

I refuted their conclusion most adamantly. In a fit of hysterics, I led the officers into our bedroom and threw open his underwear drawer. All the small holes at the seams, the stretched-out waistbands. "Do these look like the underwear of a man having an affair? Don't most people take more care with such things when they're in a new relationship?"

"Ma'am," the young one said, "I'm very sorry. I know what a shock this must be."

"Maybe it wasn't a new relationship," the older one said.

My quiet nod of acceptance ended the official visit with an appropriately subtle ego stroke. The frantic, distraught widow, subdued by the authoritative demeanor of a seasoned detective. Best to leave police business to the experts.

The most recent text messages on their phones, put everything immediately into perspective. The police had solved the case at the scene, right there in the hotel room. No need for a lengthy investigation. And with my quiet surrender to the facts, there would be no complications. Cut and dried. One for the books. Sad. So sad.

Ah, memories. They can't all be pleasant.

I'm not much of a drinker, a glass or two of chardonnay now and then, but it feels right to join the departed couple in their drink of choice on their first night back together. I raise my glass, and the chandelier casts prisms onto the rug.

"To new beginnings! Welcome home, dear."

The amber liquid burns my throat, but I have to admit, the warming sensation in my core is nice after a few minutes. I finally understand the appeal. He would be glad to know I'd developed a taste for it. It was a trait he liked in a woman, apparently. There was a half-empty bottle on the nightstand when they were found.

I wish I'd hired a photographer to commemorate this homecoming. Mementos do tend to take on more meaning as we age. I would've liked to have gotten at least a few shots, one to capture their arrival, one of our first toast. He always loved to be ballyhooed. And, well, she's still undeniably photogenic, her woolly legs aside.

His unshaven jaw is familiar against the backs of my fingers. It always amazed me how much coarser the hair felt when I stroked upward. The artist didn't skimp on a single feature. I must remember to write him a testimonial for his website. A slice of cake wasn't nearly enough gratuity for this level of skill. I'll have to come up with one of those screen names. *Hopelessly Devoted? Rose Enthusiast?*

Before I leave the lovers alone for the night, I lift one of the heavy boots from the desk, and swing it with all I've got. The hard leather toe kicks her chiseled cheekbone. It lands with more force against her chest. And then the narrow birdcage of her ribs. The first crack is subtle, but a jagged snapped-twig of bone pokes against the thin clingy fabric of her dress. She leans to one side as if trying to protect herself from the next blow. "Sit up,"

I say. "Good posture is so important for a young woman." I gently press her shoulder to straighten her in the chair, and turn my attention to my husband.

I stuff my fist down the other boot and slam the heavy tread into his perfectly stubbled jaw. A heel to the mouth splits his bottom lip, releasing a blob of cloudy gel. His twice-broken nose crunches like a corn chip. "Look at you," I say. "Breaking so easily. So weak. Such an embarrassment." I press the sole of the boot against his throat until his Adam's apple yields. His head lolls to the left like a drunkard. Well, if the boot fits.

I eye the points of impact, reposition the couple as best I can, and inspect the damage more closely. I'm pleased. Our score is far from settled. But my knuckles are sore and it's getting late.

"That's round one," I say before I toss back the last of my whiskey.

I align the boots back into formation in the center of the desk, and then turn out the lights. "I'll visit you both again tomorrow, my trophies."

The sky is mother nature's canvas tonight, streaks of tangerine slicing through the violet background, wisps of rose gold peeking out from in between—all the layers of a magnificent sunset coming to life.

I lift the bucket from the patio and head for the fence.

I'm honored to give my husband this final opportunity to feed the wildlife. Maybe some coyotes will appreciate this treat. Perhaps a bobcat will come along. If nothing else, some vultures will surely dine well. The circle of life, as he always said.

It was his wish. He'd made me promise I would ensure that his organs went to good use if he should die before me. I assume liberties in the execution of wish fulfillment go to the obligor in situations like this.

A crow caws as I hang the empty bucket on the fence.

"Feast well, my friends." I toss the lid from the bucket into the woods beyond the fence line. There will be no need to reseal it. The vessel has already served its highest purpose.

I christen the fireplace with the first flames of the season. The kettle whistles on the stovetop. My fork brings the first bite of red velvet cake to my lips, a just reward at the end of a long, hard day. The queen of my own castle, enjoying all the comforts of hearth and home.

Interrupted by footsteps in the hallway.

First one set, then two.

I take another bite of my cake, lick cream cheese frosting from the corner of my mouth, and pull his hunting rifle from the mantel. Cold steel warms in my hands, but sugar wouldn't melt in my mouth. ♜

DEATH BY SNAKE

By Jessica Lee Anderson

RAIDEN, A BALL PYTHON, GLIDED from Alona's wrist up her arm and then he slithered across her shoulder, weaving between the spaghetti straps of her tank top before settling in to cradle against her chest and neck. Alona tilted her cheek to gently press the warmth of her skin against Raiden's cool, scaled body. Some say snakes are incapable of forming relationships, of experiencing feelings or emotions, but Alona knew better. She had a remarkable gift.

Be warned, Raiden communicated.

A moment later, there was a notification on Vivarium's video and alarm panel. It was after the shop's hours, and she had no expected visitors. There were certain dealings that were never phone calls. In the security system, she caught a glimpse of a man with a muscular build. His face was turned slightly from the camera, but she could still see some of his features, like wavy, dark hair and a beard so short it was merely an extension of stubble.

Heading Raiden's warning, Alona pushed a tub and several tinctures completely out of view. Her covert projects. This man had to know about some of these secrets or else he would not be here. No one knew the totality of Alona's secrets apart from Raiden, and she was the only living one of her kind remaining who could understand him.

Alona's pulse quickened as she walked over to the door. "May I help you?" she asked the man through the door.

"I could use your skills," the man said in a deep voice. His eyes were a light blue and looked nearly as glassy as a snake's.

Alona hesitated even though she wanted to open up the door wider to get a better look. Was it possible that he had scales covering his eyes and that's why they appeared so shiny? Maybe it was his dark hair color that set them apart, especially his furrowed eyebrows. His stubbly beard outlined his strong jawline, even and clean. He looked like a model from the pages of a magazine or a tale of Roman warriors rather than someone looking for a clandestine antidote.

The man waved a stack of cash. "I'm willing to pay."

Wildlife rescues never paid in a stack of cash. Alona's shop, Vivarium, specialized in reptiles and small creatures likes scorpions among many things. She was also certified in wildlife rehabilitation, and she dedicated space in the shop to tend to rescued animals while they recovered, mainly snakes and other reptiles cast aside from the majority of society who never bothered to understand their worth. Her apartment was connected to the backside of the building, so she could frequently check on the creatures. While Alona needed to be concerned about authorities digging deeper into the dark side of Vivarium, she also needed to think about things like rent and taxes. She opened the door slowly and had to look up as the man walked inside the shop. He must've been well over six feet tall.

Vivarium had a steady enough flow of customers, and Alona remembered most everyone. She would've remembered this man had he ever been here before. He smelled like cedar chips and black coffee and seemed fit enough to stand among the elite of the ancient world. Even on the days Alona didn't work, she imagined her lone employee, Jazmyne, would've never stopped talking about someone this handsome.

Be warned, Raiden repeated.

"I've heard you can make potent antidotes."

Alona nodded, both to Raiden and to the stranger. "What antidote are you interested in?"

The man didn't answer right away but stared so intensely at her that she felt the heat rise into her cheeks. He made uncomfortably long eye contact before his eyes fell upon Raiden. Heat spread throughout her entire body.

"I heard legends of you from Xander, but you're far more beautiful than any description," the man said, his voice lower now.

Xander was one of her most loyal customers and someone Alona considered a friend, though why hadn't Xander said something to her about this? There was a protocol she required to stay in business…and out of trouble.

The man stood there awkwardly, the cash still in his hand. "That's a lovely morph. Blue-eyed Leucistic?"

Raiden buzzed against her neck though the man didn't seem to notice.

"You certainly seem to know your snakes," Alona said.

The man laughed, and if Alona hadn't already been blushing, she would've started now.

"I'm Eli Lucas, by the way. Snakes are a huge part of my life," he said, then told her how he was a herpetologist at a nearby zoo in David, Texas. "They obviously are your life as well." He looked away from Alona to study the shop, which felt small now especially compared to a zoological exhibition space. The man roamed over to see a juvenile broad-banded copperhead rescue, resting in the tank.

Alona had created a large NOT FOR SALE sign and placed a wildlife rescue logo on the tank.

"What happened here?" Eli asked.

"Human stupidity, this time in the form of a glue trap. Once he has a chance to recover a short while longer, I will release him." Alona felt like the words crashed out of her mouth at an unusual speed. She took a slow, deep breath to steady herself.

Eli moved over to look at a striped bark scorpion, another rescue from human stupidity. "When did you become interested in animals and alchemy?"

Alona took her spot behind the counter, the table and register separating them. "I'm a descendent from a long line of alchemists, though my female ancestors who fought their way into the male-dominated field never wanted to convert base metals into gold, but rather find elixirs to extend life. Turns out, they discovered how to save lives." She left out the part about how these women had the gift of telepathically communicating with animals, particularly snakes, because no one would understand. Alona herself didn't understand. "I think the word you're looking for is apothecary. That's what my family line transitioned to." There she was again, talking uncontrollably fast.

"Ahh, yes. Apothecary, not alchemy. A person selling compounds for medicinal purposes." Eli smiled, revealing white teeth with pointed canines reminiscent of fangs.

His snakelike characteristics only made him that much more attractive. As much as Alona wanted to be reckless in that moment, she traced her fingers along Raiden's spine. He had senses beyond her capabilities, and she listened to his warning. "The antidote," she said, her voice much steadier and slower now. "What are you looking for in particular?"

Eli stepped over to the counter and set the cash down. Alona noticed a white band on his left hand from where the skin remained untanned. Until recently, he must've been wearing a wedding band.

"Inland taipan. The fierce snake."

Alona felt her eyes widen. The fierce snake ranked up there as having one of the world's most venomous bites. Alona often had a variety of requests for her "medications" and antidotes much like antivenom, especially for local snakes like the coral snake. Commercial coral snake antivenom was no longer being produced, and it was hard to find places that still carried it, so her product was valuable even if these shy snakes rarely struck humans. She worked with those who handled snakes regularly, though, including vipers and even cobras. But the fierce snake, the inland taipan, was a first for her.

"Isn't this something the zoo can provide for you in case of emergency?"

"This is not related to zoo business."

Alona knew that coastal taipan venom could be substituted as an alternative, but even that would be hard to get a hold of. "Unless you're willing to pay for me to travel to Australia or can provide me direct access to an inland taipan, I will have to decline your generous offer."

The man's lips twisted into a flirtatious smile. "I've always wanted to go to Australia, and as you know, it's home to some of the deadliest snakes. I bet you would love it there."

Alona's eyes fell upon the mark of the ring on the man's left hand again.

"It's complicated. My wife left me."

Alona hadn't meant to make it so obvious. "I'm sorry," she said, not sure what else to say.

"I am, too. Your antidotes, they work?" The man seemed to lack the confidence he'd been oozing previously.

How could she rationally explain her concoctions depended on many factors including the donor snake's will and intentions? She certainly couldn't explain what had become of the importer who illegally rounded up snakes from all sorts of places including Africa, selling them in horrid conditions. His death had been ruled an accident, a careless mishandling of a cobra he attempted to import. That was only the partial truth.

Death upon him, Raiden communicated.

Alona's skin prickled as she thought back to the haunting series of events and her involvement. She hoped death wouldn't be upon Eli.

After a pause much too long, Alona spoke up. "No medication can fully be trusted, especially if you are using it for ill intent." She locked eyes with Eli as she said this, hoping to impart the seriousness of her warning.

Eli's brawny shoulders relaxed. "Xander told me you saved his life."

"He's a skilled snake handler, but he let his guard down." Alona shook her head. Xander had rescued a cottonmouth who struck when he was trying to determine the sex of the snake as it appeared gravid. The cottonmouth did in fact turn out to be a pregnant female. The antidote worked though the fang mark scars on Xander's hand would remain visible indefinitely.

Eli ran his fingers through his stubbly beard. "I can get you access to the snake at the zoo. It might be challenging because the zoo has many security cameras, but I will try."

"I never ask what my products are used for, but I have to repeat that if you're planning on using this for malice—"

Eli leaned in and whispered. "What I do, I will be doing out of love."

Raiden buzzed against her skin and slithered into a more coiled up position around her neck, though the snake didn't send any communication.

"I'll be in touch," Eli said, backing up before walking out of Vivarium, leaving the pile of cash behind him.

As soon as he left, Alona called Xander, who apologized and explained. "I should've talked to you first, but Eli seemed desperate. I am confident in his silence."

The situation made her think of a quote from Heinz Guderian: "There are no desperate situations, only desperate people."

At least Alona had cash that she planned on putting back into Vivarium and extending her rescue missions. For the next several days, the money was the only thing that kept her from thinking the entire encounter had been a hallucination. She had difficulty sleeping in the evenings, wondering how she would be able to coax the venom from a fierce snake, especially knowing none of the circumstances. It would be challenging for her to do this at the zoo if there were video cameras, and how would Eli be able to bring the snake out of the enclosure safely to Vivarium or to a different meeting place?

"Is everything okay?" Jazmyne asked as she cleaned out a cage, a beautiful corn snake who was looking for a forever home after her owner moved out of country.

"I've got a big project," she said, leaving it at that. Alona made sure her employee wasn't privy to some of Vivarium's more elusive guests and wildlife rescues.

"Like a tall, dark, and handsome project?" Jazmyne whispered when Eli walked into the shop.

"Perhaps," she said as she smiled at Eli. The less Jazmyne knew, the better. "Would you mind giving us a moment?"

Jazmyne pulled her cell phone out of her back pocket. She was always glued to that thing. She winked. "Nicely done."

Jazmyne had no idea about the apothecary side of the Vivarium, not that she hadn't been curious about the tinctures and vials from time to time. Alona had wanted to protect her from knowing too much.

Eli seemed to have not gotten much sleep the last several days. His hair was rumpled, and his beard had grown out longer. Dark rings under his eyes made them appear even more blue.

"It's nice to see you again," Alona said.

Eli's eyes were intense. Glassy. Snakelike. "You too."

Trouble. Raiden balled up tightly against her wrist, an action that gave his species the name ball python. Alona stroked Raiden's head to reassure him that she was in the control of the situation, but there was no way she could hide her slight tremor.

After confirming Jazmyne had gone into the office (and was taking pictures of herself and posting to social media), Alona moved closer to Eli. "Have you brought me the fierce snake?"

Eli laughed, his voice hoarse, though Alona was too tense in the moment to find any humor in her question, especially knowing Raiden sensed trouble. If Eli had the inland taipan with him or nearby, there could be serious consequences if it wasn't properly secured.

"No," he said. He held out a vial. "I collected the venom myself to bring it to you directly instead."

"This isn't how I work or the way the process happens!" Alona imagined the inland taipan stressed as Eli surely pinned it so it would strike the collection cup in an attempt to gather the venomous fluid.

"It was the best I could do."

"A shortcut like this could be costly. Deadly even. Have you heard the theory that water has memory? This is true with venom, and it effects the outcome of the medicines I produce." Once again, she thought of the dead snake importer.

Eli's exhausted expression stayed neutral. "I plan on being careful, and your antidote will be like insurance."

"I'll give the money back to you—"

"Please, Alona. I have a plan in place. I can get you more money if that's what it will take."

Fool.

"Money won't change the outcome. The best I can do is try, but there's no way to test out—"

"You saved Xander. I have confidence." Eli nodded, his wavy hair flopping over his eyes. Alona fought the urge to reach out and smooth his hair back. He held the vial out to her. "Please don't let it go to waste."

The snake endured much to produce the venom, and the chance of Alona coaxing it to produce more venom willingly felt next to impossible, plus it could take ages. "I'll need twenty-four hours."

"Thank you."

Alona gave Jazymne the rest of the day off as she went to work preparing the concoction using the venom, herbs, and other remedies to prevent coagulation issues and to protect the heart and the kidneys. Centuries past, some of her ancestors had been accused of witchcraft, and Alona felt like a witch now creating this serpentine brew.

Unlike scientific labs, she had no exacting machines to assess the neutralizing ability of her antidotes, but she studied instead what happened when she added her mixture to the remaining venom. Satisfied that it transformed from amber to a cloudy white like her past successes, she added drops of preservative.

Well done.

Alona had no contact information for Eli, so she sent Xander a text instead. "Please let your friend know that the package is ready for pickup."

She thought Eli might've swung by the shop that evening so she hung out a while longer, finishing up a few of the things that Jazmyne didn't get to as well as tending to her rescues. The copperhead had started moving around and got into striking position as she neared the tank.

"You're hungry. That's a great sign you're ready for release soon," she said, bringing him a tasty treat that she prepared as ethically as possible.

Alona started the day early the next morning, and Jazmyne was late to work. This worked out to her advantage as Eli showed up at eight a.m. While Alona had gotten some decent sleep finally, Eli clearly hadn't. It almost looked like he'd been punched in the nose with how dark the circles under his eyes were. Even then, he was still frighteningly handsome.

"It's ready," she said, reaching for the vial she'd specially prepared for him. She'd set inside a plain brown paper bag, the kind she used to bring on field trips as a kid. Something so simple holding something so utterly bizarre and complicated.

Raiden moved from one spaghetti strap of her tank to the next, weaving in tightly when Eli reached for paper bag. He offered her a few more hundred dollars, and though Alona refused, he set them on the counter anyways.

"Thank you again," he said, leaning forward as if to reach for her but never taking any action. "I wish things were different." Those were the last words he spoke before walking out of Vivarium.

Alona was opening up the tank to move the copperhead for release when Jazmyne burst into the shop about an hour later, holding up her phone as if it was a weapon in the middle of a hostage situation.

"It's your hot guy! The one from yesterday. He's streaming live!"

Alona raced over to see what Jazmyne was talking about. It was certainly Eli, looking even more wrecked than he had been when he'd come to the shop.

"Your boy has some problems with a woman," Jazmyne said, filling Alona in.

Eli's words sounded sharp, frenzied. "Please answer me. I'm sorry for what I've done to you. I would rather die than keep living like this."

He held up an inland taipan and allowed it to bite his finger, zooming the camera in on a trickle of blood. Tears filled his eyes. "Someone please reach Nadia so we can say our final goodbye."

Eli tried to stand up to reach something in the room. The antidote?

Before he could reach it, his eyes rolled back. He collapsed.

Alona looked away from Jazmyne's phone. She reached for her own to call Xander. "Do something!" she screamed when he picked up.

Then she called 911 to share what she'd witnessed but had no contact information to give.

In a blur, it was too late.

Alona was left to wonder if Eli had been pulling a dramatic stunt to get Nadia, presumably his wife who left him, to show up. Had he planned on murdering her by snake in this set up? Those questions would never be answered.

The only thing for Alona to do now was fight for the fierce snake to keep it from being euthanized given the cruel actions of man.

Human stupidity. What a waste. ♜

WELCOME TO MERCIFUL

By Bernadette Johnson

A BUMBLEBEE LANDED ON A purple freesia in one of the multi-colored flower beds that ran down either side of the paving stone walkway. Just past sunrise, and nature was already hard at work.

The path led to a small but well-maintained turn-of-the-century cottage with a short driveway and single car garage that appeared to have been added as an afterthought. The white wood wall slats and green shutters looked recently painted, the porch and its stone steps freshly swept. Similar homes lined the street, packed more closely together than modern zoning standards would allow, most without garages, and none that hosted such vibrant foliage.

The front door swung open, and a sensible walking shoe stepped onto the welcome mat, followed by another. Their owner wore light gray slacks and a floral blouse under a pink sweater. Her fingers bore several rings of different styles and sizes. A small jeweled cross hung from a thin silver chain around her neck. Her lips, cheeks, and eyelids all sparkled with a hint of color. A dusting of powder lay over what she called her wisdom lines. And her white neatly curled hair had been sprayed into near immobility.

"Morning, Mabel," said a man from a rocking chair on the porch next door. He sipped at his coffee.

"Morning, Harry," said Mabel with a smile and a wave as she stepped into the yard, knelt down, and fetched the paper.

"D'ya hear about Mack?" he asked.

"Ferguson? The man who runs the diner?" asked Mabel, standing back up.

"Yup," said Harry. "He passed last night. Heart attack."

"But he was so young."

"Yup. Only 47. Just goes to show, you never know when your time's up."

"I suppose not," said Mabel.

"Made terrible coffee, though," said Harry.

"It wasn't the best," agreed Mabel.

"Still," said Harry, shaking his head. "Shame."

"Yes, isn't it?"

"Hear you cracked another case."

"Oh, I just asked around town," said Mabel, with an embarrassed look. "It was the hard-working folks at our local PD who did the real work."

"You're too humble. Everyone knows you're Merciful's own Miss Marple."

"Hush, now," she said, batting the newspaper toward him. "You'll make me blush."

"You have a good day, now, Mabel."

"You, too, Harry."

Mabel walked back up the path and entered her house. She stopped at a small table just inside the door that bore a pocketbook, a vase full of yesterday's flowers, and a pen and notepad.

She grabbed the vase with her free hand, strode down the hallway to the kitchen at the back of the house, and placed the newspaper on the kitchen table.

The middle of the table was adorned with a full tea service, white ceramic with blue flowers, with a teapot, a lidded sugar bowl, a creamer, three cups and three saucers. The fourth cup and saucer set rested on the placemat nearest the newspaper, a teaspoon to the right and a strainer atop the cup.

Mabel turned to the kitchen counter, put down the vase, snatched out the wilted flora, chucked them in the bin, poured the vase's remaining contents into the sink, rinsed it, and filled it with a few inches of fresh water.

The high whine of the kettle sounded as she put the vase aside and picked up a lidded canister from which she spooned three helpings of tea leaves into the pot. She removed the screaming kettle from the stove, poured the boiling water over the leaves, put the kettle on a cold stove eye, turned off the hot one, sat down, and started reading the paper.

After a few minutes, she poured tea through the strainer into her cup, got up and shook the strained leaves in the trash, put the strainer in the sink, and returned to her paper, which she read cover to cover while taking sips of her tea.

When both were finished, she put the used dishes and utensils in the sink, took off her rings and set them aside, washed and dried everything, and blotted her hands on a towel.

She grabbed a basket from a small side table and a straw hat from a peg on the wall by the back door, donned the hat, and carried the basket out the door.

The backyard garden was more crowded than the front. Flowerbeds with clusters of similarly colored flowers in repeating patterns and greenery in between lined the yard.

She knelt next to a patch at the very back, put the basket down, took out work gloves and put them on, removed a trowel, and started pulling weeds. She placed some of them in the basket and threw others into the ivy behind the current flower bed. After a few pulls, she put the trowel away, took out a clipper, snipped a couple of choice flowers, and deposited them next to the weeds.

Halfway through the next flower bed, Mabel heard a woman's voice say, "Hello? Mrs. Clancy?" from the side of the house.

"Come into the backyard," yelled Mabel, standing up and picking up the basket. "Through the gate."

Mabel heard the gate creak open. A young woman in a burgundy knit shirt, worn jeans, and Mary Janes approached her.

"Hi," said the woman nervously. "Sorry to bother you."

"Company is never a bother," said Mabel.

"Your neighbor said you'd probably be back here."

"Old Harry. He hardly ever leaves his front porch and still manages to know everyone's business in Merciful. And your name is . . . ?"

"Janet. Janet Crane." She offered her hand, but Mabel held up the basket and clippers with her glove-clad hands.

"I'd better take these off," said Mabel, "Come inside, dear."

"Thanks, Mrs. Clancy."

"You can call me Mabel. Everyone does."

Janet followed Mabel through the back door.

"Have a seat, dear," said Mabel, motioning to the kitchen table. "I'll just be a minute."

Mabel deposited the basket on the kitchen counter, put the flowers in the vase, removed the weeds and placed them on a paper towel, took off the gloves and put them in the basket, placed the trowel and clippers in the sink, and washed and dried her hands. She picked up her rings and put them back on, grabbed the tea kettle, filled it with water, and started it heating on the stove once again.

"Do you want water while we wait for the tea?"

"No," said Janet. "I'm okay."

"You don't look okay," said Mabel. sitting down across from Janet.

"Those are some impressive rings," said Janet.

"Oh, they're mostly souvenirs from my past life," said Mabel. "Except for my poison rings," she added, wiggling her fingers.

Janet laughed.

"Are you in some sort of trouble, dear?" asked Mabel. "Strangers usually don't come to me to chitchat about my jewelry."

"Sorry," said Janet, "I'm stalling. I just don't know where to start."

"Best to start at the beginning," said Mabel, patting Janet's hand.

"I'm not even sure where that was," said Janet, sighing. "It's not me who's in trouble. It's my fiancé, Norman. Well, he's about to be. He's planning to do something . . . bad."

"How bad? Is he going to hurt someone, dear?"

"No, nothing like that."

"Well, we can be thankful for that."

"It's his job," said Janet. "He's planning to take money. Money he deposits for them weekly. But this time he's talking about taking it and skipping town."

"Have you talked to the police?"

"No. I don't want to ruin him. I thought if I could change his mind . . ."

"You might be able to do that on your own," said Mabel. "How do I fit in?"

"He gets the money today," said Janet. "If he goes through with it, maybe you can show up and ask questions. Make him think his employers might know already."

"And you think that would . . . ?"

"If he thinks you're on the case, he'll have no choice but to give up his stupid plan. Take the money to the bank tomorrow."

"I see," said Mabel. "And you think he won't get in trouble?"

"He might lose his job," said Janet. "But maybe they'll buy an excuse. He was sick, his car broke down. I don't know. Maybe you could help with that."

"You came to me thinking I would lie for you?" asked Mabel.

"I'm sorry," said Janet. "I'm just spit balling. He's put me in a terrible situation."

"It's okay, dear," said Mabel, patting her on the hand again. "I understand. This will sound harsh, but have you thought about leaving him? Letting him reap whatever he sows?"

"Yes," said Janet. "I've considered it. But even if I end up leaving, I want to help him if I can. We exchanged vows."

Mabel nodded. "So, how do you propose we spring this intervention on Norman?"

"So, you'll help me?" said Janet.

"Yes, dear. I hate to see anyone in a tight spot. And it's rare that I get to stop a crime before it happens."

"Oh, thank you," gushed Janet. "You can come to our place this afternoon, maybe at five. He leaves work at four on Fridays, and most times goes straight to the bank."

"Maybe I can say the bank sent me, worried when he didn't show up to make the deposit," said Mabel. "Might startle him less than thinking it was his employers."

"That's a great idea," said Janet with a smile. "I knew you were the right woman for the job."

"Tell me, is there any chance he could turn violent? You never know what a person will do when cornered."

"Oh, no. I know him," said Janet. "He wouldn't hurt a fly."

"Before now did you think he'd ever rob his employer?"

"Well, no," said Janet. "But I'll be there to keep the peace. And maybe you can act like you buy whatever excuse he gives. I think together we can talk him down."

"Okay," said Mabel. "If you're sure. Where is your place?"

"It's a mile or so outside of town. 101 Friendly Lane. You can just enter it in your phone map."

"Oh, I don't carry a cellphone, dear," said Mabel. "I have a landline."

Janet's eyes widened.

"I know," said Mabel with a wave of her hand. "Even my old neighbor Harry has one. He thinks I'm a crazy Luddite. I still use cash, too."

Janet gave a slight chuckle, and said, "That's okay. I can write out directions. Do you have a paper and pen?"

"Yes, dear. Back in a moment." Mabel grabbed the flower filled vase on her way, walked up the hallway to the table next to the front door, and put the vase back in its place.

Janet got up, walked into the hallway, and looked at the pictures on one wall as Mabel grabbed the pen and notepad and returned.

"Is this you and Mr. Clancy?" Janet asked about a picture of Mabel and a distinguished looking man in front of the Eiffel Tower.

Mabel looked where Janet was pointing, "Oh, no, dear. That's husband number one. Taken on our first wedding anniversary. I was Mrs. Mitchell back then."

"Paris is pretty great for the paper anniversary," said Janet. "Did you divorce?"

"No," said Mabel. "He passed. Not six months after that trip."

"Sorry," said Janet.

"It's all right," said Mabel. "Like they say, time heals all wounds."

"Not all of them," said Janet. "Husband number two?" she asked, pointing at a picture of Mabel with a different man.

"Yes," said Mabel. "*That* was Mr. Clancy."

"Was?"

"I'm afraid so," she replied. "I can't seem to keep them alive."

"I'm so sorry," said Janet.

"It's okay, dear," said Mabel. "You didn't kill them."

Mabel waved them back into the kitchen, said, "Here you go," and placed the pad and pen on the table. Janet sat and started writing.

Mabel put the teapot back in its place and set up two sets of cups, saucers, and spoons. The kettle went off as if on cue. She spooned three spoons of tea into the pot, grabbed the kettle, and poured.

The doorbell rang. Janet jumped.

"It's Grand Central Station here today," said Mabel, grabbing a third set of tea things, spooning in a little more tea, pouring in more water, and setting the kettle aside. "Finish your directions. I'll be right back."

Mabel answered the front door. A man in a dark blue suit, light blue button-down shirt, and carefully polished shoes greeted her with, "Sorry to bother you, ma'am."

"You're not bothering me, Detective Ross," said Mabel. "Come in."

"Thank you," he said, following her down the hallway.

The tea kettle whistled. "Would you like some tea?" she asked.

"Sure, if it's no trouble."

They entered the kitchen and Mabel said, "Janet, this is Detective Ross."

Janet stiffened, put the pen down, and turned over the pad.

"It's Tom," said the detective, extending a hand. "Don't worry. I'm not here on official business."

She shook his hand and said, "Janet," with a meek smile.

Mabel poured tea through the strainer into all three cups in succession, handed one to Janet and one to Tom.

"Anyone take sugar?" asked Mabel, taking the lid off the bowl.

Janet shook her head.

"Yes, please," said Tom. She spooned a little into his tea as he stirred. "That's plenty."

"Milk? I can fill the creamer."

"No, thanks," said Tom.

"That's okay," said Janet, taking a sip and wincing as she burned herself.

"Careful now," said Mabel. Then to Tom, said, "What can I do for you, detective?"

"Mr. Shepherd called us," he said.

"The drug store owner?"

"Yes. There was money missing from his cash register. And a couple of bottles of barbiturates from the pharmacy."

"I thought this wasn't police business," said Mabel.

"It's unofficial business," said Tom. "The chief would tear me a new one if he knew I was talking to you."

Mabel looked at Janet and said, "Chief Brady doesn't approve of me sticking my nose into their cases."

"No," said Tom. "And you know I don't normally come to you. But this one's a bit . . . delicate." He blew on his tea, then sipped.

Janet fidgeted with her teacup and listened, looking back and forth between Mabel and Tom as they spoke.

"Spill," said Mabel.

"Should we maybe speak . . . ?" started Tom, looking around at the exits.

"We can trust Janet to be discreet," said Mabel. "Can't we, dear?"

"Oh, of course," nodded Janet.

"I'm helping her with her own delicate situation," said Mabel.

"Nothing serious, I hope," said Tom.

Janet's mouth opened, but before any sound could escape, Mabel interjected, "Relationship troubles. Nothing that requires police intervention."

Janet gave an embarrassed smile and nod.

"Ah, well, speaking of relationship troubles," said Tom, "Mr. Shepherd's wife is . . . missing."

"That sounds an awful lot like official business," said Mabel.

"Thing is, I don't think she, the money, or the pills are really missing," said Tom. "The bartender at Skipper's saw her with a man. I'm thinking she took them and spent the night with the guy. I'm hoping to track her down. Get her to call her husband before I have to fill him in. I believe you know her."

Mabel rolled her eyes. "Yes, I know Edna. I was just there yesterday. She did say something about wanting to get away for a while." To Janet, she added, "Edna does my hair."

Back to Tom, she asked, "When did all this happen?"

"Last night," said Tom.

"And you don't think this guy could have harmed her? Buried her out in the woods? Things like that have been known to happen."

"I don't think so," said Tom. "It was Jack Brady."

"The chief's son?" said Mabel. "That would explain the pills."

"Yes," said Tom, looking down at his tea. "You see why I want to clear this up quickly."

"Spare Mr. Shepard his feelings and the chief a fresh scandal," said Mabel.

"Exactly," said Tom. "Do you have any idea where they might be? I checked his place and all his normal hangout spots."

"There's a place Edna talks about sometimes."

"Where?" said Tom, feeling his pockets for his notepad.

"I think I should go," said Mabel. "Without a police escort."

"But—" started Tom.

"You came to me for a reason. Don't want to scare them off, do you?"

"Perhaps you're right," said Tom. "You'll keep me apprised?"

"Of course, detective," said Mabel.

He finished the rest of his tea in one gulp and got up to leave. "Well, I'd better get back to the precinct. I'll see myself out. Thank you, Mabel. Nice to meet you, Janet."

Janet smiled and nodded again.

"Have a good one, Tom," said Mabel as he walked down the hall and out the front door.

Janet let out a long breath.

"Sorry about that, dear," said Mabel. "You never know who's going to show up here. You okay?"

"Police make me nervous," said Janet.

"Been in trouble with the law?"

"No. Not me."

"Finished with the directions?"

"Yes," said Janet, turning the pad back over, ripping off the top page, and handing it to Mabel.

"Thank you," said Mabel. "Well, I'd better go find Edna. Wait, I have a thought. Want to come with? We have some time before your husband comes home."

"I . . . doubt I'd be much help," said Janet.

"Doesn't hurt to have backup," said Mabel. "Even if it's just for show. Maybe we can come up with more ideas for Norman's predicament on the way."

"Okay," said Janet, standing, but not looking so sure.

"Is your car here, dear?"

"No, I took a taxi."

"Then I guess we'll take mine," said Mabel, grabbing her pocketbook from the front table and taking out her keys.

They walked out the front door and to the garage. Mabel pulled the door open manually, revealing an old brown station wagon with fake wood paneling

"You don't keep it locked?" asked Janet.

"No, dear. I don't keep anything of value in here."

"Except the car," said Janet.

"A car thief might be doing me a favor. I think I'm the only one who can get it started. I just can't justify getting a new one while it runs."

Mrs. Clancy got in the driver's side, and Janet tried the passenger side door. Unlocked, just like the garage. She got in.

"Mind if we put this at your feet?" asked Mabel, holding up her purse.

"Oh," said Janet. "No. It's fine." She grabbed it and put it on the floor.

Mabel turned the key and the engine turned over several times. "You have to hold it just right." A moment later the engine sprang to life and with a triumphant smile, Mabel said, "Here we go."

She pulled out of the garage, stopped, got out, closed the garage door, got back in, and fastened her seatbelt.

"The place looks better with the door shut," said Mabel by way of explanation.

"Where are we going?" asked Janet as they pulled away.

"Someplace shady," said Mabel.

#   #   #

They parked underneath the flickering neon Shady Grove Motel sign, which looked like it had seen a lot over the past fifty years or so, as did the single-story stucco-sided building.

"Do you really think she'll be here?" asked Janet,

"She talks about this place while she does my hair," said Mabel. "She really isn't very discreet. But that also makes her a good source of info."

"Helpful in your line of work, I guess."

"It's more of a hobby, but yes, exactly."

"Where do we start?" asked Janet.

"Ah, so you do want to help?" said Mabel.

"While I'm here, I figure . . ."

"Come on," said Mabel, grabbing her pocketbook, opening the car

119

door, and getting out. "Follow my lead."

They walked across the lot to the motel lobby.

An unkempt man in a baseball cap and worn T-shirt slouched behind the front desk, flipping through the pages of a *Penthouse* without bothering to hide it. He didn't look up until Mabel coughed.

"Mrs. Clancy," he said, sitting up straight and stuffing the magazine under the desk. "If this is about . . . you know . . . I've been keeping my nose clean. I swear."

"Don't worry, Bob. I'm not here for you."

"Oh," he said, relaxing a bit. "How can I help you then? Need a room?" He looked back and forth at the two women.

"Close," said Mabel. "I need a room *number*. Specifically, Edna and Jack's."

Bob opened his mouth, closed it, opened it again, and said, "I can't legally give you that."

"Oh, I wouldn't want you to break the law," said Mabel. "Not again. Tell you what. Book a room for my friend Janet and me. And if it just happened to be right next to a certain couple, it would be ever so helpful. We won't even mess it up."

Mabel pulled out two fifty-dollar bills, well over the daily cost, and handed it over. Bob looked at the money for a couple of seconds then pocketed it.

He pushed a clipboard toward Janet and said, "Here, fill this out. Just the name's fine." She started to write, scribbled the first couple of letters out, and finished signing. Bob pulled a red plastic keychain with a single key dangling from it out of the desk drawer and said, "Room seven."

"Thank you, Bob," said Mabel, taking the key. "Come on." She pulled Janet out of the lobby.

"So, they're in six or eight," said Janet as they walked down the line of rooms. "In theory."

"And likely in reality," said Mabel. "He was evasive. If they weren't here, he would've said so."

"How do we figure out which one?" asked Janet.

"We knock," said Mabel. "You take six. I'll take eight."

When they reached room six, Janet looked at Mabel with an uncertain look, then knocked on the door. A hairy man in a towel answered and said, "What do you want?"

Janet looked at Mabel again, who shook her head.

"Sorry," said Janet to the man. "Wrong room."

He slammed the door without a word.

"Here goes," whispered Mabel, she knocked on eight.

They heard a woman say, "See who it is first." The plea went unheeded as a man in white boxers and a black T-shirt opened the door.

"Mr. Brady," said Mabel, pushing into the room. "Edna," she said nodding to the woman under the covers of the first double bed.

"Mabel!" said Edna. "What on Earth are you doing here?"

"You know this bitch?" said Jack.

Janet stifled a laugh from the doorway, and Edna said, "Jack!"

"It's okay, Edna," said Mabel. "I'll ignore his bad manners for now. I did bust in on you two."

"Did my husband hire you?" asked Edna.

"No," said Mabel. "Let's just say there's interest in clearing this up before word gets out."

"My dad, then," said Jack, pulling on a pair of jeans. "This is none of his business."

"Not him, either," said Mabel. "But do you want to scandalize him?"

"I couldn't give two shits what happens to that jerk," said Jack.

"The apple doesn't fall too far from the tree," said Mabel. Before he could retort, Mabel said to Edna, "Your husband thinks you've been kidnapped by whoever took the money. And the drugs."

Edna looked embarrassed.

"I don't know nothing about no money," said Jack.

"I can see from your pupils that you at least know about the pills," said Mabel.

"I needed the money to get away for a while," said Edna. "It wasn't even that much. Only enough for a room for a few days."

"I don't care about the money," said Mabel, sitting down next to Edna. "Or the pills, even. But can you at least call him? Let him know you're alive? If you have to break up over the phone, so be it."

Jack stepped into a pair of shoes by the door, looked Janet up and down and said, "Who the hell are you?"

"Just Mrs. Clancy's backup."

"It's just so hard," Edna continued. "He's not interested in me anymore. I mean physically. And he's clueless how that makes me feel."

"So, clue him in," said Mabel. "Have you tried couple's counseling?"

"Oh, he wouldn't be into that," said Edna.

"He might be after this," said Janet, still in the doorway.

"Who is . . . ?" started Edna, pointing at Janet.

"A client who obliged an old lady," said Mabel.

"It doesn't matter," said Edna with a sigh. "Guess the whole town knows by now."

"Probably everyone but Mr. Shepherd," said Mabel.

"That's what I mean," said Edna. "Clueless."

"Please," said Mabel. "Just call him and let him know you're okay. If not for him, then for me. You have the police showing up at my door. And besides, who's going to do my hair if you never come back?"

"Oh, all right," said Edna. "I didn't mean to cause anyone else trouble. Least of all my best customer." She picked her phone up off the nightstand

and dialed.

"I'm out," said Jack, snatching his keys and wallet from the TV stand and pushing past Mabel, then Janet.

Mabel glared after him for a moment, then said to Janet, "We should probably go, too. Take care of your Norman situation."

"What?" said Janet. "Oh, yes. Norman."

To Edna, Mabel whispered, "Call if you need me."

Edna nodded in reply.

A millisecond later, Mabel could hear a frantic, "Hello?!? Honey?!?" from Edna's phone.

"Hello, Fred," said Edna. "No . . . no . . . I'm not telling you where . . . I'm okay . . . I know . . . Just listen for a minute . . ."

Mabel stepped out beside Janet and shut the door behind her.

"Think they're going to be okay?" asked Janet.

"Who knows?" said Mabel. "But maybe this will keep the peace for a bit. Could I borrow your phone, please? I need to fill Tom in."

"Sure," said Janet, handing over a flip phone as they walked to the car.

Mabel looked at it, and said, "I thought *I* was the only throwback."

"Oh," said Janet with an embarrassed laugh. "That's a prepaid temp. My real one is in the shop. Got it wet."

"That's too bad," said Mabel. "After the call, we'll go to your place. Wait for Norman."

Janet smiled as Mabel opened the phone and keyed in the detective's number from memory.

#   #   #

Mrs. Clancy and Janet pulled up a gravel drive and parked in front of a double-wide mobile home on a cinderblock foundation. No garage and no vehicle were present. The closest neighbor's house was just visible a ways down the road.

"This place is off the beaten path," said Mabel as she retrieved her purse. "Do you two share a car?"

"Yes," said Janet. "He's not due home for a little while."

They got out. Janet pulled a small keyring with only two keys out of her purse. She opened the door, and said, "After you."

Mabel stepped into the dingy but clean living room.

"It's not much," Janet apologized. "And I don't have tea, but I can make us both some coffee."

"Sure, dear. Coffee would be great."

After Janet walked into a nearby room that Mabel presumed was the kitchen, Mabel snooped around the living room, looking in every corner, opening and closing a couple of shelf cabinets. She found some paperwork in a drawer and held it out to read for a moment, then put it back and closed the drawer.

It hardly looked like anyone lived here. No pictures. No plants. No books or magazines. None of the bric-a-brac people tend to acquire over time. No TV, even. Just old furniture that probably came with the place.

After a few minutes, a drip coffee maker sounded from the other room, and a few minutes after that, Janet came out with two steaming cups. She handed one to Mabel.

Janet sat on the couch and Mabel took the spot next to her, causing Janet to scoot closer to the couch armrest.

"Do you have a coaster?" Mabel asked.

"Oh, no need," responded Janet, motioning to the coffee table. "It won't hurt anything."

Mabel took a sip, raised an eyebrow in surprise, and said, "Good coffee."

"It's the little things in life," said Janet, taking her own sip.

"How long have you two lived here?" asked Mabel.

"Just a year or so. A rental. I haven't done much with it."

"How do you live without television?"

Janet laughed. "I don't. There's one in the bedroom."

"How long has Norman been at his job?"

"Three years," said Janet, looking at her coffee.

"And how long have you been married?"

"Two years, give or take." Janet put her mug on the coffee table.

"No kids?"

"Heavens no."

"How'd you two meet?" asked Mabel, putting her cup down right next to Janet's, placing an elbow on the couch back, and observing her client.

"At a conference out of town," said Janet, shifting slightly away from Mabel and facing the front door. "In a hotel where I was working."

"Was it a long engagement?"

"No. We married after two months."

"Church wedding?"

"Justice of the Peace."

"So, you'd never seen our quaint little town until then?"

"No," said Janet with a slight nod of her head. She looked at the door.

Mabel picked up Janet's cup, proffered it to her, and said, "I can see I'm taxing you. Let's fuel up for the confrontation to come."

Janet glanced at her with a crinkled brow, looked at the cup, took it, and drank.

Mabel picked up her own cup and followed suit, then patted Janet on the hand, and said, "We can just wait for Norman for a while."

They finished their coffee in silence except for the occasional slurp.

"Now," said Mabel, putting her empty cup down. "Why don't you tell me why I'm really here?"

"What?" said Janet, "For . . . Norm—"

"The imaginary husband?"

"He's not—" started Janet. Her expression went blank, cold. She looked Mabel in the eye and asked, "How'd you know?"

"For one, you're showing signs of lying. Different for everyone. But you haven't looked me in the eye much while answering my questions. Your answers have been devoid of detail. You turned to face the nearest escape route. And you nodded when answering in the negative."

"What else?"

"Your whole story. Skipping town with a stolen deposit. The names Janet and Crane. Brought to mind that Janet Leigh played Marion Crane, a character who did just that. And the pièce de résistance, Norman, who wouldn't hurt a fly. Did you watch *Psycho* recently?"

"I did, actually," said Janet, reddening a bit and putting her cup down.

"You have good taste in movies. But a career criminal you're not," said Mabel. "Unlike your father."

"What?" said Janet, eyes widening, breath leaving her.

"You're Zoe Jacobs," said Mabel. "Daughter of Ted Jacobs."

"You remember him," said Zoe.

"Yes," said Mabel. "He was tall, handsome. And an embezzler. From his dear old boss of ten years, Mr. Simons."

"Do you have any idea what you did?" asked Zoe.

"I helped catch a guilty man."

"My mom was a broken woman after that. She didn't deserve the shame, the financial ruin."

"I don't doubt that, dear," said Mabel. "And I felt a sort of pity for you and your mother."

"Not enough to just let it slide?"

"Your father would've been found out eventually. He didn't cover his tracks all that well."

"We were going to leave the night he disappeared. The suitcases were in the car already. Mom waited all night. Obsessively looking at the door and at her watch. She thought he must have been arrested. But the next day, the cops came looking for him."

"That must have been tough, dear," said Mabel.

"And that's when we found out that the nice woman who had come by the day before and talked to us, and then to dad privately, was actually a sleuth working for the police."

"Not for the police," corrected Mabel. "For Mr. Simons. He was shocked, and hurt. He trusted your father and didn't want it to be true. He sent me ahead of the police to find out. See if it was some sort of misunderstanding, which I could tell from Mr. Jacobs's reaction wasn't the case."

"You showing up tipped him off, and he ran," said Zoe. "He left us there."

Mabel pursed her lips and shook her head.

"Wait," said Zoe. "I was a child when you saw me. There's no way

129

you'd recognize me now. How . . . ?"

"I kept tabs on you and your mother. Found out where you landed. Where she got a job. Where you enrolled in school. I have friends on the force and in the PI world who are quite helpful when they think I'm on a case. It's been even easier since the advent of social media. People really do put too much of themselves out there. It's a treasure trove for someone like me."

"How'd you do all that without a smartphone or computer?"

"Oh, I have a laptop at home. And I use library computers, and other peoples' phones from time to time."

"I thought you—"

"I don't carry a cellphone because I don't like to be traced," said Mabel.

"Same with the cash?" said Zoe.

"Yes. Use plastic and you leave a trail," said Mabel. "Pay cash and there's no record. Except for security cameras and eyewitnesses. But still, it provides a level of privacy."

"You knew the whole time we weren't doing well," said Zoe.

"Yes."

"And you didn't step in to help." Zoe's expression hardened.

"Wasn't my place, dear," said Mabel.

"Do you know about Mom?" asked Zoe.

"Yes, dear," said Mabel. "My sincere condolences for your recent loss."

"You ruined our lives," said Zoe. She leaned down, reached into her purse, pulled out a handgun, and pointed it at Mabel. "And she killed herself."

"Your father shares much of the blame," said Mabel, unshaken.

"Shut up! He was a good dad. A good husband to Mom. He was just trying to give us a better life."

"Through theft?" said Mabel. "There are less risky ways to do that. He was drawing a decent paycheck. And you were probably too young to notice, but I doubt you or your mother's life improved much during that time. Do you want to know what he needed the money for?"

"It was for us."

"No, it wasn't."

"He was talking about moving us to a better place."

"There is no better place than Merciful," said Mabel with a smile. "For me, anyway. But your father *was* rather fond of Shady Grove."

"Shady Grove?"

"Especially the motel," said Mabel. "You know the place."

"What about it?"

"That's where he took his piece on the side."

"You lie!" shouted Zoe.

"Not very original, of course," said Mabel, shaking her head. "But kind of a tradition with Merciful's philanderers."

"I don't believe you," said Zoe, her gun hand shaking.

"She was Mr. Simons' secretary," said Mabel. "Also not very original."

"He couldn't have," said Zoe.

"What reason do I have to mislead you?"

"You took me there?" asked Zoe. "Why?"

"Oh, it was just dumb luck that Tom showed up and that that's where we had to go to find Edna. She's not too original, either," said Mabel. "But since I was going there anyway, I figured I could use the trip to find out what you knew."

"I hardly said anything," said Zoe.

"Your actions did most of the talking. You didn't react to the location, so I figured you didn't know about your father's extracurricular activities. But that wasn't the important bit. It was you getting in the car with me in the first place that told me all I needed to know."

"What did that tell you?"

"That you didn't know enough about me."

"Get up," said Zoe, standing and stepping to the side of the couch. "Go to the door. We're going for a drive."

"Whatever you say, dear." Mabel grabbed her purse, stood, calmly walked past the coffee table, went to the front door, opened it, and stepped out.

Zoe followed, and said, "You drive."

Mabel obliged, got into the driver's seat, and put her pocketbook on the floor again as Zoe got in.

"You don't need yours?" asked Mabel.

"We're not going far," said Zoe.

Mabel started the car and said, "Where to, dear?"

"Go that way," said Zoe, motioning down the street with her left hand while keeping the gun leveled on Mabel with her right.

Mabel backed onto the road and took the car in the direction indicated.

"Where are we going, dear?"

"Someplace secluded."

"The little dirt track past the old barn that leads into the woods?" asked Mabel.

"How'd you . . . ?"

"Good place to murder someone," said Mabel. "Did you do any prep?"

"I dug a grave," said Zoe. "Off the trail in the woods."

"How are you going to get back?" asked Mabel. "My car would be a little conspicuous."

"Mine's parked off the trail already."

"Ah, so you do have a car. And a plan."

"Since Mom died, it's all I've thought about."

"You should really take up a hobby," said Mabel. "Maybe knitting."

"Why are you so calm?" asked Zoe.

"You're not going to kill me," said Mabel.

"You don't think I have it in me?"

"You might," said Mabel. "You're fixated enough on this blame idea.

But you're not going to make it to the secluded spot. Maybe not even to the old barn."

"What do you mean?"

Zoe squinted and rubbed the spot between her eyes.

"Feeling okay, dear?" asked Mabel.

"What? I'm fine."

"You don't look fine."

"You should be worried about yourself," said Zoe.

"And you should have paid closer attention to your coffee," said Mabel.

"What?" Zoe shook her head. It was getting hard for her to keep her eyes open. "What did you . . . ?"

Zoe's right arm fell to her lap and the gun bounced to the floor.

Mabel slowed down, turned the car around on a side road, and started back the way they had come.

"It really is lovely out here this time of year," said Mabel.

Zoe tried to shake herself awake, but to no avail. As the seconds ticked by, it got harder and harder for her to move or speak.

"Where . . . ?" said Zoe.

"Home," replied Mabel.

Zoe noticed the cheerful *Welcome to Merciful* sign as her head slumped to the right and thudded against the window.

#   #   #

Zoe opened her eyes. When they adjusted, she looked around at what seemed to be a sort of warehouse with cinderblock walls and a concrete floor. She was in a chair in the middle of the floor. To the left she saw rows of shelves of canned and boxed goods. To the right, a couch faced a small table against the front wall with an old television on it. A wire ran from the TV's antenna to the ceiling. A few feet behind the couch was a small door.

A tarp lay underfoot. She sat across from two shelves that held lots of small items she couldn't quite make out.

Between those shelves and the food shelves she noticed a stairway. She tried to stand, but wrist and ankle restraints that affixed her to the heavy chair stopped her. She struggled against them for a moment.

"Help!" shouted Zoe.

"Pardon my absence," said Mabel from somewhere behind. "Had to go to the ladies."

Zoe looked back and saw Mabel coming from the direction of the now open door.

Zoe faced forward again and screamed, "Aaaagggghhhhhhhh!"

"There's no point screaming, dear."

"Aaaagggggghhhhhhhhhhh!" shrieked Zoe, louder this time.

"Suit yourself," said Mabel.

"Where am I?" yelled Zoe, tugging against her restraints.

"I told you," said Mabel. "Home."

"This is your basement?" said Zoe. "It's bigger than the house."

"Oh, no," said Mabel. "We're not at the house."

"You said . . ."

"I said home."

"A second home?" said Zoe.

"More of an underground bomb shelter. Just inside the town line," said Mabel. "Built by a paranoid gentleman decades ago. Mr. Lambert. He didn't get permits or tell anyone official that it existed. Water's from a well he dug himself. Electricity's provided by a gas-powered generator in a little room that vents to the surface. Perfect, really. He shouldn't have confided in me, of course. And really, I think of the *other* place as my second home."

"You live here?" asked Zoe.

"No, it's not that sort of home," said Mabel. "I sleep at the cottage. But this is where I *feel* at home. The place I get to be me."

"And who are you?" asked Zoe.

"According to you, the person who ruined your life."

"You . . . ," said Zoe. "You poisoned me?"

"Drugged, dear, not poisoned. I *poisoned* Mr. Ferguson."

Zoe's eyes widened, "The . . . the diner guy?"

"He was a sad little man who made a sad cup of coffee, which, unfortunately for him, he also drank."

"You killed a man over coffee?"

"It was truly vile," said Mabel matter-of-factly. "A town is like a garden. To keep it healthy, sometimes you have to pull a few weeds."

"How . . . how many people have you killed?"

"Oh, I've lost count over the years. I'd have to go through my trophies."

"Trophies?"

"Yes, dear," said Mabel, motioning to the shelves with the small items. "I keep a little knickknack from each one."

"All those people," said Zoe. "How can you . . . how do people here not notice?"

"Some are from my time *before* here. Starting with husband number one," said Mabel, picking a man's wedding band off the top of the left-hand shelf and putting it back. "And I mix up the methods. Sometimes I use a poison that causes a heart attack and dissipates before autopsy time. They might not even check for anything if a person is old enough. Sometimes I drug people, turn on their gas, and they die of asphyxiation. And you'd be surprised how many house fires the Merciful fire department responds to. Often too late, of course."

Zoe just stared at her.

"And some special cases I bring here," continued Mabel. "Hold on a sec." She walked over to the second shelf, grabbed something off the middle, and returned dangling a small shiny object on a chain before Zoe's eyes.

"That's . . ."

"A Saint Christopher medal," said Mabel. "Your father's. Not that it did him a lot of good."

"What?" said Zoe, the breath leaving her lungs and the color draining from her face.

"Like you, your father blamed me for his troubles," said Mabel, replacing the trophy.

"What . . . what did . . . ?" Zoe stammered, tears forming.

"He came to my house in the middle of the night. Caught him tearing up my backyard flower beds. I got him to calm down. Offered him a cup of tea."

"Tea," said Zoe.

"Yes. Who won't take a cup of tea from a sweet little old lady? Although I was more a sweet little middle-aged lady at the time, I suppose."

"You poisoned him. Like that Ferguson guy."

"I drugged him. Like you. Wouldn't do to have him die in my house."

"Then?"

"I got him into his car," said Mabel. "He could still walk, sort of. The dose was low. I drove him out here. Put him right where you're sitting. Kind of a nice symmetry to it."

"What did you do to him?"

"Put him out of his misery."

Zoe looked at the shelf holding her dad's medal.

"Had to walk home before sunup," Mabel continued. "Came back later with the car to clean up. It was a mess."

"Why'd you kill him?" asked Zoe, looking at Mabel again. "Why not just let him get arrested?"

"It took me years to get the roses to that level. I couldn't let that slide."

"Roses," said Zoe in disbelief, "Coffee."

"Like you said, it's the little things in life."

"Dad didn't abandon us," said Zoe.

"No, dear. And if it makes you feel any better, turns out you were right. It *was* my fault. Just not how you thought."

"Where . . . where is he?" asked Zoe, looking at Mabel.

"Buried," said Mabel. "In the woods not too far from the shelter. Still on Mr. Lambert's property.

"And Mr. Lambert?"

"Not too far from your father."

"All those cases you solved," said Zoe. "You killed them all?"

"No, dear. That would be *crazy*," said Mabel. "I really am good at finding clues and making deductions. And I read up on all things criminology every chance I get. Comes in handy. Plus, this is a gossipy little town. It's not hard to get people to flip on their neighbors. I help the police tidy the town. And lead them astray when I need to, of course."

"How'd you drug me?"

"The poison rings," said Mabel. "You thought I was kidding about that. I carry a little something in each, one for sleep, and one for the big sleep. Just tipped the former into your cup when you weren't looking."

"What are you going to do to me?"

"What I did to your father," said Mabel. "And I must say you made it easy on me. You rented your place under an assumed name. You carry a burner phone. And I'd be willing to bet the car in the woods isn't in your name."

"I paid cash," said Zoe, stricken.

"And didn't change the tag or title so no one could trace you? Smart. Under normal circumstances."

"Don't do this," said Zoe.

"I understand your effort and your rage, as misdirected as they are," said Mabel, taking a knife off the shelf. "In some ways, you remind me of a young me."

"I'll leave. Never come back. Never tell anyone."

"I'm afraid not, dear," said Mabel, prying a ring off Zoe's finger. "I haven't flown under the radar this long by showing mercy."

"Let me the fuck out of here!" screamed Zoe, tugging at her restraints again.

"Language, dear," Mabel said as she flicked the knife across Zoe's throat, dropped it onto the tarp, and stepped back.

Blood flowed and spurted, soaking Zoe and dripping onto the tarp. As Zoe struggled to hold on to life, Mabel walked to the shelf and put the ring next to Ted Jacobs's medal.

She then took Zoe's phone out of her pocket and dialed.

"Hello. Can you connect me to Shepherd's Drug Store? . . . Thank you."

Zoe tried to make a noise. Alert the person on the other line that something was wrong. But it came out as a weak moan and gurgle.

After a pause, Mabel said, in a different accent, "Mr. Shepherd? I thought you might want to know where your wife is . . . Shady Grove Motel. Room eight . . . Just an interested party." She listened to him for a moment, then hung up.

Mabel looked at Zoe and said, "Now that Mr. Shepherd's whereabouts are in flux, time to pay a visit to a certain rude chief's son. Really, I'll be doing Edna two favors."

Zoe's head slumped down onto her blood-soaked chest. Her struggle, and her breathing, ceased.

Mabel picked up and put on a pair of gloves, grabbed a large pipe wrench, looked back at Zoe and said, "No time to dilly dally. I'll clean up later."

She walked up the small set of stairs, flung open a trap door, and exited.

#   #   #

Mrs. Clancy walked out between the rows of flowers and grabbed the morning paper from the end of the walkway. Harry was on his porch as usual, sipping his coffee.

"Morning, Mabel."

"Morning, Harry."

"Did you hear about Jack Brady? Dead."

"Oh, my God," said Mabel. "How?"

"I'm up on you twice in one week," said Harry with a satisfied smile. "Found behind Skipper's with his head bashed in."

"Poor Chief Brady. I hope they find whoever did it."

"Police think it was Mr. Shepherd."

"No!" said Mabel. "I can't believe that. He's such a nice man."

"Just goes to show," he said. "You never can tell what a person's capable of."

"I suppose not."

"You have a good day, now, Mabel."

"You, too, Harry," she said with a sweet smile. ♜

POKER

By S. de Freitas

SARAH DONNER DESPERATELY WANTED HER night to be anything but normal.

She had claimed the seat in the corner of the bar; far enough to not be disturbed by the cliques laughing about office politics over margaritas, but close enough to feel the pulse of the band. They weren't bad, better than most bands Sarah had heard in the many hotel bars she knew well. A local group called Pussyfooting; all women except the drummer, but Sarah guessed he was just filling in for the night. He kept looking at his band mates like he couldn't believe his luck.

Their classic rock, with a bit of punk thrown in, fit Sarah's mood, and the way the women were pounding across the small stage, was a salve to Sarah's need to just sit still. She could sip her Femme Fatale while letting out her extra energy vicariously through them.

It had been another long day. The women doctors dismissing her; the male doctors giving her too much attention. She had given her pitch twenty-nine times, handed out thirty-eight boxes of samples, and broken one nail when the wheel of her sample case tripped on a prescription pad someone had left on the floor. Hopefully it was worth it and she was heading for a decent month of commissions. She sure had sucked up enough.

But she was done worrying about that for today. She'd be leaving—where was she again?—in the morning. Onto the next town and the next doctors; she'd have to check her schedule for where. Tonight, Sarah wanted to relax. A cocktail or two before she'd grab a vending machine snack for dinner and call it a night.

She closed her eyes, ignored the talking around her and felt the music boom boom boom through her body.

"They're great." The voice was deep. A man. But also tentative. He was anxious.

Sarah opened her eyes. The man had squeezed himself into the small space between her stool and a stool occupied by a leggy blonde. He probably preferred the blonde, but she was with her pack and Sarah was alone. Easier prey.

"The band, I mean," the man clarified. He wasn't bad looking. Icy blue eyes, beckoning to Sarah from beneath long mousey bangs. His suit jacket had been left on a chair, or perhaps up in his hotel room, but he'd kept the tie, pointing down, just loosened it around his neck a tad. He wanted to portray business and pleasure.

"Mmmm." Sarah's lips didn't part for him, but she allowed a small nod of agreement.

The man glanced at the stage, where the singer was waving her long red hair in circles. He tapped his shoe loudly to the beat, rapped his fingertips on the bar.

Sarah could taste his nervous anticipation of what this night would bring.

She wasn't about to give him security.

She downed the last of her Femme Fatale, relishing the warmth of the vodka, the bite of the martini bitter and lemon, and the sweetness of the lychee juice and raspberry puree. She could never decide what she liked best about this cocktail: its taste, its sunset coloring, or the way it made her feel. Whatever it was, she was ready for more.

She gave the bartender a wave, and the man leaned even closer. "I'll get it," he said, slapping a worn twenty-dollar bill on the bar before she could protest.

Sarah lifted the corner of her eyebrow. She had wanted an un-normal night.

"What is this drink? It looks good." Too much enthusiasm dripped from the man's words. "I'll have one too." He tossed his last line to the bartender.

Sarah bopped her head to the music, and the man followed with the heel of his hand on the bar, anything to break through the awkward silence. Until, finally, two tattooed arms dropped the tumblers in front of them and swiped up the money.

"We should make a toast," the man said, holding up his glass.

"Oh really? To what?" He was trying awfully hard. Sarah thought she should throw him a bone.

The man smiled slyly. "Actually, I'm kind of celebrating. I made a big sale today. So how about a toast to Pierce Plumbing Supplies? Thanks to them, I'm going to make my quarterly quota."

A fellow salesman. Sarah knew that life. It didn't matter whether you were shilling pills or pipes, the dance was the same. She lifted her glass in solidarity. "To Pierce." The Femme Fatale slid down her throat with ease.

The man gave Sarah a grin, then a hand. "I'm Joseph, by the way. Joe to my friends."

"Good to meet you, Joe?" She left the end a question to give the man, Joe, the opportunity to say she wasn't a friend. But he smiled and didn't correct her. Of course, he didn't.

She wondered whether she should tell him her name, how far she should let this go. He was staring at her expectantly. She exhaled. Fine. "My name's Sarah."

Sarah wasn't sure if it was the boom boom boom of the music, the warmth of the liquor or the icy blue eyes of Joe, but the next few hours passed by quickly. Before she knew it, the tables around them had cleared out and even the leggy blonde had left with her pack.

The bartender's tattooed hands cleared away the empty tumblers, a clear sign that she was ready to go.

"This has been fun, Joe," Sarah said. And it had. They'd swapped sales-on-the-road stories, and Joe had even turned out to be funny. Bonus. "I should get going. Got an early morning."

She slid off her stool. Her stiletto buckled, making her trip, but Joe caught her, one hand on her wrist, the other on her waist. He was strong, his touch firm but gentle.

"I don't know how you women wear those things," he said with a light laugh.

"Me neither," she agreed. "Or why. But I can tell you my sales go down when I wear flats." A fact she hated but had accepted as reality.

"That's not fair at all," Joe said. He slid his hand down to hers, hot fingers entwining as he helped her steady herself.

"Nope," Sarah said, "but it's as you said, you do whatever it takes to get the sale, right?" She smiled at him. He didn't have boobs to be stared at and could wear comfortable shoes, but he knew at least some of what her job entailed.

As Sarah stood, the room spun into a kaleidoscope around her. She swayed, and Joe's hands tightened.

"Woof, those drinks were strong," she said.

Joe chuckled. "I'm feeling them too."

Sarah waved a hand, trying to show that she was okay, but her fingertips slapped the edge of the bar. "Ouch! Actually, I just realized I didn't have anything to eat tonight. I had planned to have one drink while I listened to the band, then walk back to my hotel and grab something from their vending machines." She stared at the icy blue eyes. "But then you came along and ruined my plans."

"I won't apologize for that. I just couldn't resist talking to you." He smiled. "Let me make it up to you. The restaurant here is closed now, but my room is just down the hall on the first floor and we can order whatever you want. My company gives me a big expense account, and after the sale I closed today, they won't care if I order the whole menu."

Sarah narrowed her eyes.

"No strings attached," Joe said, lifting his hands away from her as though that proved his intentions. He wriggled his fingers in the air, like he was trying to emphasis his hands-off offer.

And that's when Sarah noticed it.

A thin tan line on his wedding finger. Could be an old tan. He could be divorced. Except for the indent where the skin missed the ring that normally lived there.

Sarah sighed inwardly. She had wanted an abnormal night. But then again, she was hungry…

She swayed a little, then slid back onto the safety of the stool. "I do need to eat." Her words couldn't disguise the slur within them.

"Perfect," Joe said, his icy blue eyes twinkling. "We'll order appetizers, big entrees, dessert. You name it. Let's go."

He had been right, his room was just down the hall. It was also twice the size of Sarah's. His big expense budget must extend to the room too. As well as a king-size bed, the room had a desk, chair, and large TV sitting on top of a wide dresser.

"You take the bed," Joe said, guiding her onto the crisp white comforter, then flipping off his shoes. "I'll be fine on the chair. What do you want to eat?" He opened the thick room service menu on the desk and thumbed through the pages as Sarah kicked off her stilettos. His eyes flicked to them as they gave a thud thud when they hit the floor.

"I'm easy," Sarah said, leaning back on the bed. It was more comfortable than the one in her hotel room down the street. "I eat everything."

"Perfect," Joe said, then into the phone, "Let's get the Angels on Horseback for two to start. Steaks with grilled asparagus. Rare. And for dessert, the warm chocolate lava cake. That has a topping, right?"

His voice got lower and lower with each item he ordered, but Sarah could hear and everything sounded fine.

"Yes, that too," he said. "Ummm, whatever you recommend."

He hung up the phone and turned to Sarah. "This will be a meal you'll never forget."

She smiled. "I'm sure it will be."

The knock on the door came about twenty minutes of sales talk later. The waiter was older, glancing at them like he'd seen everything before as he pushed the cart to the center of the room. Sarah noted a bottle of wine and glasses had made it onto the menu.

Joe made a show of getting his wallet and passing a ten-dollar bill to the waiter like it was a prize. Then he hurried the waiter out and shut the door firmly behind him.

Sarah heard the deadbolt click.

"You have to try these Angels on Horseback." Joe clapped his hands over the dinner cart as though he had cooked every morsel himself. "They're bacon-wrapped oysters with aged balsamic. I have them every time I'm here." He picked one up and brought it to Sarah's lips.

She gazed at his icy blue eyes then parted her lips so he could slip the roll inside. He watched her expectantly.

"Mmmm." The approval reverberated from her throat as she swallowed the salty and smooth goodness. "Another," she said, sitting up. And Joe obliged.

"It pairs beautifully with this merlot." Joe didn't look at her as he grabbed the bottle and poured two glasses.

"I've really had enough," Sarah said, knowing full well she was going to drink a glass… or two.

"You can't eat a meal this good without wine," Joe said, handing her a glass. "And besides, you're eating now. It'll soak up all the alcohol."

"Sounds like good logic to me," Sarah said, taking the glass then her first sip.

Before long, they were both lounging on the bed, dishes spread out between them and small talk disappearing faster than the lava cakes.

Sarah allowed the conversation to turn from giggling glee to a pregnant silence, and as she expected, Joe filled it quickly.

"You play poker?"

Sarah shook her head, letting her dark curls fall coquettishly in front of her eyes. "I'm terrible at cards." She took a long sip of wine. "But you could teach me to be better."

Joe's icy blue eyes twinkled. "I can do that."

He scurried to the briefcase on the desk, clicked it open and pulled out a worn pack of cards. Sarah raised an eyebrow. He had done this before. But, of course he had.

"What should we bet with?" he asked, as though he didn't already have something in mind.

Sarah shrugged, letting the shoulder of her blouse fall a little down her arm. "We're all out of oysters."

The icy blue eyes surveyed the landscape of the hotel room, trying not to focus too long on the curve of Sarah's neck. "Hmmm," he said, then his eyes lit up. "We could play for clothes."

"Strip Poker?"

"It's okay. I'll be helping you. The betting is just for fun." He grinned. "I tell you what, I'll even give you a head start."

His fingers fumbled with the buttons of his shirt until they were all undone, then he peeled away the fabric like he was peeling off his work skin.

Sarah appraised his bare chest. He had a little fat on him, but only enough to make him not look like a Ken doll. His pectoral muscles were broad and smooth, abs pulled in tight, and arms swollen in all the right places.

Joe tossed his shirt on the desk, his biceps flexing, then lay five cards in front of Sarah and five in front of himself, face down.

Sarah stared at the intricate red design on the back of the cards, innocent enough at first glance, until you looked closer and caught the naked women sitting like models in the corners—and the tiny symbols they were holding that told a trained eye what's on the other side.

"So you have to get a flash or blackjack or something, right?" Sarah sat up, downing more wine.

Joe's chuckle rumbled low out of his throat, as though he was laughing at more than her naiveté. "Something like that. Pick up your cards, but don't show me. You don't want me to have an advantage, right?"

He winked. Sarah pulled her shoes back on with a thin smile. "Definitely not," she said, her voice feigning shock.

"You can swap up to three cards to make your best hand." Joe placed the rest of the deck on the bed between them, then rattled off the different types of winning hands as quickly as an auctioneer announced cracks he wanted bidders to ignore. Yeah, he really wanted her to do her best.

Sarah took in her 10 of clubs, ace of spades, 2 of diamonds, jack of clubs and king of diamonds. She had a good hand.

Joe must've noticed. His icy blue eyes narrowed slightly, but he spread out a quick smile as he looked back up at her.

"Hmmm." Sarah downed the last of her wine, then Joe immediately topped up her glass. "I can swap up to three, right?"

"Yep." He nodded, pushing the glass back into her hand.

"Okay." She swayed a bit, but pulled the ace, king and 2 out of her hand, laying them face up on the bed.

The corner of Joe's lips twitched at her choices, then he quickly turned her cards over as though protecting their modesty. "You don't want to show me these either," he said, pointing at the deck for her to claim three new ones.

When they'd both done their swaps, Joe said, "And now we see who wins," then placed his cards proudly in front of him: 6 of diamonds and four 9s.

Sarah shook her head. "I don't think I did well at all."

"Let's see." Joe lifted his voice to make it appear surprised.

Sarah showed him her 10 of spades, jack of spades, 3 of hearts, queen of spades and 4 of diamonds. "I was going for the same suit thing."

"A great try," Joe said, with a little too much encouragement.

Sarah sighed. "I guess you get to tell me what to take off now."

The icy blue eyes grazed over her body as Joe tidied the cards for the next round. "Let's start small. How about one of your shoes?"

Sarah gave him a side-eye look that whispered a thank you, but she didn't miss the hunger in his eyes as she slipped her toes out of her heels and let the shoe drop to the floor.

Five hands and another glass of wine later, Sarah had lost her other shoe, her watch, her bracelet, her skirt and her blouse. She sat in front of Joe's covetous eyes wearing only her gold earrings, red panties and black bra.

"I'm not very good at this," Sarah said, with a short laugh, one arm draped protectively over her stomach as though it could hide her whole body.

"That last hand was so close," Joe said, still only his chest bare. "You'll get the next one. I'm sure of it."

And magically he predicted right. Sarah watched the tell-tale design on the back of the cards and knew before she picked them up that he had dealt her almost a straight flush. She only needed an 8 of hearts.

He wanted her to win this hand.

He wanted her to think she had a chance.

He didn't want her to give up and go home.

Yes, Sarah, thought. Maybe it was time she won. Her eyes were hungry too, after all.

She gathered up the cards, showing him her smile, then showing him how she tried to hide her smile.

He smiled too. His cards were duds, but Sarah knew he didn't care.

It was Joe's turn to swap cards first, and he swapped two, giving him nothing.

But now, the card lying on top of the deck, waiting for Sarah to claim it, was that 8 of hearts. Yeah, Joe was good. He was practiced.

But so was Sarah.

She slid the card into her hand and gave a little jump of glee, catching Joe's eyes on her bouncing breasts. She had to keep him interested too.

"I think I got one," she said, doing her reveal.

"Wow." Joe dumped his cards out, shoulders making a show of deflating for his loss. "That's a fantastic hand. You're getting good at this. So, what do you want me to take off?"

His act of disappointment was over. His lips were pulled into an excited smirk. He wondered if she was ready to stop the game—this pretense—and move on to the real fun of the night.

But Sarah knew she had to take it slow too. She didn't want to scare him off too quickly either.

"Ummm." She sipped her wine delicately, her eyes browsing his body, then she pointed at his sock. "Like you said, it's best to start slow."

He pulled the sock off with a relish, swung it over his head like he was on a stage, then let it fly into the blinds across the room. She gave him a giggle, letting him know the game was on.

He just didn't know yet which game she was playing.

Sarah watched his face carefully as he dealt the next hand. She knew it wouldn't be in her favor, but that didn't matter. She saw the twitch of his cheek. His small frown. The wriggle of his bare toes.

"You okay?" she asked, downing more wine.

He shrugged. "Sure! My toes are just cold I guess."

"It is chilly in here." Sarah leaned her chest forward, showing him her own proof.

He smiled in approval. "But I like cold."

"Good," she answered, and picked up her cards.

Joe was going in for the kill now. His icy blue eyes rested on the round cups of her bra. With his next win, there would be no pretense of protecting her, no asking her to take off her earrings. He was ready for business.

And his smirk showed it when he laid down his full house.

Sarah almost felt sorry for him when she turned over her four 7s. His face contorted in confusion, but investigating how she'd got those cards would give away his own secret.

"You won again! I told you you're getting good at this."

"Your other sock, please." Sarah's voice was silky smooth, and the glint in Joe's eyes told her he liked that she was enjoying her part of the game. This time, though, he whipped the sock off without ceremony and dealt the next hand.

His icy blue eyes were hungrier still when he laid down four kings, but they fell when, with a giggle, Sarah turned over her four aces.

"How—" Joe began, but didn't finish. Perhaps because he knew he couldn't give away what he knew. Or perhaps because his feet needed attention. He rubbed the skin, the toes, the heels.

"Everything all right?" Sarah asked, as she gathered up the cards for him.

"My feet feel like they're burning."

"That's too bad. You want to stop?"

The icy blue eyes glanced at her, at her bra, and he quickly shook his head. "No, they'll be okay. I'll deal." He put out his hands for the deck. He wanted to win this time, to break past her barrier. He needed the control.

And he was a master. He dealt himself a winner first time. His face was alight with anticipation as he plopped down his 3 of diamonds, 4 of diamonds, 5 of diamonds, 6 of diamonds and 7 of diamonds. "A straight flush. Too lucky."

"Very lucky," Sarah said, laying out her 10 of clubs, jack of clubs, queen of clubs, king of clubs and ace of clubs. "I got one too. But wait, isn't this the other one you had talked about? What was it again? Oh yeah, a royal flush. That's the strongest hand you can get, right?"

Joe's jaw dropped. His mind couldn't comprehend how she'd got these cards. He flipped one over, icy blue eyes searching for the tell-tale symbol.

"I guess it's time for your pants." Sarah's voice was a sing-song, and Joe's face softened. He was still getting what he wanted, even if the game was turning out differently than he'd planned.

"You're sneaky, you are," he said, as he slid off the bed. He unzipped the fly and the waistband slid to his ankles.

His legs were as built as his torso and arms, and Sarah got a little shiver. He would taste good.

"Ow!" Joe suddenly doubled over, rubbing his hands over his legs.

He dropped to the floor as his toes curled into themselves and disappeared. "No!"

He grasped the ends of his feet, but they began to shrivel. "What's happening?"

Fear filled the icy blues as he looked at Sarah. "My toes!"

She shrugged. "I get to keep the parts I unclothe. Isn't that how you play?"

"What are you talking about? NO!" His feet disappeared.

Sarah licked her lips.

Joe's hands grappled with the space where his feet should've been. "What is happening to me?"

Sarah leaned back on the bed, feeling the warmth rushing into her.

The stumps of his legs were shriveling now too. Joe screamed as his ankles disappeared.

Sarah sipped more wine. This merlot went with him surprisingly well.

His legs shrunk farther, and Joe's scream turned into an exhaustive pant as he tried to stay conscious, tried to stay alive.

"I don't... I don't..." he said between breaths. "I don't understand."

Sarah stood slowly. "Of course you do. You wanted to devour my body, didn't you?"

She knelt down next to him, her red panties in line with his mouth. "You wanted to ply me with alcohol, get me drunk, trick me out of my clothes."

She cupped his chin in her palm and lifted his icy blue eyes to hers.

"You wanted to make me your meal. I just beat you too it." She rubbed her belly. "Every fat cell, every muscle, even... mmmmm... even your tasty . bone marrow."

Joe writhed on the floor as his legs shriveled.

"I... I..." His icy blue eyes widened.

"Sshhh," Sarah said, standing over him now. "You wanted to get inside me, and in one last gulp, you will be."

She closed her eyes, breathed in deeply, enjoying the heat rolling up and down her body as every ounce of life from Joe spread out inside her.

And then it was done. All sign of Joe and his icy blue eyes was gone. All that was left was a pair of pants and briefs on the floor and a sock in the blinds.

Sarah exhaled.

She got dressed, picked up her bag, and smiled satisfied. She wiped her lips as she opened the door, then let the lock click into place behind her.

Outside in the night air, she walked down the street to her hotel. She had wanted a quiet night, just her, a cocktail and some music. But she couldn't bypass meals when they laid themselves out in front of her.

She passed an all-night bar, the swirl of music, laughter and alcohol seeping out the open door. She stopped and peered in.

It was late. She had an early flight.

But maybe there was time for one more Femme Fatale. After all, she had already eaten. ♜

THE LIVING AND THE DEAD

By Madeline Smoot

"SO THIS IS WHERE THE first victim was found?" My question was purely rhetorical. My death sense could already feel, concentrated in the far corner of the hotel's ballroom, the lingering aura of a violent death. The body had been removed days ago, and a guy that gets frozen from the inside out isn't going to leave tell-tale bloodstains on the mid-priced hotel's industry-standard beige carpet. The rest of the room was equally dull with the vintage Eighties crystal chandeliers hovering above us, the uncomfortable fabric-covered chairs set up in too-close rows surrounding us, and a carpeted dais complete with generic podium looming over us from the front of the room. There was nothing that the five normal senses we all learned about in kindergarten could grasp onto, and yet there was a feeling of malevolence in the room that could be sensed even by non-mediums like the man behind me.

161

"Can you do it, Ms. Poe?" the man asked instead of answering my question.

I turned away from the corner to face the hotel's General Manager and the small committee of people hovering behind him. "It's Artemis, not Ms. Poe. Just Artemis." When no one said anything, I held in a sarcastic comment and instead addressed the metaphorical elephant in the room. "Can I do what? Figure out what paranormal visitor keeps killing your guests?" I shrugged, ignoring the manager's wince. "Probably. I can also dampen the psychic energy emanating from the different murder sites." As soon as the clients left me in peace, I'd pull back the carpet in the corner of this room and salt the subfloor with the good Himalayan pink salt. Based on the way the area had too many shadows when I glanced at it out of the corner of my eye, something had to be done, or this place would have one doozy of a haunting about a month from now. If the other sites were as bad as this one, I was going to be spending most of the afternoon sowing salt and smudging sage.

The group of people before me gave each other little glances, but they nodded.

"But can you do it in time?" a woman in a demure grey skirt suit with elegant ghost-revealing glasses perched on her nose asked me. She'd been introduced as the head of the weeklong conference being held at the hotel. I'd already forgotten her name. "Can you fix things before the keynote speech at lunch tomorrow?"

My attention had been wandering back to the corner with the shadows, but I snapped quickly back into focus. "I'm sorry. Did you say you wanted this done by lunchtime?"

"The keynote is actually in sixteen hours," said some other flunky.

I have been often accused of resting bitch face, but in actuality I possess a blank stare that unnerves even the toughest client. I turned this full force on the group assembled before me. Some of them actually took a step back. After a moment, I glanced down at the double-barreled shotgun I had cracked open over my left arm. I tapped one of the salt laden shot casings already loaded in place before looking back up. More than just a few of them had taken a step back at that point. The pack was in full retreat out the main door. You'd have thought a full-scale specter had manifested behind me, but the sun was still up, keeping us all safe.

"Just to get this straight," I said in my softest, deadliest voice to the only two people brave enough to remain, "you're giving me sixteen hours to find a supernatural serial killer that's preying on your conference attendees?"

The hotel manager flinched again, but the conference head squared her shoulders as if daring me to go on.

I dared.

"Over the last three days, fourteen men—all part of your conference, all white guys with brown hair and blue eyes between the ages of twenty-six and forty-two—have been ghost-frozen in various sites all over this hotel."

The grey woman's lips drew together in a hard little line, but I couldn't decide if it was my blunt speech or the use of the term "ghost-frozen" that bothered her more. This conference boasted the largest gathering of paranormal academics in the world. That type preferred jargon over slang any day. She would have said the victims had experienced "phantasm-induced hypothermia."

"And instead of closing the hotel," I ignored the manager's little gasp of horror, "or at least sending all the men home, you expect me to solve this problem for you in," I consulted my watch, "fifteen hours and fifty-six minutes?"

At this point the woman looked about as put out as me. "That about sums it up. Yes. Considering the price we're paying you, I don't consider this unreasonable."

I gave a small snort. "Quality is not cheap, and results are not always fast." I took a deep breath in order to get my irritation back under control. Something was being drawn to the emotions releasing into this room. The small chill I felt warned me of that, and any ghost strong enough to coalesce even slightly during the day was powerful indeed. Whatever was stalking and killing those men, I didn't want to draw its attention before I was ready.

"But you'll do it?" the hotel manager finally spoke up. "You will help us, won't you, Ms. Poe?"

"It's just Artemis," I reminded him. I flicked my shotgun up and shut with the satisfying click that strikes terror in even the most hardened hearts. "And if I'm going to meet this deadline, I best get started." I gave them my sharpest smile.

Perhaps it was the smile or perhaps the loaded shotgun held ready at my waist unnerved them, but the living finally had enough and scurried out of the room, leaving me to the dead.

#　　#　　#

Of course, I didn't need a loaded shotgun to salt a room, not during the day. I sat it down, pulled my jumbo-sized saltshakers out of my rolling luggage, and got to work.

It did take me all afternoon, but I got all fourteen sites cleansed of psychic residue. It helped that several of the deaths had happened in the same rooms. I then did a quick tour of the hotel using my death sense to search out any other psychic anomalies, but the fourteen new deaths and the half-dozen ghost specimens on display in one of the small conference rooms drowned out any potential clues.

I saved the ghost specimens for last. I wasn't a big fan of keeping ghosts locked behind salt-impregnated glass any more than I liked seeing lions in cages or lizards in terrariums. Every ghost was created by a soul with a purpose, and even though that purpose might seem sort of pointless to the living, it didn't give us the right to lock the more harmless ghosts up in portable zoos.

Still, I needed to make sure that none of the ghosts had somehow found a way to escape its display case and spend its nights celebrating its freedom with an epic murder spree. With an expression even blanker than normal, the moment the sun dipped below the horizon, I squeezed past a crowd of academics in suits.

Each case had been labeled with the ghost's living name, their *nom de morte*, their academic classification, and a brief summary of their death and after-death activities. It only took a glance to rule out all six ghosts. Four of them were nothing more than visual echoes of some souls' past lives, and the two stronger souls couldn't have been more than shades. None of these ghosts could manifest a corporeal form, not even at the darkest part of the night on the longest night of the year. The echoes were so weak, I could have banished all of them with a single smudge pot of sage or lavender. The shades were stronger, and one was even able to make some nasty faces, so it at least knew about its captivity. Still, a simple flaming torch would have banished even that shade back to the Otherworld for at least one hundred years. Whatever was killing those men, it wasn't the sad bits of the past floating in the glass boxes for the academics' amusement.

I had the irrational urge to use my shotgun like a baseball bat and smash each of the cages open, not that it would have done any of the ghosts any good. What they needed was to be returned to their original hauntings. I glared at the oblivious people around me before heading for the door and the hallway. I was not in the best of moods, so I all but snarled out a "What?" when someone said my name just outside the door.

Some dude was pushing off the wall he'd been leaning up against. Like everyone else I'd seen, he was dressed in a sober suit with a conference badge hanging from a lanyard in front of his non-descript black tie. "Artemis Poe?" he said again.

I nodded but didn't pause. I wasn't in the mood for academic chit-chat. The sun was down, and the ghost I needed to find could manifest anywhere in this place at any moment. I needed to narrow down the most probable spots if I was going to get it banished tonight.

"Artemis Poe of Poe Paranormal Industries?" The guy joined me, his long legs easily keeping up with the brisk pace I was setting.

I frowned at the mention of my family's company. "I'm strictly freelance," I told him. It wasn't entirely true. I had a ton of PPI tech on me and my brother's number saved in the favorites section of my phone for worst-case hauntings. I might not agree with my family on a lot of things, but I'd be a fool to ignore valuable help when I needed it.

The guy looked disappointed for maybe half a minute before getting over it. "Still, you're here about the ghost murders, though, right?" He glanced at my T-shirt and jeans and messy bun on the top of my head, at my backpack and carry-on suitcase I dragged behind me. "I mean, you aren't here for the conference."

I wanted to rip the condescending smile off his face. "I dunno. I have that nice little BBA in business management and an MS in Paranormal Psychology and of course my PhD in Russian Literature, but that was just for fun. I've been known to attend conferences."

"Russian literature?" Behind his ghost glasses, the man blinked twice like he was trying to realign his world view.

"My tastes are eclectic. Do you want something, or did you just feel the need to be an asshole to a random stranger?"

If anything, the guy's smile got even bigger. "Sorry, I'm not at my best with the living. I think I got off on the wrong ectoplasmic trail." He gave a small laugh like he thought he was being charming.

Now, I'm not exactly known for my people skills either, but this dude made me look like a social adept. The look I gave him wasn't even kind of encouraging, but he opened his mouth to start talking again. I held up a hand before he could get more than a word out. I stopped dead in my tracks. "Wait. Do you hear that?" My question was purely rhetorical. I'd heard the sound with my ghost sense not my ears.

Mr. Shit-for-Brains went a few more steps before stopping too. His head cocked in the same direction as mine, like his ears were straining to catch the sound. "Is that ... crying?" he asked in a low voice.

Interesting. Not many people could hear ghosts. There were way more visual mediums in the world than auditory ones. I was one of the few that could do both. There weren't many of us outside the family.

The annoying dude pushed his spook specs further up his nose and peered down the hallway even though there was nothing supernatural to see. And he wouldn't have been able to see anything anyway if he hadn't been wearing salt impregnated glasses.

The crying sort of intensified into a heart-rending sob before dropping back into a lighter sniffling sound. I let go of my rolling suitcase and snapped my shotgun shut again and started running for the sound. I paused at the doorway of each conference room, yet I heard nothing but the drone of some academic speaker. The guy kept pace with me, checking the rooms on the other side of the hallway. He shook his head. Finally, we broke out of the hallway into the hotel's main lobby. Normally, the place was bustling with activity. People checking in at the front desk usually stood in front of helpful clerks. There was always a family or two waiting to speak to the concierge. But right now, the place was emptier than a high school classroom on a Saturday evening. Even the doormen and valets seemed to have vanished from their posts just outside the doors. Nothing living occupied the space.

I took two deep breaths in an effort to slow my racing heart. Some ghosts feed on emotions, using our ramped-up energies to make themselves stronger. Since fear is such a powerful emotion complete with powerful physiological reactions, most of the lesser sentient ghosts like shades and spirits relied on fear to anchor them to the living plane. The one manifesting in the lobby though wasn't a lesser ghost.

"Fully corporeal less than an hour after sunset," the guy next to me said. He jotted down something in a pocket notebook he'd unearthed from somewhere. Because when confronted with a murderous wraith that had already killed fourteen people in the last three days, this dude felt compelled to take notes. Amateur.

"A true wraith," the guy added, awe in his voice. "Fully formed with only the faintest sheen of ectoplasmic reflective glare to give away her true nature."

"There are a bit more clues to her paranormality than that," I muttered. The temperature in the room had dropped a good twenty degrees since I'd passed through the lobby less than an hour ago. There was a faint hint of decay in the air as if someone had set a plate of fish out for a few hours too long. The ghost itself was not quite the right color for a living human. She—and the ghost was definitely appearing as a woman—was a bit like a washed out sepia photograph. Her skin, the colors on her grey suit, even her shadow were fainter than they should have been. Her clothes were wrong too. Contrary to popular belief, not all ghosts inherently look exactly how they appeared when they died. This ghost's clothes were similar to the suit the conference director had worn earlier in the day, but the cut was off as if the person designing the suit had been used to different patterns and clothing silhouettes.

And if all of that hadn't been enough to clue me in about her "true nature," the woman hovered three inches off the floor.

The goober next to me seemed to be oblivious to all of these nuances. "And just feel the compulsion she's sending out," he said, making another note. "I can barely stand in the room. I have this weird urge that I badly need to be somewhere else. Anywhere else. Fascinating." He turned to me. "Do you feel it too?"

"I feel something." I spared a second to glare at Oblivious Man before focusing again on our Otherside visitor. He was right though. The ghost was sending out a strong "Go Away" vibe that, coupled with the existential dread all wraiths naturally inspired in the living, made me want to flee the room. However, I'd been withstanding ghost compulsions since my mom started taking me out in the field when I was six. There was no way though that this dude had been raised to be immune to ghosts like I was. I knew all the members of the prominent medium families like mine, and this guy wasn't one of them. So, to have him still standing beside me meant this guy had one serious force of will to combat the compulsion. I was secretly impressed although I would have preferred getting ghost-frozen to admitting it to the guy.

Instead, I scanned the room, my heart sinking as a figure appeared from the hallway leading to the elevators. A man, just the right age, race, and type to be a victim, wandered into the room. I was too far away to be sure, but I suspected his pupils were dilated, his hearing fuzzy. His lurching walk indicated that he'd been fully ensnared.

"Not everyone is feeling the compulsion."

The guy next to me looked up from his notebook and frowned. "Oh no."

I started walking forward, raising my gun to aim.

The man ran after me. "Wait. No. Let me talk to her for a second."

The ghost's crying increased in volume and intensity. The victim took another confused step closer. "Ma'am?" he asked. "Are you all right? Can I help?"

The ghost's tears transformed into a strange hiccup-laugh that ran across my skin like icicle needles. I resisted the urge to shiver or retch or both at the same time. The ghost reached out her arms and began pushing her hands into the victim's chest.

"No time." I aimed my shotgun and pulled the trigger.

I hate shotguns. They're loud and bulky and hell to take on a plane. But they are also the most efficient way to spread salt shot over a large area in a very short amount of time. The spray of salt sliced through the ghost's ectoplasmic body shattering her into a puff of slimy smoke.

The droplets fell to the ground, narrowly missing the man the ghost had been attacking. With a sort of gurgled gasp, the man collapsed over onto his side.

The annoying dude from the hall tore past me and dropped to his knees next to the almost victim. "Is he dead?"

"Not likely." I didn't lower my gun, and I scanned the room for a moment. The ghost shouldn't be able to re-form that quickly after such a blast of salt, but wraiths were strong and tricky. "The ghost didn't have her hands in him for more than a second. No way his insides froze quite that fast." When the temperature started to return to normal, I propped my gun against the concierge's desk and pulled a spritzer of sacred spring water out of my backpack. I'd need to get my suitcase out of the hall and in here as soon as possible. The spring water would make it harder for the wraith to coalesce, but it wouldn't stop her. We had maybe five, ten minutes tops before she was back. Already I could feel the dread starting to push at my psyche again.

"Not the ghost," the dude said in exasperation. "Did you kill him when you shot him?" He was pawing at the victim searching for a pulse.

"Saved his life more like it." I sprayed the last ectoplasmic blob then joined the dude by the victim. "The gun is loaded with rock salt. It stings, but I was too far away for it to do much more than that." I sprayed spring water on the two burns on the guy's face where drops of salted ectoplasm must have hit him. "Those might leave a small burn, but nothing serious."

The victim started to gasp a little and come around. I helped haul him to his feet. While annoying dude stood around staring at the supernatural mess soiling the lobby's marble floor, I helped escort the victim to one of the conference rooms. While the people in the back of the room started to make a fuss over him, I slipped back out into the hall and grabbed my bag and headed back into the lobby. The dude was sitting cross-legged on the floor once again making notes right next to the ectoplasmic globules.

"Dude!" I yelled from the doorway bee-lining for him as fast as I could. "Get back from there before she corporealizes again. Do you want to be her next victim?"

The guy's face reddened with embarrassment. "Of course." He scooted back but didn't really get far enough before he started taking notes again.

I wanted to scream from exasperation. Instead I asked, "Why are you still here? Who are you?"

"I'm Anthony Milton. Maybe you've heard of me?"

I gave a reluctant nod, trying to match this eager noob with the famed paranormal psychologist. I failed, but then Anthony Milton had a reputation for a decided idealistic slant when it came to human/ghost relations, so maybe the child-like enthusiasm fit. Milton had written a couple of popular science books on ghosts. In some ways, he'd done more in the last few years to normalize the paranormal for the general population since Cricket and Sonnfield definitively proved the existence of ghosts and the Otherside. However, he was also a kook who thought all ghosts were lost souls that just "needed counseling" to help them "Move On." Don't get me wrong, I think most ghosts are harmless and should be left in peace. If Milton wants to waste his time chatting with the ones sentient enough to carry on a conversation, that's his business. Only there are some ghosts that can't be reasoned with, that are too dangerous to the community to just leave manifesting around. Those need to be banished. Period. The ghost around here that had killed fourteen people and just tried for a fifteenth. That was an excellent case that proved my point.

"I think I may have an idea who's haunting the hotel," he said.

That brought me up short, and I turned to look him full on in the face. He pulled his pair of spook specs to the top of his head like an unneeded pair of sunglasses.

"How?" I asked. "I did a cursory search on the plane ride here, and there hasn't been so much as a blip of supernatural activity at this hotel until this week."

Milton's smile got even bigger. It almost made him attractive. "I thought so too, but just on a hunch, I spent yesterday evening trolling the microfiche at the physical archives for *The Sun Belt Times*."

I nodded. If I'd had more than one day for this job, I would have gone there too. Only the editions from the last decade of the paper were online. I still thought the man was a kook, but I respected his research instincts.

He pulled his phone out of his suit jacket's inner pocket. Tapping on the screen, he showed me a picture he'd taken of an article displayed on a microfiche screen. "Ever since 1960, this hotel has averaged two or three deaths every decade or so. Some of them were obvious accidents and one was a confirmed heart attack, but the rest were single men found dead in public rooms of the hotel. And since phantasm-induced hypothermia only became an accepted cause of death seven years ago, all the other deaths were put down to unknown causes. All eight of those men were between the ages of twenty-five to forty-five." He gave me a significant look before swiping and bringing up a table noting all the hotel's deaths and causes.

I all but snatched the phone out of his hand, scanning the data. "You're right." I glanced back up at his satisfied smile. "How has this pattern been missed all these years?"

Milton shrugged. "No one was looking." He pointed at the first death on his table. "But I think this is our culprit." The entry was for a woman named Marlena Martingale who had died in the bath in the late fall of 1959 just months after the hotel first opened.

I wrinkled my nose. "Drowning. What a crap way to die."

"Indeed." Milton reached over my shoulder to open a different app. This one was full of notes on Marlena. "I did some research on her. Her death was listed as an accident, but there were bruises on her shoulders according to something her sister told a reporter."

"Like she'd been held under and killed." I nodded again. It made sense.

The fury and impotence that comes with being murdered usually led to a stronger form of ghost like a specter or a wraith. You didn't get many wraiths from people dying peacefully in their sleep at the end of a long life. I flipped back to the list of deaths. "But why now? If you're right ..."

"I am."

I ignored his satisfied smirk. "If you're right, then why the sudden body count? Marlena's been comfortably killing one dude every decade or so for sixty years. Why suddenly go full on Jack the Ripper now?"

Milton started to shrug then froze as if he'd seen something behind me. I turned half expecting to see Marlena's ghost materializing. There was nothing there. The lobby was still as empty as it had been when we first arrived. I checked the thermometer app on my watch, observing as the numbers dropped one degree at a time. She wasn't here yet, but she was coming. Then, I realized Milton wasn't wearing his spook specs. He wouldn't have been able to see Marlena anyway.

"Put your glasses back on if you don't want to be blind when Marlena gets back."

Milton seemed to come back out of his half-trance. He ignored my comment and pointed at the list of deaths—although he pulled his glasses back down onto his face. "Marlena had already started escalating a bit as she got the taste for revenge."

"Or just enjoyed the high of killing. We don't know what motivates her."

"True. But why do serial killers suddenly increase or start sending notes to the police or taunting videos to the media?"

"For attention," we both said at the same time.

"Of course," I added. "A whole conference full of people talking ghosts, and no one has mentioned Marlena once. No one even realized she existed."

"Until now." Milton shivered. "We're all talking about her now."

I shook my head. "Not really. In fact, I think that's why more bodies are showing up each night. She only killed three that first day, but five the second and six last night. Yeah, we're talking about the killings, but we still aren't talking about HER. Not until now."

"We will be after tonight." Milton took back his phone and pocketed it.

I shrugged and opened my carry-on. I pulled out the very latest PPI magnesium flare lantern, the big one that creates a short-lived and contained fire hot enough to banish even a score of wraiths back to the Otherside for a century or so. I started setting it up next to the bits of ectoplasm. Since most ghosts have a limited energy to draw from, they usually chose to coalesce in the same place every night. As the strongest type of ghosts, wraiths could materialize anywhere within the bounds of their hauntings—in this case the hotel—but it still required massive amounts of energy. It would be easiest for Marlena to reappear where her psychic signature remained strong. Each of those little globs of ghost guts represented a connection to our physical world. I hoped they would draw her back here. I didn't want to play the world's deadliest game of hide and seek all over this hotel.

"Wait, that's a flare," Milton said.

"Top of the line," I said with some pride. "This one isn't even in production yet."

"But you can't banish her!"

The distress in his voice caught my attention. The dude looked distraught. "Excuse me? What do you mean I can't banish her? I've been banishing ghosts, even wraiths, for years."

Milton flushed. "No. I don't mean you can't do it. I'm sure you're a banishing pro."

"Yeah." I was literally a banishing pro. The conference was paying me to banish the ghost.

"I meant, don't banish the ghost."

It was my turn to look appalled. "Why wouldn't I banish it? Marlena has killed fourteen people. You watched her nearly kill someone else. We can't let her find a replacement victim."

"But if I can just talk with her—" Milton began.

I cut him off before he could go any farther. "Wraiths aren't the type of ghosts you talk with, at least not outside controlled conditions." I gestured around at the empty lobby, trying to convey my shock at such a hare-brained idea. Sure, I knew Milton had a soft spot for helping to counsel ghosts, but I hadn't assumed it would extend to ones he had just watched try to kill someone.

Milton tried to give me an ingratiating grin, but from the way his face had flushed, it was safe to assume he was equally irritated. The temperature dropped in the room, but I barely noticed. My anger heated my blood.

Milton gestured at the empty lobby too. "It's about as close to lab conditions as you can get," he said. "The place is deserted."

"Only because the wraith is keeping it that way." My voice rose, and my fists clenched around the flare lantern I hadn't finished setting up. "Hundreds of people are only steps away crammed into conference rooms. She changes her mind about an audience, and we could have tons of traumatized, if not flat-out injured, people littering these floors."

Milton crossed his arms, preparing to be stubborn. The problem was, I was just as stubborn. The bigger problem was that our anger filling the room gave Marlena the extra energy she needed to materialize between us.

One minute I was staring at a pissed off dude, the next it was a pissed off ghost.

When she had been attempting to ensnare her victim, Marlena had been all delicate boned and overtly-feminine and helpless. She looked nothing of the sort now. She'd dispensed with ghost flesh to appear as some sort of leering skeleton with hair jutting from her skull and whipping in a fierce wind only she could feel. She still wore the suit from before, but with ectoplasmic bloodstains all over it as if she'd been the victim of multiple stab wounds, not a drowning. The effect would have been terrifying if I wasn't so annoyed with Milton and just so over ghosts at this point in my life. I reached for the iron truncheon-baton in the back pocket of my jeans.

Marlena gathered her energies together and lunged for me, her outstretched finger bones grasping for my throat. I ducked, pulled my baton out, flicked my wrist to expand my baton to full length and in the same motion, delivered a stunning forehand swing that would have made any Grand Slam tennis champion proud. My iron passed through the wraith, depriving me of a satisfying thwack, but it did disrupt her manifestation. She flickered back to the Otherside, but she wouldn't be there long. A minute at most.

I fumbled for a second trying to get a salt grenade out of my backpack. We were too close to safely fire my shotgun again, and besides I'd stupidly left it over by the concierge's desk when I'd started setting up the flare. I looked over at Milton, expecting to see the academic cowering from the recent manifestation or feverishly taking notes. Instead, he stood in a guard position with an iron dagger in each hand. I had no idea where the weapons had come from, but maybe the pencil pusher wasn't completely useless after all.

"Heads up," I yelled and lobbed the salt grenade at him in a gentle underhand throw. He dropped his right blade to catch the small ball, but never let down his guard with his left. Interesting. The dude had more practical field training than the average paranormal psychologist. I didn't have time to mull over the contradictions that Anthony Milton possessed. The ectoplasm had begun to glow again as Marlena attempted to cross over onto our plane for the third time.

"Press the red button and throw it at the wraith the second it coalesces," I said.

Milton nodded but didn't take his eyes off the glowing goo. It was beginning to steam slightly as Marlena pulled herself together. There was always a little warning before a ghost manifested, and if the two of us had been paying attention instead of fighting, she wouldn't have been able to get the jump on us a moment before.

I smacked the last support into place and backed away from the flare. I pressed the control button on its remote, activating the device.

Once more the temperature of the room dropped, and a pale light began forming over the ectoplasmic drops. A fury like I'd never experienced beat at my psychic senses. On the other side of the ghostly remains, Milton winced.

"Still want to try talking with her?"

Milton gave me a crooked smile. "Yes, but I'm coming around to your way of thinking. This isn't the time or place."

Marlena reappeared with a high pitched screech that stunned even my battered senses into immobility. For a second, both Milton and I stood locked in place while Marlena flew at him. Then, I came back to myself, screamed, "Fire!" and punched the flare's activation button.

I dove for the floor with my arms over my eyes, but it still felt as if the sun had exploded in front of me. Marlena's scream morphed from one of fury to terror as the brief flame bit into her very essence, cutting her off from this plane of existence and permanently consigning her to the Otherside. The light of the flare enveloped me and heat seared my arms and back of my neck for a moment of eternity before I landed face first on the ground in what was now a freezing darkness. Like all PPI tech, the flare was designed around protecting the living. It had almost impregnable light and heat shields, so it hadn't hurt me. That didn't stop the thing from disorienting me for a minute or more, leaving me defenseless. It was a good thing no wraith could survive such an intense fire, even one so short. No one knows why ghosts are banished back to the Otherside by flames, we're simply grateful they are.

I stayed on the floor for a moment, sending my psychic senses out over the room. Nothing. The room was free of Marlena's fear and anger and that psychic barrage she'd assaulted us with only seconds before. The temperature in the room began to climb back to normal, and even the very air seemed easier to breathe. Marlena was gone. The conference could go on without any more paranormal interference. I'd banished the ghost before the keynote address, as requested.

When I could finally see more than dazzling stars, I looked over to see how Milton had fared. He'd been farther from the ghost when she'd gone for him, so I didn't think she'd had time to ghost freeze any part of him. Unlike me, he still stood, but just barely. As I hauled myself up, he sort of toppled onto his knees, his head bowed, and his eyes still shut.

"She's gone?" he asked.

"Oh, definitely. No way a single wraith survived a flame like that."

Milton shook his head and rubbed at his eyes for a second. "It couldn't be helped." He seemed genuinely sad, like the murderous wraith hadn't been trying to kill him right before she'd been banished. Milton frowned for a moment, staring unseeingly at the floor, before he visibly brightened. "Well, there's always the next one. There's no shortage of ghosts for me to help."

"And no shortage of the living to protect." I started taking the flare back apart and packing it carefully back into my bag. When I looked back up, Milton stood next to me, shaking his head at the mess on the floor.

"Such a waste of an afterlife," Milton murmured, more to himself than to me.

I shrugged on my backpack and zipped my suitcase shut. When Milton made no sign of quitting his morose reverie over the ectoplasmic glop, I gave him an awkward pat on the back that he didn't seem to notice. With a shrug, I left him with the dead while I went off to rejoin the living. ♜

MARLA REINVENTED

By Carmen Gray

"COME, MY DARLING," SHE HEARD him whisper thickly. Her whole body surged, her muscles spasmed uncontrollably. She woke to find her thighs slippery and warm again. Faint puffs and snorts came from the other side of the bed. Luke was dead asleep. She was beginning to wonder if or even when he might start to notice what was happening. It wasn't clear what exactly was happening to her.

She relaxed and melted further into herself, allowing the continued sensations of expansion to engulf her. "Mmmm . . ." she moaned aloud, savoring the orgasm.

Luke stirred. "What time is it?" he muttered sleepily.

Marla pretended to be on the verge of waking up. "Hmmm?" she murmured and then yawned, "I think it's eight."

"Good, just enough time." He reached over to brush her hair off of her cheek, which was still flushed. "You're so warm."

She smiled secretly. "Really? Must be humid out."

He pulled her to him and pushed himself against the curve of her belly. "So warm . . ." She felt him, hard and ready, as he was most mornings. She guided him into her easily. "You're so wet!" he groaned as he pushed into her, providing that fullness she had needed just minutes ago.

Or had she felt *him* inside of her, too? It seemed like he was right up until she came each time. She couldn't feel bad about it, she had no control over it, really. It was a dream she kept having. And she wasn't even exactly sure who *he* was.

"Marla, you feelin' this?" he asked while he put his hand behind her back to an arch.

She felt it alright. She rolled him onto his back and straddled him, moving hungrily on top.

"Yes, get on me," he whispered underneath her. "This'll get you pregnant!" He slapped her ass.

As she rode Luke, thoughts of *him* licking her just moments before brought her to climax. She cried out with pleasure. Luke finally released himself and groaned heavily. She slumped over him, feeling his chest rise and fall and the robust thumping of his heart against her chest. All at once, she noticed a light, tingly sensation on her foot, as if someone's fingers were brushing against it.

She turned and noticed a white glimmer of light shoot across the room.

"Marla, you okay? You seem distracted this morning," Luke said, "Although, damn, that was some hot sex! What's gotten into you lately?"

Marla smiled at him, her amber colored eyes lowered. "I just had one of those dreams, that's all."

"Ooh, you naughty girl. Was I in it?" he asked, puffing up his chest a bit.

"Yes," she lied.

He smiled, more to himself. "Alright, hon, it's time to get moving." He got up, ensuring that she could view his erection, still slick and arrogantly on display. She watched him head to the bathroom and grabbed a tissue to wipe herself.

They were obligated to go to church, Luke's mother was very strict about that. That was the understanding when they got married last summer. Luke was a good catch for her. He was stable and had a good job. He was a traditional man. She'd always wanted that. And he was all about pleasing his mother, who was extremely domineering. Since she had not grown up with a traditional family herself, having lived with an unreliable single mother most of her childhood, Marla willingly accepted that aspect of him. Until now. Now, she was starting to feel a bit confined by the intense demands Willa had. Willa wanted to be a grandmother.

When Marla and Luke became serious about their relationship, Willa had insisted that Marla take catechism classes at their church to become Catholic. Jonathan, Willa's reserved husband, encouraged it as well. He seemed to be the type of man to just do what he was told. It kind of reminded Marla of herself—of who'd she'd become. Marla, who had grown up wandering from one place to another with her meandering mother, did what was expected of her to remain a part of Luke's life. She was relieved to be in a stable situation, after many years of fluctuating circumstances.

Luke was handsome, strong and had been the high school prom king in their little town high school. Everyone had been in love with him during high school at one point or another. Luke hadn't given any of them the time of day, except Denise, the next door neighbor's youngest daughter. When Luke met Marla while he was away at college and when he'd brought her home to meet his mom, his mom insisted it would not last. But it did. And even though Willa had always hoped Luke would marry Denise, that hadn't happened. Denise instead had hastily married Jesse, the altar boy who was now the deacon, after a family tragedy while Luke was away at college.

Now the only thing that would make Luke's mom happy would be if Marla had a baby.

It was not lost on Marla that Willa fawned over Denise. Nor that Luke was probably still in love with Denise. Willa was always complimenting Denise, and now that Denise was pregnant, she was especially attentive to her.

As Marla got ready for church, she was careful to pick out clothes in styles similar to Denise. After all, Marla had survived her tumultuous childhood by being a good observer. She knew how to mimic her surroundings in order to be inconspicuous. With a mother who frequently uprooted them, it made readjustment easier.

She chose a modest collared white button-down shirt and an A-line blue skirt. She slipped on her brown penny loafers and observed herself in the bathroom mirror. Her dark brown hair was short and flat. She fluffed it up a bit with a brush. Put on some lip gloss. She had a pretty mouth—full bow-shaped lips—just like her mother. Still, what did Luke see in her? She looked nothing like Denise, who he talked about incessantly.

Denise was tall and willowy. She had long, wavy tresses and striking, ice-blue eyes. Denise somehow managed to look elegant and sexy, like that secretary Marla remembered from the posh New York City law office where her mother had worked as a cleaning lady for two years. That was probably the longest stretch of a time they had lived in one place.

She tried to smooth down the front of her buttoned blouse, but it kept popping open at her breasts. They were full and pendulous. Luke didn't approve of her wearing anything that brought too much attention to her body. He preferred the good girl image that Denise presented. She decided to change bras to bind them back a little. That would help to keep everything in place. She put on some dark mascara, which made a nice contrast with her golden-brown eyes. Lastly, she put on the silver cross pendant that Luke's mother had given her. The closure pinched her finger as Luke was calling to her.

"Come on, Marla. We can't be late! Mother's going to be waiting for us!"

"Dammit!" she hissed at the necklace. She rubbed the red mark the clasp had made on her fingertip and felt a strange sensation, as if someone was watching her. She looked around. Must've been imagining things, she thought to herself as she scurried out the door.

When they arrived at the church, Denise was already seated next to Willa and Jonathan. Jesse was busy welcoming parishioners. Although he was very involved in the church community, he creeped Marla out. He always stared at her too long, not that she could figure out why. He was married to the beautiful Denise. Wasn't that enough? It was as if he felt she could be lusted after because she was an outsider. He came in close to usher Marla and Luke into the pew where Denise, Willa, and Jonathan sat. She noticed him staring unabashedly at her silver cross one second too long which lay right above her breasts. She wanted to feel her blouse to ensure that there were no gaps but resisted the urge. Discretely, she tried to wipe the gloss off of her lips with the back of her hand. Maybe she should have left off the little bit of make-up she had chosen to wear. Denise was always bare-faced. She'd told Marla that it was a sin to be vain. Maybe Jesse disapproved of her, but the look he was giving her seemed to reveal a different sentiment. Marla wished he'd stop. She cleared her throat and glanced up at the light refracted from a sunbeam off of the stained glass window behind the altar. Maybe it was sinful, but she imagined the sunlight shining directly into Jesse's eyes so that they would promptly close.

Suddenly, his gaze was broken. He began to rub his eyes. When he opened them, they were red and irritated.

"What's wrong, honey?" Denise asked her husband soothingly, as he was drawing attention to himself inadvertently now.

"Don't know, feels like I just stared at the sun."

Thank goodness, thought Marla . . . and . . . weird. Had she spoken her thoughts aloud?

Denise reached into her purse and pulled out a handkerchief. She tended to her husband. "Go rinse them out, sweetie," she suggested and off he stumbled.

Forgive me for wishing ill upon Jesse, Lord, Marla thought. Even though she was trying her best to think good and pure thoughts, she stifled a snicker. It wasn't like he didn't deserve it.

Marla sat next to Denise and they hugged briefly. Marla truly liked Denise. She was not just beautiful, she was kind. She could understand why Luke could be in love with her. She'd been the first to accept Marla in when Luke introduced her to his family and close friends. And because Denise had suffered the death of her oldest brother five years ago, she felt they had a commonality of loss. No, Marla had no siblings, but she had an estranged mother that was very much a real and deep loss. They always had heartfelt conversations and Denise seemed to be one of the only people in Luke's circle of "family" that seemed genuine. Denise had an easy way about her, and she was extremely patient. She'd helped Marla memorize all of the church doctrine and shown her a good example of how to be an obedient wife. She even shared secrets about her poor oldest brother, who had been the life of the party, once upon a time. He was fun loving and always up for meeting new people. He had died unexpectedly after a night out with a strange girl from a different town. Denise didn't think he'd truly died of an accident with a drunk driver on the way home, like the sheriff asserted. Denise told Marla there was something up with the woman he had been with, but they never found any evidence of foul play, so they'd put it behind them and the girl was never heard of since.

Willa glanced over at Marla and smiled politely. Her smile broadened greatly when her eyes found Luke, and she embraced him heartily. There was not much Marla could do to make Willa love her. She'd never be Denise and she'd never be good enough for Luke. She sighed and opened the missal to the opening prayer. While she did, she felt *his* presence. *He* was here. She had only noticed his presence at night, in vague dreams up until now. But she knew it was *him* because she felt the distinct sensation exhibited in the beginning of those dreams—a light tingling that started in her toes and ran up to the top of her thighs. She wriggled uncomfortably and felt the heat begin to build inside her.

Denise noticed and leaned over. "Is everything okay, Marla?"

"Yes, I'm fine. Just a little hot in here," she responded, smoothing out her blouse. The sensation continued up to her breasts, where she felt *him* suckling her, as *he* did in her dreams.

Her nipples became erect and the bra seemed unable to keep her breasts bound as they swelled. The button between her breasts popped open on her blouse. She fixed it quickly and began to fan herself with the church bulletin. Willa looked over at her, clearly annoyed. Luke was oblivious, as was his father. Jesse looked over at her and licked his lips as his eyes rested on her breasts.

That did it. How could she discreetly leave?

As if she'd heard her thoughts, Denise touched her arm gently. "Let's go get some fresh air, shall we?"

Marla gratefully left the pew with Denise by her side.

They stepped out into the balmy morning air, the clouds opening a bit for some sun to come through. "Are you okay, sweetie?" Denise asked, looking intently into her eyes.

Marla took a deep breath. "Yes, I think so. It's just that . . ." She hesitated. The sun felt stronger than it was on her skin. Her head pounded. Could she trust Denise? She didn't really have any friends in this tiny little town to confide in, and she really wanted to figure out what was going on. Denise seemed like a safe person to talk to about this. Denise peered into her eyes, and encouraged her to continue. "Well, it's just that it feels like there's a guy . . . a guy having his way with me."

Denise's eyes widened. "Who? Luke will kill him! What's his name?"

Marla took another deep breath. "That's just it. I don't know. I don't know anything about him or who he is or even what he looks like."

Denise looked at Marla quizzically. "What do you mean? That doesn't make sense." She stepped back to look at Marla fully. "You need to tell me more about this. Tell me everything."

Marla squared her shoulders and tried to hold it together. "Okay, at night, I have these dreams. There's this guy in them. Only I can't see him. I can only *feel* him. He….he…well, he *does* things to me that Luke would never do."

They heard a rustling nearby and looked around. But there was no one there.

"Go on," Denise said, shifting her weight.

"Well, so he begins at my toes and moves up to the top of my body . . . with his tongue."

Denise looked both disgusted and shocked. Her jaw dropped. "What do you mean by that? He's licking you? Everywhere?"

Marla drew in another deep breath. "Everywhere," she whispered.

She decided not to go into any more detail, as Denise looked horrified, her expression clearly displaying that this was very inappropriate. There was a lot more that he did. His tongue was amazing, he gave her the most intense orgasms. When he licked her, it felt as if he consumed her. It was intoxicating and passionate. And she often felt him opening her up in other places, too, his tongue finding its way into every part of her. She'd once felt warm liquid spurting onto the small of her back after one such episode. And another time she had woken up with a sticky pool of warmth all over her breasts, which she'd rubbed in greedily, wanting more. Luke was always snoring beside her, completely unaware of these nocturnal dalliances. It had started to happen so regularly that she looked forward to going to sleep. *He* made her feel. *He* opened her up. *He* made her feel like life was more than just being a wife or living in this tiny town. *He* made her feel restless and alive.

"I knew it!" Willa's voice seemed to appear out of nowhere, surprising both Denise and

Marla. Willa grabbed Marla's arm. "That's why you can't get pregnant. I know who he is."

Marla stared, absolutely aghast that Willa had snuck up on them and eavesdropped on their conversation. "You do?" Marla's face was hot with shame.

"You've got a demonic incubus visiting you! I'm not sure why . . . hmm," Willa declared with an eyebrow arched, making the sign of the cross.

Denise gasped and stepped away from Marla. "It's like that woman with my brother!" Denise exclaimed and slapped her hand over her mouth. Willa looked at her and began to mumble a prayer.

Marla drew a deep breath and asked, "Why do you think that?"

"Because he told me things like you're telling me, Marla," Denise responded, wiping tears from the corners of her eyes. "The dreams, the . . . the . . . stuff about the tongue . . . you know . . . That girl my brother was with brought that on. That's what I think."

Willa nodded her head and gave Denise a hug. "Your poor, poor thing. Sweet Denise, you've been through so much . . . I just don't know why Luke . . ." Her voice trailed off.

Incubus. Where had Marla heard of that word? She'd grown up reading every bit of literature she could find to escape her chaotic life.

The Epic of Gilgamesh! That was it!

She could still picture the front cover. In the story, Gilgamesh's father had been an incubus, hadn't he? Her favorite teacher from her childhood, the only one in fact she could remember, had been an English teacher named Miss Penny in sixth grade. Miss Penny knew Marla was an avid reader and had noticed her among the group of rowdy students she taught. She'd given Marla *The Epic of Gilgamesh* to read as an extra credit assignment. Didn't she still have that book somewhere? She was going to have to dig around and find it.

Marla steadied herself. Could there really be such a thing as an incubus? And why had it chosen her? Somewhere in a quiet corner of her mind, she felt a kernel of passion tug at her. Someone had chosen *her*. She'd been the one to chase Luke. In fact, she'd never even had a boyfriend before him. She had just been too busy trying to survive. And her mother, well, she had always just been a burden to her. She didn't even know who her father was.

Willa spoke up. "You're going to need an exorcism, right away. That incubus needs to be excommunicated from you. I'm going to let Father Klein know after mass." Before Marla could say a word, Willa turned around and marched straight back toward the church's entrance. "Ladies, get back into mass."

Denise kept looking at Marla as if she were the incubus herself. When they returned to their pew, Denise moved closer to Jessie and kept a noticeable distance from Marla.

That would be the last time she shared anything with Denise. She had deceived herself thinking she could ever blend in with anyone. She belonged nowhere. She really had no family. She slumped her shoulders as she sat next to Luke, who still seemed completely ignorant to everything that had just happened. She went through the motions of genuflecting, taking the Eucharist, listening to the final blessings and finally leaving the pew with Luke.

What was he going to think about her when she told him? She already knew. He'd be just as upset as his damn mother. Maybe he'd distance himself from her, like Denise was doing. She felt like a leper. Would she really have to go through with an exorcism? This meant . . . it meant these nights of passion could end if *he* really was an incubus. And *he* would no longer be with her. Her life would continue with Luke, who was in love with Denise. And she would grow old in this tiny town because she really had no choice. She had not finished her degree when Luke had. She had run out of scholarship money and she had no family to help her. Luke was a good catch. He wanted to be the big man. He wanted her to be a stay at home wife and mother. She wasn't even sure if she wanted children. But that's what he wanted, because his mother wanted them. They'd been married almost a year, and still she could not get pregnant. Willa had made an appointment for her to see the doctor that next week. Never mind how Marla felt. It was as if her body was not her own. Nor her mind, nor her emotions. But at night, this thing, this being...*he* made her aware of her body. Fantastically aware of every part of it. And she felt things she had never in her life felt before.

"Don't worry, darling, I will never leave you," she thought she heard a voice say.

Willa insisted that they all meet at her house with Father Klein that afternoon. She'd spoken to Father Klein right after mass. They ordered some fried chicken and sat around the kitchen table, discussing the problem very matter-of-factly. Marla could barely touch her food. She was not hungry. Father Klein explained that he'd had to perform an exorcism on a succubus, but never on an incubus.

Willa pursed her lips and nodded her head in acknowledgement, while Jonathan stepped out of the room. Luke looked from his mother to Father Klein and asked, "Who was it on? Somebody in this town?"

Willa looked at Father Klein, waiting for his direction. "Son, your father was visited upon by a succubus," Father Klein said.

Luke looked horrified. "What? What does that even mean?"

"Oh honey," Willa interrupted, "it's the female version of a demon—a succubus. They visit at night and do nasty things with a person. They can kill a person! Father Klein helped your father. You were away at college. We think it was the same one that took dear Donald, Denise's brother. Only this time, we got to it in time! Thank heavens for Rosemary Gibbons. She took care of it. She has the ability to call in angels. That's what works when an exorcism fails." She patted Luke's hand as if he were still a child.

Rosemary Gibbons was the head librarian at the local library. Marla had met her plenty of times when she'd checked out books. Rosemary always gave her the stink eye. She couldn't believe cranky, old Rosemary Gibbons was the town Angel Caller or whatever name there could be for such a role. It made Marla laugh out loud.

All eyes turned to her, not one of them had a smile on their faces.

"Have you noticed anything different about Marla lately?" Father Klein asked Luke. They were talking about her in third person. As if she didn't exist. As if she had no agency, because she did not.

"As a matter of fact, I have," Luke said, looking at his wife now with new eyes. It was as if she were a stranger to him now. His mother nodded her head in agreement. Marla was shocked. She could not believe trying to share her feelings with Denise had led to this. She noticed Jonathan had slipped back into the kitchen quietly. He seemed to be the only one looking at her with any sympathy.

"What have you noticed, Luke?" Father Klein asked.

"Well, she seems to be a lot more interested in the bedroom arena. And, she's been telling me about some strange dreams she's had," he managed to say. It was as if this was a blow to his ego, nothing more. Never mind that his wife could be having an extramarital affair with a demonic being. Or that her soul could be in mortal danger. That really irritated Marla.

"Hmmm . . . Why did he pick her, Father?" Willa asked, sizing Marla up while Jonathan shook his head, as if disagreeing with what Father Klein was about to say.

A tear slipped down Marla's cheek. She was even more of an outcast than she'd ever been in her life. These people did not seem to care about her. But this demon did. Why?

"Well, you know, it's always the ones who are a little different that they like," Father Klein answered.

For the first time since the conversation started, Jonathan spoke. "Marla, it's going to be okay. It's not your fault. This happened to me."

Before Marla could thank him for his kindness, Willa cut her off. "Jonathan, we don't need to talk about that. Let's move on. We have to protect our Luke and his future. That's what we need to focus on. Father Klein, how should we proceed? What do you need from us?"

"We need to place Marla in your living room to sleep so I can keep an eye out for the incubus. Luke, I need to bless your house. You will need to say a full Hail Mary in your bedroom. I suggest you stay at a friend's place for the time being."

Luke got up quickly, not even bothering to bid his wife goodbye. Marla knew he'd be upset, but this was unbelievable.

"Can you at least bring me my old chest that's under the bed?" she called out to him weakly.

"A chest under the bed," Willa said. "Best to not keep anything from under the bed. Bring it here, Luke. I'll have Father bring it in for the exorcism."

So much for that idea. At least she'd have some books from her chest to read during this exorcism.

As Father Klein and Willa began to prepare the living room for the evening, Jonathan stepped closer to Marla. "You know," he whispered, "It really wasn't so terrible."

Marla looked up at him. "What do you mean?"

"I think you know what I mean, Marla. She made me feel alive," he said, a faraway look in his eyes.

The rest of the evening consisted of Father Klein drawing a pentagram on the floor around the mattress that Marla would sleep on and saying about one hundred Hail Marys. He lit a white candle and ordered Marla to take a salt bath.

Marla obeyed. She got into the warm bath and closed her eyes, exhausted from the events of the day. Finally, she had a moment to herself. There was a soft knock on the door. "Yes?" Marla whispered.

"I have your chest of books. Do you want anything from it?" It was Jonathan! He was truly the only decent person in this town.

"I would love it if you could see if *The Epic of Gilgamesh* is in there," she said. A tingling sensation began on the tips of her toes. So familiar, so nice. Had she noticed this sensation back in Miss Penny's class? Her life had been such a mess, she could hardly remember all of the details. But this feeling…it was familiar.

There was another knock on the door. "I found your book, Marla. I'm setting it outside of the door for you," she heard Jonathan's soft voice.

She stepped out of the warm bath and opened the door a crack. There on the floor was her old book! She retrieved it gently and slipped back into the bath. She opened up to the inside cover and in Miss Penny's perfect cursive was written, "*To Marla, a hero's journey that stands the test of time. Always remember that the great Gilgamesh was supreme in his dualistic nature. You'll understand this one day. You're a special one, Marla. Much Love, Miss Penny."*

She flipped to a page describing Gilgamesh's father, Lilu. He'd visited the women of the city and taken advantage of them by night. She set the book down on the floor and closed her eyes for a long moment, trying to conjure up how Gilgamesh became a benevolent king and what he looked like, as part god and part man. Miss Penny had told her this book was the most important one to read because it was the oldest, with ancient creatures and great and terrifying gods from the beginning of time.

A buzzing noise disturbed her thoughts. She opened one eye and noticed a flickering of light. The familiar tingling sensation moved up to her thighs, a heavy warmth enveloping her belly. She could hear Father Klein in the other room mumbling his Hail Marys. She opened her legs as she felt *him* parting her even more. For the first time, she felt him inside her all the way. It was a beautiful feeling. She opened her eyes wide and saw a pair of ice-blue eyes looking back at her. It looked like Denise' beautiful face, only masculine, with sharp features and a square jaw.

He nodded his head, listening to her thoughts. "Yes, darling, I'm Donald." He lifted her chin toward him and kissed her mouth, every part of her feeling aroused by him. His pointy tongue reached all parts of her, every crevice, all at once. She was enthralled. How did he get here? Hadn't he died?

She heard a knock on the door. "Marla, you almost finished? It's just about time for Father Klein to bless you before you go to bed," Willa's nasally voice came through the other side of the door.

Marla mumbled, "Yes," then ducked under the water to wet her hair.

He suckled her, caressed her, and brought her to orgasm when she came up for air. Then he held her and softly whispered, "They can't touch you, darling. You're not fully human."

"Who am I, then?" she asked with her mind.

"You're a cambion. Your mother slept with an incubus and he did wear her energy out quite terribly. She couldn't love you because you reminded her constantly of her weaknesses. There are powers you don't even realize that you have, darling," he whispered again.

She noticed a tail on the back of him, whipping silently behind him. She smiled. She had powers. Her mother didn't love her because she could not. This was such a relief to her. Her shoulders straightened. She felt alive. She was like Gilgamesh.

"So are you a cambion, too?" she asked, again with her mind, looking deeply at his sky colored eyes.

"No, darling," he hissed. "I'm an incubus. I just took Donald's body after I used him. We can do that, darling. We are shape-shifters."

She wondered if she'd want to keep her body or change into someone else. What fun this would be. "He liked men?"

"No, darling, but we can be whatever they want us to be. I looked like a beautiful young lady to him. He was easy. This town's ripe with people wanting something new."

She smiled dreamily. Life was changing for the better for her. "Where's my father now?" She wanted to know.

"He sent me to find you, darling. So now, now you have to choose," he whispered into her ear while he rocked her body gently. It felt so good to be with him.

"Marla! Come on, dear. It's been almost an hour. Father Klein has to get back to the church soon. You need to get out," yelled Willa, twisting the doorknob.

"Coming!" Marla called.

Yes, she was coming . . . again. He made sure of that. He lifted her chin to kiss her mouth once more. She felt known. She felt whole. "You have to choose. You get a choice, because of your dual nature, darling."

Dual nature! She thought about that. She had a choice. It wasn't a hard choice. This human life hadn't been so great. There had been an awful lot of bad luck. And suffering. Her husband, Luke, was in love with someone else. His mother was awful. His father was emasculated, an empty shell of a man. Maybe that succubus had taken his spark from him?

But her? She had powers! Who knew what they were? Maybe it was about time for her to find out. She kissed him passionately and thanked him for the visit. She wrapped herself in the fluffy towel, drying off every bit of her human body. She examined herself in the mirror. Her flat, brown hair. Her amber eyes. Her pendulous breasts. Her small waist and round, shapely bottom. Her small feet. This had been a good human body.

"Thank you," she whispered to her body. "Thank you, mama for these pretty lips you gave me." She kissed her hands. "I've enjoyed these hands and these eyes." She forgave her mother for not loving her. After all, she could understand why now.

She practically bounced out of the bathroom and into the living room with just the towel wrapped around her. She bumped into Jonathan in the hallway, and her eyes met his. She'd never noticed before how vibrant they were. Obviously, Luke was a handsome man, but she'd never considered where he'd gotten his looks. But she could see it now. Jonathan had the same square jaw line. In fact, he had really broad shoulders, now that she thought about it. He'd always just seemed so *small* next to Willa.

He reached down and touched her shoulder, gently. A rush of electricity passed between them that took her breath away. Without Willa near him, Jonathan was downright powerful. She'd never considered this quiet, reserved man to be like this. She lifted up her eyes to meet his.

"Take me, Marla," he whispered. "Take me with you."

She had choices. She had powers she never even realized she'd had before. A burst of light came pulsating out of her fingers as she pulled him close to her. The towel fell to the floor and she wrapped her legs around him. He grabbed her hips and pushed her up against the wall, his techniques much better than his son, she thought to herself. He was gentle and savored touching her body. Yes, this would be her first, she decided.

"Are you certain?" she asked. She would be a benevolent succubus.

His eyes said "yes," and he smiled down at her. She began to expand, feeling as if she took up the space of the whole hallway with his confirmation. She noticed claws beginning to appear in the place where her fingernails had been.

Somewhere between Jonathan sliding his tongue from her clitoris to her ass, Willa and Father Klein had come into the hallway. Willa began screaming as Father Klein ran to get the white candle. Jonathan looked up at Willa and shrugged his shoulders. A tale sprouted from Marla's lower back. She growled at Willa, who was now running out the front door screaming for Rosemary Gibbons.

Within a minute, Marla devoured Jonathan in one gulp, licking her lips as she disappeared into the beautiful night, taking Jonathan with her, just as he'd asked her to do. ♜

COMFORT WOMAN

By Jess Hagemann

"WOULD YOU TELL ME?" I asked him, my heart rate quickening at the prospect. "If you had a plan to kill yourself, would you tell me?"

His smart—too smart—dark eyes blinked back at me. Chilo had always spent more time in his head than was good for him. "I'd tell you if you asked me," he said.

Okay, then. I sat up, squared my shoulders, made direct eye contact. Asked as matter-of-factly as I'd been taught to during my training. "Chilo, do you have a plan to kill yourself?"

He smiled. Nodded. "I know exactly how I'd do it, actually. I've thought about it a lot."

"And how would you do it? Kill yourself, I mean." Apparently, part of the key to preventing suicide was to say the phrase over and over again. *Kill yourself.* Not to talk around it by just saying *it* all the time.

"Inert gases," Chilo answered. "Nitrogen. Helium."

At my blank look, he elaborated. "It's the build-up of carbon dioxide and other waste products in the blood that causes the body to panic, to think it's drowning. Inert gases don't break down. No waste products, no panic. You go out on a high."

"Hypoxia," I said, recalling a documentary I'd once watched about the death penalty. Hypoxia, or death by lack of oxygen, was, according to that filmmaker anyway, the "most humane" way to kill someone. There's no pain. But in its place, something like euphoria.

"To be honest," I said, "that sounds like what suicide is meant to do. Take away the pain. Make everything better."

I'm sure it wasn't the type of comment one is *supposed* to make in these situations, but it was honest. I respect an individual's right to choose. If we don't own our own lives, what do we have, really?

"I agree," Chilo said, like he'd heard the thought I hadn't voiced. "In abortion, it's the woman's body, and in suicide, it's mine."

He was fiddling with his paper cup of coffee. Raising it to his lips just to set it back down without drinking. He had enough caffeine in his system, if his jiggling legs were any indication.

"But I won't," he said. "I can't. Not with Max."

Max was Chilo's thirteen-year-old son. I'd often heard Chilo remark that children "complicated everything."

"You won't kill yourself," I clarified, slipping the phrase in again intentionally. "Because of Max."

Chilo's look grew distant. "I was thirteen, you know. When my dad tried to kill himself."

Maybe I'd known. Maybe he'd dropped that factoid the first time we met. But clearly it hadn't resonated with me then the way it was doing now.

"I found him," Chilo said. "I told my mom, 'We need to see what's under those bandages on his wrists.' She didn't want to. She said he was fine. But I insisted, and when we saw what he'd done, I said, 'We need to go to the ER. *Now.*'"

The man before me was forty-something years old, but in that moment, I could almost see the teenager he'd been. Was that the experience that had taught him to distract everyone with jokes? Chilo was one of the funniest people I knew. But I often got the impression he was covering for something else.

"If we hadn't gone," he said, "my dad would have died. I look at my son now, and I think *He's a child.* But I had to be the fucking adult in that situation."

A fly landed on Chilo's arm. He scratched at it unconsciously. I noticed the red track marks reaching up his arms. He'd been scratching again. I wondered at the extent to which trauma is inherited.

"And that's not even the ironic part," Chilo continued. "The stupid part is that he died anyway, three years later."

"Because he successfully killed himself?" I prompted.

Chilo shook his head ruefully. "Nah. He was diagnosed with terminal cancer."

I couldn't be sure—because Chilo would never have *let* me be sure—but I thought I saw his lower lip quiver just the slightest. What's that they say? That each of us has a hurt little kid inside?

"So when are you going to kill yourself?" I asked. "When Max is sixteen? Eighteen? Thirty? What age is old enough?"

Chilo shrugged, smiled again. Like he'd been caught and was on the verge of masking it with a joke.

"Why not now?" I said, before he could change the subject. "Max is not you. You are not Max. You don't *know* that he'll respond the same way you did when you were thirteen."

Chilo's eyes grew a little watery. Sadness at the prospect of a son without a father? Happiness at the thought of being free?

"I could help you," I said. And now those eyes laser-focused on me.

Leaning forward, I let the V-neck of my shirt fall open just a bit. A tiny invitation. "Have you ever heard of a comfort woman?"

It took Chilo a second to process my words. To draw his eyes back up to my face.

"Like, in Korea?" he asked, confused.

"Mm-hm." I waited for understanding to dawn.

During World War II, the Japanese Imperial Army operated a network of brothels across Asia intended to "entertain" Japanese soldiers. In the system's original iteration, the women staffing them were meant to be volunteers. But when not enough women signed up to be prostitutes for their country . . .

"I'm confused," Chilo said.

"Never mind then." I smiled graciously. "What matters is that if you want to kill yourself, I can help you do it. I've done it before."

"You've killed yourself before," Chilo repeated, misunderstanding my meaning.

I needed to be explicit. To use the phrase over and over.

"I've helped men kill themselves before."

He raised an eyebrow.

"It's easy. It's quick. It doesn't hurt. Anyway," I said, gathering my stuff to leave our weekly coffee break. "Think about it, and if you want to talk more, you know where to find me."

#   #   #

It was Damien who came up with the nickname comfort women. I figure he thought the name made it sound like he was our pimp and the six of us females his harem, and he liked that notion, the illusion of power it gave him. In reality, Damien was just the IT guy, the one who built and kept the website up and running that allowed our clients to find us. It was hosted in another country to skirt around FOSTA-SESTA—legislation intended to deter sex trafficking, but which really just made it harder for clients to hire professional sex workers. Sex with any one of the comfort women was on the table, and indeed, sex was how and why most people who found us did. It was far from the only service we offered, though. We specialized in all flavors of pleasure and release, some of which ended in orgasm . . . some of which ended in death.

Each of us—June, Pauline, Clarissa, Stacy, Maeve, and me—had our specialties. All of us knew how to talk someone off a ledge, how to push someone to the brink who needed pushing, how to offer an experience a client would never forget, and/or how to help them permanently forget. The way we did it, though—the difference between us—was in the details. June was brash and domineering. She took decisive action and didn't wait for a client to think twice. Pauline was submissive, never speaking unless spoken to. Perfect for those who wanted to maintain control, but still have a witness to their deaths. Stacy reminded me of a tree frog blending in with its environment. Whether the part of a nurse, a cheerleader, or a mother, she effortlessly assumed whatever role her clients wanted her to play, and she gave a convincing performance every time. It was Stacy, more than any of us, who believed in the essential morality of what we did, Stacy who taught me that fantasy and reality are but two sides of the same coin. When it came to helping a client kill themselves, she said, "Keep it as simple or get as creative with it as the client wants. Not every fantasy is elaborate. Not everyone wants to draw the thing out."

The first time I shadowed kind, intuitive Maeve, I watched as she prepared a lethal dose of a barbiturate for a sixty-year-old man dying of pancreatic cancer. Tumors were pressing on the nerves in his abdomen, causing such excruciating pain that even the two months doctors had given him seemed like two months too many. The man was jaundiced and skinny in a way that made me nauseous. I didn't want to look at him, much less the open, weeping wound on his back where the cancer had started devouring him. Maeve, however, seemed totally unfazed. She had greeted him warmly, asked how he felt, whether there was anything else he wanted her or the world to know. When he was ready, she inserted the needle so gently, kissed the dying man's forehead so sweetly, that I understood why we sometimes call death's harbinger the Angel of Death. Maeve didn't have wings, but she was wearing white. Soft, bridal white, not clinical white. The kind you get lost in on your honeymoon. The kind we should all be so lucky to be enveloped by as we leave this world.

My style, refined by first learning from, then adapting, the techniques of the others, was heady. Immersive. I liked to draw on all six senses—

the five usual ones, plus the power of imagination—to make a client's most personal dreams come true. It didn't matter if they needed saving or, alternately, sundering. They gave me a seed and together we made it bloom in Technicolor.

As for Chilo, I didn't yet know which camp he fell into. Would he fall or would he fly? Regardless, I hoped he would call me again.

One year later, he did.

#   #   #

Almost a year to the date exactly that Chilo and I had last talked, he sent this text to my work phone: *You might not remember me, but I'm hoping you do. You said something during our last conversation that stuck with me. About how you help men kill themselves. Did I hallucinate that? Well. I'm ready.*

Obviously, I remembered Chilo. People in my profession don't easily forget a body.

The next time we met, he filled me in on the previous 365 days. How he'd spent them all with his young son, Max. The important conversations they'd had. The places they'd traveled to together. How wonderful and intentional that time together had been . . . and how Chilo's depression had nevertheless cast a dark halo around the edges of every happy memory. We discussed his vision for the end, the role that Max would play. We set a date.

Late March—the first day of spring. On that date, I made my client's wildest dreams come true.

Looking back on it now, I can safely say that euthanizing Chilo was the honor of my life. We found ways to incorporate everything he wanted—a quick exit strategy, no pain, the continued physical and emotional well-being of Max. Chilo and I had already enjoyed each other physically enough times for me to have memorized his body, its heft and muscle. I knew exactly how much Nembutal to administer to put Chilo slowly to sleep, leaving plenty of time for his and his son's last goodbyes. It was Max who helped me pull the thatched raft bearing his father's body into the pond on their property. Max who notched the flaming arrow in his dad's bow, who set that arrow to flying. Where it landed, we watched the flames lick at the edges of the bridal white sheet draping Chilo's remains. Tentative at first, the fire soon caught, engulfing the man-shaped mound on his floating pyre. Tears streamed down Max's cheeks, and once again I found myself wondering. Sadness at the prospect of a son without a father? Happiness at the thought of setting that father free? The tears gathered beneath the boy's nose, dripped off his chin and to the ground. They formed a little puddle. The puddle ran to meet the pond. On the raft, Chilo became a small inferno. Acrid smoke reached up to the sky. The fire sucked all of the oxygen from the air, making it hard to breathe. Forming, for a moment, Chilo's idyllic hypobaric chamber. Heat drifted toward us in oppressive waves. A cool breeze chased it off; in its place, something like euphoria. ♜

WHY NOT OPHELIA?

By Britta Jensen

CAN ANYONE GO BACK TO who they were before? Ophelia asked before Hamlet woke beside her. His arms were tied in front of him, his breathing still punctuated by soft snores from the drugs she'd laced his wine with the day before. Her brown index finger stroked Hamlet's still brow, his indigo-black skin and her umber dullness looked incompatible next to each other. Maybe here their difference in pigmentation, in status, in everything that had separated them before wouldn't matter. She inhaled, the air stale and dry, and turned away from him to open the viewfinder of their sand crawler. If it had stopped, as it had an autopilot function—the smugglers had assured her—she'd reached Five Lakes.

Hamlet's face was dotted with rays from the early morning sun, and she was eager to leave the cramped vehicle to explore the area. She had been convinced by the quick talking merchants that it was a shorter journey under the sea that separated Rendvik from the northern deserts than to attempt passage by boat. She peered through the sole window of the crawler, and only a cloudless sky and dunes were visible. The pod wasn't as roomy as advertised, the dual seats joined together haphazardly with a thick chain and bolted beam. The sun heated up the cabin, and she reached over Hamlet's thick torso to unlatch the window hatch. *Is this still the person I love most in the world?* A horrible tension rose in her gut, making her skin clammy. She knew she had to do something about the oppressive fear of him waking and not knowing what came next.

She leaned into his cheek to check that he was breathing. Slow and steady, in and out, his bare chest still rising and falling. She put one hand on his heart, then removed it, feeling ashamed. She wanted him to wake and feel that stirring energy, that skip in her pulse that had never left her, despite everything that had happened before. When they'd made their promises four years ago, before the ship took him away from Rendvik, the sea had been as rough as her mood that day.

She would probably never see the ocean again. Looking over Hamlet's sleeping form, she was resigned to losing one love for another. *When he wakes up, I won't force it.* She would accept whatever lay behind the eyes of Hamlet as he was now. She wasn't sure that she could keep that promise to herself, though.

When she stepped outside the vehicle, the auto engines on the pod still going, black smoke plumed behind. The crawler had been designed to both bore and travel through massive layers of earth, but the area around them looked nothing like Five Lakes, the nearest oasis in the northern deserts. She was at least a thousand kilometers from Rendvik. This way, the army didn't come after them or claim the neighboring states had kidnapped them. The priests had said it was the cheapest form of transport out of Rendvik. She reached into the cockpit to the engine button and hit the release to kill the engines. She wished she'd paid more attention to other forms of transport.

Piles of sand drifts surrounded her while the sun bored down from a searing white-blue sky. There weren't any visible lakes or insect life. Instead, it looked like they had stalled in the middle of the barren Sand Sea. Behind the crawler was a pile of sand where the crawler had surfaced. Maybe she could get it to run for a few more kilometers. She checked the fuel settings. The gauge showed the crawler was nearly empty. She didn't know how to restart the autopilot navigation.

She walked around the vehicle, attempting to still her panic. Had she been duped by the smugglers? The abbesses, who had been her surrogate parents, wouldn't have entrusted her with someone who couldn't get her across the desert. Yet, here she was, waiting for Hamlet to wake, stranded in the middle of a foreign desert, when she'd grown up her entire life surrounded by the lush green of Rendvik, her harbour city. She fought against the bile rising in her esophagus, causing a fine sheen of sweat to break out across her forehead. She was about to run her fingers through her hair, except it had all been shorn off to pay for passage. Few women in Rendvik could grow hair down to their calves, and hers had fetched an even higher price than her beloved dog, Musket.

"What the hell?" Hamlet roared and shook the entire vehicle climbing out. His large form towered a whole head over her before falling into the sand. Maybe tranquilizing him hadn't been necessary . . . but with the wild accusations he'd been throwing around the kingdom, she knew getting him away was the only way she could save him from his murdering uncle and her father sending him to the front of their next war. Hours earlier he had been curled into her, and she felt foolish thinking this journey could equalize and restore them. She rushed over to untie his hands. Once he figured out this was her attempt to save his life, maybe he'd see reason. *Maybe he'd come back to me. No, best drop that thought.* She saw the rage building in his eyes as he writhed to break his wrists free of the rope before she untied the knots.

He rubbed his wrists, narrowing his eyes to look past her at the dunes surrounding them. "What have you done, Ophelia?" It was the first time he'd said her name in months. It had been "girl, you, O" but never her actual name.

She had been so accustomed to long periods of silence in her house, or while working in the gardens surrounding the manor, that her voice felt like it wasn't fully attached to her body. Her words came out bird-like and chirpy. "We're supposed to be at Five Lakes, but there's a problem with the crawler."

Hamlet rubbed his head. "You're joking. This something you and Laertes came up with?"

"No, just me," she said.

She couldn't remember the last time her brother had taken any interest in anything she created. No, this was all her and the abbesses, particularly Sister Pride's doing. She looked up at the cloudless sky, sand blowing gently with the breeze. The morning was already heating up.

"Look around. Nobody but us here," she kept her distance, just in case. "They were going to kill you, so I paid to get us out on a crawler."

Hamlet's eyes focused for the first time on what she was saying. "Are you completely mad? How did you even . . . ?"

He stormed around the crawler, checking the systems and the fuel canisters, then held up a frayed fuel line.

"We can't stay here, we're going to need to make our way south for water," she said.

"I was going to . . . how did you . . . ." He sat on the front of the crawler, head in hands. "I need some answers here, Ophelia."

"I overheard my father talking to your uncle. They were . . . they were going to kill you. Send you off again, like before, except this time say you were lost at sea, like they hoped would happen before."

There. She'd said it. There was no going back on the truth that she'd been trying to drum into his thick skull while he played hero all over Rendvik.

"I could've stopped them," he said softly, still clearly exhausted from the potion she'd given him. He looked up at the sky. "You didn't have to do this. Not without telling me."

"You wouldn't listen—we used to be so close, but then you came back . . . different." She'd seen that dull sheen to his eyes, the way he avoided her gaze, yet sought her out in the dark, like that was the only time she was worthy of him.

Now, with him meeting her gaze, his eyes bloodshot, she wasn't sure that she wanted to go back to the more blissful times, the easy conversation between them. Maybe it was easier to see all the garden walks as something from a dream, not a reality worth revisiting.

He sat down, sand grains blowing over his head making him more beautiful.

She had to look away from him, do something useful. This wasn't at all like she'd planned. "I'm going to try to get this going. If it won't move, we have to," she said.

Hamlet stood up and paced in the sand. "We have to go back."

"We're a thousand kilometers from home." She checked the fuel canisters and they were all empty, including the reserve compartment.

"I had things I was supposed to do. My father . . . my uncle is going to . . ." Hamlet trailed off.

"Kill you. Or send you to the front line with Urla and Sebric's armies surrounding Rendvik. Both of us were dead either way." Rendvik's neighbors had become restless since Claudius rose to power.

Hamlet stood up, holding the damaged line. "If I can't stop Claudius, he's going to destroy everything we know. Do you honestly want to let that happen?"

Ophelia felt all the anger from the past month rile up inside her like a coiled snake. To think she'd taken him instead of Musket. Her beloved dog wouldn't have been questioning her like this. They would be at least twenty minutes into finding water by now. Maybe if she hadn't been worried about Hamlet's sorry ass she'd have made it to Five Lakes. Perhaps this new, angry and methodical Hamlet always brought destruction in his path.

He walked over to her, the anger receding, only a hurt there she recognized. It had been what she'd first seen in him in the abbess's gardens where she'd caught him stealing a ripe pomegranate all those years ago.

"You can't take that," she'd said to him, keeping her voice low in case one of the sisters was walking nearby.

"Give me something better in exchange," he had said, holding his hand out. He'd had a sincerity in his dark eyes she'd never experienced before.

223

Filled with loss and something else that had drawn her to him, his white tunic open at the neck. She hadn't been afraid to touch him, her fingers brushing his clavicle before he took her hand and kissed it.

Those same dark eyes now looked defeated. "I ought to thank you," he said, holding her shoulders before whispering in her ear. "I know you did what you thought was best, Ophelia." He let go of her. "I wish I could explain how twisted I've felt inside, how it made it hard to be around you when I saw it hurt you to see me like that. Fighting against all of them."

She looked into his eyes' hardened, onyx surface, watching how they were still looking beyond her.

"You can't go back." She walked away from him. "There's no way to get there from here."

She gathered her things from the crawler, flipping her sun veil on, throwing her cross-body satchel and waterskin over her shoulder. She took a tiny sip, anticipating it could be a long journey to find water again.

"What are you doing?" he asked.

Her fragile heart had imagined, once removed from all the dangers of Rendvik, he would fall in her arms again. That they could build a life on equal terms in the small desert oasis. But they had to get there first. She had to make it up to the ridge of the next dune so she could get her bearings. It was no use imagining their lakeside cabin and everything that could have been possible in their previously bright future. They had to get out of the desert first. The flimsy map she'd been given was only useful if they were within twenty kilometers of Five Lakes.

When she reached the peak of the closest hill, the sun was in the east over the neighboring dunes. There wasn't anything that resembled water or plant life. She regretted not packing an eyeglass. The Sand Sea was north of Five Lakes, so if she headed south, she ought to be heading in the right direction.

She called out to Hamlet, who had gone back into the crawler. "We need to go. Do you have your compass?" As a kid, he had at least two on him at any given time.

"I think so," he replied, searching his pockets. "Wait, why don't we try to see if we can't get this thing going?"

"It's hopeless, Hamlet. Trust me—I checked all the gauges already."

He turned the engine, and it started, black smoke blowing out the back until it sputtered and died. Hamlet jumped out of the crawler, coughing as the wind shifted and blew sand and smoke in his face.

Ophelia snapped down her sun veil and started her journey, hoping he'd follow. The dunes reminded her of camels turned on their sides at night. She tried not to think about the fact she would probably still be sleeping at home, if she hadn't left. She had to keep going, up one dune and down the other. *Simple, easy*, she consoled herself.

The cloudless sky and barren, ochre landscape mirrored her scalded mind. Hamlet called out to her, following behind while she drove herself forward between the dunes. She was going to need to find shade by midday, and there wasn't anything suitable nearby.

Her mouth and skin were parched in the heat of the day, and she found herself walking diagonally up the dunes and sliding down, sometimes tumbling in the fine sand to save energy to make it over the next ridge. At the next peak there weren't any more hills to climb for at least five kilometers. The sun was at its apex, and she needed to rest.

Hamlet caught up with her, casting his long shadow over her. She crouched with her back facing away from the sun, lifting her veil to drink from her water skin, trying to take small sips. She'd heard the abbesses talking about digging for water in the desert, but she would need tools to do that. Although, in desperation, she was certain her hands would do. Hamlet gently put his hand on her forearm and she passed the skin to him.

"It's all we have," Ophelia said.

He nodded, looking too tired, like her, to say much else.

When he closed the cap on her waterskin and handed it back, something winked and sparkled in the distance. She watched it, letting her breath and heartbeat settle. She made a frame around her eyes, shading them to see if the object that was winking moved. It didn't. She took out the map, drawing a compass on it, then ripped it in half, poking holes in the second sheet of paper for the sun to peak through. She was hoping it could help her keep a relative sense of direction.

She wanted to take Hamlet's hand, but she was afraid of what she might feel from the way he touched her. If she reached for him and he rejected her, her heart might fail her. It might be the last thing she could handle losing. If Musket were with her, he would undoubtedly sniff out water for her. She tried to push down the regret of not bringing him, refocus her energies on surviving, all the while still wishing her dog were there.

She followed the blinking object, only for it to disappear when she came close enough. Another one appeared in the southwest, and she followed that until the sun dipped down and the shining stopped. The air was cooler, and she was glad of the relief from the heat. She was also aware that she didn't have sufficient cover for night-time desert temperatures.

Hamlet had their only blanket draped around his shoulders. "Are we stopping?" he called out. His dark face shone, dressed in white, like her, his sun veil pulled down. His benign appearance reminded her of how he had been the only one in Rendvik to accept her in all her unfeminine pursuits.

How had the boy who had helped her get lessons with the priestesses and abbesses, who had refused to wear the courtly saffron and green robes with her become someone she was sometimes afraid of, but still loyal to? The last four years of solitude on her father's estate, with only the neighboring priests and abbots to keep her company, had suited her because she hadn't had any other choice. Court life had never interested her or Hamlet. It's what had brought them together as children: their love for being outside with Yorrick in the ocean, or taming the gardens with him before he died.

"It's going to get cold, and you're walking in the wrong direction." Hamlet's face was shadowed in the dying sun. The whites of his eyes were the only part of his face with dimension in the dusk. She pushed down her veil, exposing her bare head.

"What happened to your hair?" Hamlet asked, his voice cautious and tentative. "I'm sorry. For earlier." He took her arm tentatively, then stopped when she didn't move toward him.

The boy you've known has disappeared, she thought for the first time. *Don't listen to this stranger.*

"Are you saying that because you want to steal my water?" She stepped away from him and he didn't come any closer.

"I wouldn't do that."

He sat on the ground and she stood above him, searching for a better place to camp for the night, her legs and back sore from the journey. She looked out for the winking lights again, but they'd stopped. Her stomach was empty, but she wasn't sure she could eat. She was too upset. Maybe as she came closer to dying, her emotions would leak out of her pores like the last remnants of living moisture before the desert consumed her.

It sounded comforting to not be obsessed with thinking about him, for her body to finally focus on her survival above his.

"I have a compass for you." He came closer, but she turned away. "I don't know how to make it better." He edged closer and she held out her hand.

"Don't touch me." She took the compass. "Don't suddenly change your mind because it's convenient and I'm the only living soul you can talk to." It felt nice for her voice to feel like it was back in her body. "I gave up everything to bring you here."

The last rays of light were slowly leaving the purple sky, and he kneeled in front of her, his hands outstretched. "How did you manage it? Did you have to steal?"

She didn't know if answering him would change anything and she was afraid it might. "I sold my hair, jewelry, even Musket. At first it was going to be Musket and me."

"You should have brought him instead," he said gently. He smiled, his teeth glowing white pearls that matched the brilliant whites of his eyes.

For once she agreed with him, imagining her red-furred Rhodesian Ridgeback curling into her body. No complications.

"We would have died if we stayed. Urla's king was already cutting off the fuel reserves, and Sebric had messed with the upriver water supply. Your uncle and mother were poisoning your food. I tried to tell you."

"And I only stirred up trouble, trying to play hero and acting the fool." Hamlet exhaled, folding into his knees. He held out his hand again. "I shouldn't have come back to Rendvik. I should have sent for you."

229

"Why didn't you answer my letters?" she asked.

The sun was gone and he was a mere shadow, amorphous and less threatening. "They never came. I assumed the war had already begun and I needed to be there."

"I wish we could go back to what we were before," she finally said, the words smoother than she'd expected.

He didn't say anything for awhile, the silence like a like drawn-out apology his mouth wasn't capable of forming. "Since I arrived back there wasn't room in me for anything other than finishing what Claudius started."

She waited for him to say something reasonable, to explain all the weird confrontations, his attempt to get the abbesses to take her away. But he'd gone silent, and when she moved closer to where he was, he threw his arm around her and curled into her, like their secret nights in the gardens before he left. A half-moon was rising, shining light on Hamlet curled up on his side, facing away from her, like Musket, not wishing to be covered with a blanket, no matter how cold. They both preferred neighboring heat. She moved closer, covering them both in his blanket and he didn't stir.

The next morning, the same sparkling woke her when the sun peaked over the dunes in the distance. They looked closer than the night before. Hamlet was already up, crouched, digging in the desert floor.

"We have to find water. Take this." He handed her a biscuit that was hard and salty. The food woke her up and helped fuel her trek with him while he took steps too large for her to keep pace.

"Let's follow that shiny bit over there. It could be water," Ophelia suggested, and Hamlet changed his route to follow her.

"Must be a mirage," he said when the blinking stopped.

She knew mirages were wavy; they didn't blink. There had to be something below the surface that was causing the objects to retract. She searched for the next series of blinking. Instead of one, there were several of them. "Look!" she said, but Hamlet pushed his sun veil over his eyes and set off in the direction he'd originally been moving.

"I don't want to die out here following nothing. Come on, Ophelia."

She watched as more of the objects moved along the trail as she and Hamlet cut across the desert, the dunes and rocky hills increasingly surrounding them the further they walked, but the trail ahead stayed flat. She didn't want to admit Hamlet had picked a better route.

By midday the wind had picked up, and thick, fast-moving clouds rolled overhead. They reminded her of the thunderheads before an ocean storm. "It looks like it's going to rain."

He grinned. "Maybe. We certainly need the water. My canister is almost empty. What about you?"

"Same," she lied. If they got desperate, she didn't know what he'd do to survive. The clouds blocked more of the sunlight the further they walked. The sparkling objects had doubled, and she was desperate to change course.

"The weather is getting worse. Let's go toward that one there. It's only a few minutes away."

"Until it disappears like all the rest."

She sat in the sand, sipping water, while Hamlet appeared to drain what he had left. She caught a sweet scent on the wind. Then it was gone. The wind blew and she caught it again: grass mixed with mint. She rose and followed where the scent could be coming from.

"I'm staying out here until it rains, so I can refill the skin," Hamlet said.

Ophelia knew he'd need a larger-mouthed canister to catch enough liquid. "I'm going."

Hamlet stopped in front of her. "Don't. It's safer if we stay together."

"Oh, you've decided that now?" She took her veil off, securing it on her shoulder straps, the warm rain dropping intermittently on her bare head.

"Ophelia, I'm sorry. I didn't mean to leave you. I cared for you then. Even now, I still care." He took her hands. "I know I've been beyond stupid. I can see that now, and I'm sorry you went through so much trouble to save me, and still—here I am. Being stupid. I don't know how to love you like I did before, after everything my uncle and mother put me through. It's like they stole something away from me I can't get back."

She saw how he looked past her and couldn't meet her eyes. She couldn't stay another moment near him. "You know what the worst thing is? I left everything behind because you had promised me. I don't expect your love, after everything that happened," she lied, feeling the tension of the untruth rising out of her, "but I do need you to trust me about where we go next. Please, Hamlet."

He looked up at the rain, canister outstretched. "I am not a pearl without price, Ophelia." He closed his eyes and let the droplets fall on his face. "My uncle sent me away to make a man out of me. Claimed you were turning me into a sissy. It looks like I can't please anyone, most of all myself." He peered at her through red-rimmed eyes. Something of the boy she knew shone through.

"You're already a man." She cupped his cheek with her hand and stood there as the rain washed over both of them. She leaned in to kiss his rough cheek.

He nodded, took her hand, and followed her toward the winking light. The beacon rose with a glassy dome atop a tower sticking out of the desert floor. When she came within two steps of the tower, she found a rounded doorway in the cement walls. Hamlet took a step back, appearing unsure. In the deluge of pounding rain, the surrounding dunes folded with the water. Ophelia grabbed Hamlet and scurried down a stone passageway, the scent of grass and mint filling her nostrils. Within seconds they were below the surface of the desert. She wasn't certain if she was hearing water running, or if it was the distorted crashing of rain outside.

The entranceway without a door let in the howling rain and gusting sand pelted the dome above them. Hamlet charged back up the stone stairs looking for something to keep out the rain. In the dim light she saw something of who he'd been before.

Maybe he had always been that person and she hadn't noticed, because she believed in a Hamlet that didn't exist. She'd been too seduced by everything around them: the white stone arches of the manor house where she'd lived, the large gardens, the fresh scent of mint every time he was near, the soft pressure of his lips. Perhaps the promise of giving birth to his children who would be more blue-black than her muddy skin was more a dream than anything else. The wind howled outside, and it matched her own turmoil when Hamlet had returned and broken his promise to her.

"Where are we?" he asked her.

"Somewhere safer than out there." She had to try again, that feeling of needing him welling up inside her. He reached for her before she could think how to start again. The sound of water rushing below them drowning out the fearful thoughts trying to protect her from what came next. His arms wrapped tightly around her. The scent of mint faded, the dusty smell of him mixing with the earthy wet aroma around them. He swayed side-to-side, humming an old tune she hadn't heard in ages.

His tenor voice rose and fell, and he held her out from him. His face beamed pleasantly, his cheeks showing two bright spots. She looked at her own muddy skin and wasn't ashamed. Leaning into him, she kissed his dry lips once, testing out the warmth that surged through her and lit up his eyes.

It wasn't over after all. He took her hand and followed her down the steps to the underground cavern. She dipped her water skin into the river and drank slowly so she wouldn't cramp. She looked at the boy she had loved for too long. Then she imagined all her sorrows being carried down that dark, fast-moving cavern of water, away from the land she would never see again. ♜

THE CARPENTER

By S. N. Rodriguez

IN A SMALL CLEARING SURROUNDED by an evergreen forest of pines and cedars, was a rugged log cabin. Inside the main room was a stone-lined hearth and beautifully carved furnishings. There was a wall lined with cedar shelves and upon those shelves were masterfully carved wooden statuettes meticulously dusted and displayed. It had one bedroom and a large workshop that made up the opposite side of the cabin with its own front door for patrons. The carpenter's home was located two miles from the main village alongside a deep river. Its location made it easy to access cut trees sent downstream toward the neighboring mill. Villagers came from miles around to have custom pieces crafted by the master carpenter. From commissions of ash wood combs and picture frames, whittled carvings, keepsake boxes, to rocking chairs, bed frames, and cedar wardrobes, the carpenter crafted them all.

One morning, a woodsman entered the carpenter's workshop. A wooden bell rattled as the door closed behind him. He was tall and fresh-faced with a short, golden cropped beard and shaggy, sun-soaked locks. He waited at the counter as he heard the hammering from the back of the shop cease.

"Hello, I've come to request a commission, and I've heard you're the best in these parts," said the woodsman.

A chair scraped against the floor, and the boards creaked under the weight of the carpenter's approaching steps. From out of the doorway, stood a woman brushing her sleeves and apron of shavings. She was slender and petite, with sandpaper hair flecked with shaved curls of wood framing a pair of green eyes.

"Of course I am, considering I'm the only one to be found for miles," she said with a smile.

"Isn't there another workshop near the mill?"

The carpenter huffed. "He's no carpenter. He's a butcher."

The woodsman crossed his arms and nodded his head, smiling. "You're not at all what I was expecting," he admitted.

"You were expecting a man?" She threw her head back and laughed. "If I was paid for every soul I heard that from, I might be able to put down my tools and retire." She approached the woodsman and placed her olive palms against the black walnut counter. "Is it a problem for you?"

The woodsman uncrossed his arms and shook his head. "Not in the slightest. I'm merely impressed, is all. From what I've seen and heard, you're a master and just the person I need for this job."

"And that would be?" asked the carpenter.

From his pocket, he produced a block of white wood and handed it to the carpenter. "Would this make a good bed frame?"

The carpenter examined the block with her fingers. "It's a lovely shade." She placed it to her nose and sniffed. "This came from an ash. It's a hardwood and it's very durable when dry. Yes, I've worked with its kind before. It would do nicely."

"Perfect. I'm envisioning trees and forest creatures carved along the head and footboards. I would need it completed by autumn. Is that possible?"

"It will take two, maybe three months and be quite expensive, but yes. I can have it completed by then. Fortunately for you, I'm completing a wardrobe at the moment, so I won't have any other large projects. I'm assuming you will supply me with the wood?" she asked, returning the ash block to him.

"Of course, with trees I've felled myself. They've been stacked and seasoned for over a year now."

"Wonderful. You can start bringing the wood tomorrow, woodsman."

He gave her a nod before walking out the door. "I'll be here, carpenter."

#   #   #

The following day, the woodsman unloaded his wagon and delivered a large tree trunk to the carpenter. Gradually, she worked it with her hand tools and transformed it into posts. She planned all of the pieces she would need for assembly, and when she was finished carving, she would wait for the woodsman to bring her more material. When he arrived with new trunks and planks, he would stay to chat and check on the progress. To keep her fresh cut wood from drying, the woodsman helped the carpenter fetch water from the river.

"Thank you for your help, woodsman," said the carpenter as she picked up two brimming pails. "You've saved me a few trips."

"I'm happy to help. I wonder, wouldn't it be easier to work with dry wood?" the woodsman asked, hefting the buckets of water at his sides as they walked toward the cabin.

"For smaller projects, I like to cover the wood in damp cloths to help keep in the moisture. Carving green wood feels better to me. Besides, the wood could crack if it dries too quickly."

They stepped into the workshop and placed the buckets of water beside the elevated logs.

"Do the trees really need to drink all of this water?" the woodsman asked, staring at the four buckets.

"No, actually," the carpenter laughed. "Those two are for my basin. Would you mind bringing them inside?"

The woodsman smiled. "Quite the opportunist, I see. Go on, lead the way."

They left the workshop and walked into the main room of the cabin where the woodsman noticed a wall display of wooden figurines.

"Wow, did you make all of those?" he asked, passing them as he followed her to a small back room.

"Yes, I did," she gestured at the washbasin in front of her, "You can put the pails here, please."

He placed the buckets beside the basin and walked back to the figurines on the wall. The carvings were made from different woods and showed various stages of aging. They depicted men and women throughout the ages. Romans in tunics and togas, Vikings in furs wielding spears and shields, a woman at work on her loom, a pilgrim in his doublet, a barefooted pirate in baggy trousers ready to strike with his cutlass. "These are stunning. You can even see the strands of their hair—the texture of their clothing. How did you get into carpentry?"

"I come from a family of artisans. My father and grandfather were carpenters. I learned the trade by watching them work. When I was seven, I took my father's whittling knife and made wood carvings to sell to our neighbors." She smiled at the recollection. "I even made this." She reached for a small piece of leather on one of the top shelves. She handed the leather to the woodsman. "It's a leather thimble. My father and grandfather were impressed and knew there was no use trying to dissuade me. Many girls preferred music and painting, but carpentry was my art."

He slid the thimble onto his little finger. "It's a perfect fit," he laughed, wagging his digit.

"Hey, be careful. That's a relic now." She pulled the thimble from his finger and placed it back onto the shelf.

"Are any of these for sale?" he asked, eyeing a female archer.

"No, these are a part of my personal collection. I've had them for so long I can't part with them." The carpenter picked up the archer and ran a finger along her hair. "She was a fun one."

They walked back into the workshop and the carpenter resumed her work. The woodsman inspected the designs and shapes of the carpenter's furnishings and creations, the smoothness and color of each grain. "I would love to be able to make furniture. I've only ever cut the wood down."

"Well, if you're so inclined, perhaps you can have a hand in it with me. I could introduce you to the grain on a more intimate level."

The woodsman smiled. "Really? You wouldn't mind teaching me? I wouldn't want to be in your way."

"No problem at all. I'll let you know if you get in the way. You won't be doing any of the fine carving, that's for certain."

"I suppose it would mean all the more to my wife knowing that I helped build our bed."

"Oh." The carpenter paused to brush her hair aside with her wrist, chisel in hand. "You're married?"

"My betrothed. We'll be married in the fall. This project is for her—well, for us—but inspired by her."

"*Inspired*," the carpenter raised an eyebrow. "I'm sure. Well, congratulations are in order for you and your beloved. We'll make her the most splendid bed. Now come. Take this file and let's begin."

#   #   #

As the bed took shape, so too did their friendship. Over the next few weeks, the woodsman would work alongside the carpenter twice a week after delivering more materials, and she would teach him new techniques in measuring, planing, joining, and shaping.

"I daresay, you are on your way to becoming a carpenter after all, woodsman. You'll develop a lighter touch with time." She watched him as he gripped the wood in one hand and sanded with the other using long, gentle strokes.

"You think so?" His eyes met hers from across the frame as he shot her a smile. "That's high praise coming from the master." He winked and continued concentrating on his sanding.

"The frame is nearly complete, and then all that's left will be the carvings. I will see less of you and miss you, dear apprentice."

"I'm excited to see your artistry. I'll still visit to admire your progress."

"Yes, the progress." The carpenter felt as though she had shrunken into herself. He would continue to come only until the commission was completed, and then? What then? She would only ever see him in passing, like any acquaintance on the road, hand in hand with his new bride? His beloved? This realization overtook her. "Well, I'm feeling a bit winded. How about we call it a day?"

The woodsman wiped his brow with his arm. A mix of sweat and sawdust. "Oh, alright. I'll come by next week to finish up and then leave you to it. My, it's hot in here, even with these windows open."

"It is," said the carpenter, removing her apron and placing it on the hook in the doorway. With her back turned toward him, she unbuttoned her blouse so that the tops of her breasts peaked out for air before turning to face him again. "I am going to soak in the bath as soon as you leave."

He stood up to remove his apron and noticed her blouse, damp with perspiration, her breasts lightly dusted. His eyes instantly looked up and caught hers. He blushed. "Perhaps we should leave the doors open next time, too, for more air."

She watched as he took a sip of water and gathered his things with flustered movements.

"Good day, carpenter. See you next week."

"Good day, woodsman. I'll see you."

As the door closed behind him, the carpenter smiled and watched him through the window.

I will have you, woodsman.

#   #   #

"Knock, knock," said the woodsman. "I brought you some spare cedar today. I noticed last week you were running low. Where should I put this?" he asked, hefting a section of tree trunk over his shoulder.

The carpenter smiled and placed her hammer down. "Ah, more precious than roses." She stood up and ushered him into the workshop. "You can lay it there beside the pine. You are so good to me."

He lowered the trunk onto the ground and looked at the carpenter. "How's our bed going? May I see it?"

He said our bed. Yes. We've created this together. It will always be ours. "Nearly done, I think. Come with me."

When they arrived at the headboard, the woodsman inspected the carvings of the pine forest scene. Hidden throughout the trees were squirrels, porcupines, raccoons, and other woodland dwellers.

"Extraordinary! So much detail in such small carvings. It must be those tiny hands of yours," he joked, casting her a glance before admiring her work again.

"I'm working on the hart last."

The woodsman looked confused. "A *heart*? I only wanted plants and animals depicted for this commission."

"Oh," the carpenter said, "*hart* is another word—an old word—for a great stag. I learned that from my grandmother."

"Ah. Is that what this spot is reserved for beside the doe?"

"Yes, beside the doe, or *hind*. I envisioned the hart and the hind together there in the middle of the forest. The king and queen of their domain. Long may they reign," she said in a mock bow.

"Long may they reign," mimicked the woodsman. "These are beautiful, carpenter. My beloved will be awed."

Beloved. "I believe she will be, especially when you tell her that you helped conceive it." She moved to sit on a stool beside the bed opposite of him. "How are the wedding preparations going?"

"All set. We are hoping for fair weather. She wants the ceremony and celebration to take place in the woods. We found a lovely spot near the river. Which reminds me," he said, reaching into his back pocket, "this is for you."

He stretched across the bed and handed her a brown envelope. Her fingers brushed his knuckles and she opened it. "A wedding invitation?" Holding it made it all the more real. He really was going to be married soon. She realized she was scowling, and summoned a smile right away. "How lovely. Of course

I will come." The words felt like sawdust in her throat. "I would like to meet the woman who has stolen your heart. She must be delightful."

He placed his hands in his trouser pockets and beamed. "She really is. She's always quick to put me in my place and has such a great sense of humor. You'd like her. She makes me a better person. Those amber eyes of hers just locked me in."

Inside the carpenter was furious. She should protest. Tell him how he was making a grave mistake. Didn't he see that? Confess to him how much her body craved his—how her very *soul* craved his. She should kiss him until he loved her, until his body entered hers on the hardwood planks beneath *their* bed where a soft mattress should be. Proof that they belonged together, but instead she replied, "How endearing."

She walked over and pressed the invitation onto the counter. "After the craving is done, all that's left is the sealing and staining. It will be ready for her next week, woodsman."

#   #   #

The day had finally arrived. The bed frame was completed. Carved vines climbed and wrapped themselves around the bedposts and extended along the rails. Oak and pine limbs stretched across the footboard, their fertile branches bearing pinecones and acorns. The stag, with his great chiseled antlers, stood beside the elegant doe in the center of their forest.

"Thank you, carpenter. You've done a magnificent job. It's a work of art."

"You're welcome, woodsman." She walked up beside him and slid her arm under his. "Don't forget, you helped...a little."

The woodsman looked down at her arm then at her face, its expression soft, but he saw wanting in her eyes. He placed his hand over hers, held it, and slid his arm from beneath hers. Turning to face her, he cupped her hand between both of his. "Thank you, carpenter. You are a true artisan and a wonderful friend." He lifted her hand to his lips and kissed it.

This is it. This has to be the moment. As he released her hand, she wrapped her arms around his neck and kissed him. Her fingers dug into his golden hair. For a moment, he savored her lips in return, his hand behind her neck, the other on the small of her back. She led him out of the workshop and into the main room.

He could feel her hunger, her desire as it flowed into him. As he began unbuttoning his shirt, memories of his beloved laughing with him and kissing him colored his vision. He tried to push the images away and stopped. He bit his lips and pulled himself gently away from the carpenter. "I'm sorry, carpenter, I—I can't do this."

Her verdant eyes were wild, her breathing fast and deep. "Yes, yes you can." Her hands ran up his chest beneath his cotton shirt. "And you should." She embraced him. "I love you, woodsman. I've craved you for so long."

She bit her flushed lips. "You must have felt it. I know you did."

She stepped back and unbuttoned her blouse. "Claim me, woodsman." She unclasped her brassiere. She stood before him bare-chested letting his eyes take in her image. He did not move, yet he burned inside. He could smell her. His animal soul beating against him, begging him. She saw his struggle and stepped toward him, never taking her eyes off of his. She guided his hands to her breasts. "Claim me, woodsman," she commanded again, her fingers finding the clasp of his trousers, "or I'll claim you."

His hands fell onto hers and he pulled them to her sides. "I can't, carpenter. Heavens above, I want to, but I can't. You're the most difficult temptation I've ever fought. You're beautiful, talented—a true masterpiece like your work. If my heart didn't belong to another, I would let you claim it...but this....this is lust. I love her. Please." He retrieved her blouse and brassiere from the floor and handed them back to her. "Please." He turned his back to her, his hands running up and down his face, and back into his hair.

"Are you certain? Can you not be swayed?" She walked up behind him. "Look at me," she pleaded and he turned around to face her. "Can you ever love me?" Her clothes were tightly gathered in her hands as she spoke, her grip tightening as if willing him to comply.

"As long as my beloved lives, I swear to you, I cannot."

Tears formed and fell around her olive cheeks. "Cruel fate. Then there is nothing to be done. I had hoped you would resign yourself to me." She walked away toward the bed and began to dress herself. "I believed we were destined for more together, but it appears I've been mistaken." She slid her hand into her pants pocket, her palm finding the sharp corner of her chisel.

"I'm sorry if I misled you. You have become such a dear friend to me, carpenter. That is how I see you, although now—now that may be complicated and perhaps ill-advised."

"You're right. Look at the mess I've made. I've soiled our friendship. I suppose this will be the last we speak to one another."

"It doesn't have to be." He took a step toward her and stopped. "I—I don't know. Perhaps it is."

She turned back to face him. "Then this is to be our farewell." She walked up holding her right hand with her left, palm clasped.

"I suppose so. At least for now."

She gazed into his brown eyes and held his hand in hers.

"'Tis the blood that binds us

and makes us whole.

Our actions then defined thus,

solidify thine soul."

She kissed his hand and let go before stepping back.

Bewildered, the woodsman looked down at his hand and saw that it was wet with blood. He looked at hers as it bled. "Your hand!" He took a step forward to help, but froze.

"I claim you, woodsman," she cried.

He felt a snap. He gasped and clutched his chest before falling petrified onto the floor. "What's...happening?" He couldn't move.

The carpenter locked the doors and started a fire in the hearth. When she returned, her hand was wrapped with linen and she carried a bucket with water. She placed the bucket on the floor and knelt beside the woodsman.

"I claim you," she said, her lips touching his. "Yes, you are mine." She removed his shirt and traced his muscles with her fingertips. "You are mine, woodsman," she said as she kissed his chest, "from now...," she kissed his neck, "...until always." She kissed his lips and watched the transformation begin.

He writhed against the planks unable to scream. His bones cracked and creaked as his body convulsed. His muscles began to cramp and seize. The carpenter carefully arranged his limbs and brushed his hair with her fingers as one would pose a doll. She pulled a cloth out of the water and wrung it over the pail. His body stiffened as he struggled to breathe. She pressed the dampened cloth against his skin. Only his eyes could move. His vision blurred and refocused. Behind her, he noticed the wall lined with cedar shelves and the weathered figurines of men and women perched upon them. The room began to grow.

"You are so very special to me, woodsman. I want you to have this." She wiped her blood from the chisel against the cloth around her hand and placed its handle into his hand. "A gift for my favorite apprentice." With tears in her eyes, she rested her forehead against his. "You should have claimed me, my love."

The woodsman's eyes locked into place. He shrank into a miniature version of himself as the last of his breath left his new wooden body. The carpenter sighed and padded over to the cedar shelves where she dusted and shifted the figures in the center around to make a space for her new woodsman. She picked up his wooden effigy and slid him onto an amber shelf. She ambled across the room to the fire with his shirt. Before she could toss it onto the eager flames, she hesitated, and pulled it on over her head instead. As she sat on the settee, she held his shirt collar up to her nose and wept. ♜

ROUNDUP

By Miracle Austin

Priority #1:

Pushing the button, so I could exterminate all of them.

Priority #2:

Leaving Cydrastearea-S709 as fast as I could to prevent mass infection.

"RAIN! I CAN'T LET YOU kill them!" Shane shouted.

Staring at her, I thought back to over four months ago, when I lived on Earth with Mrs. O and the bunch. No worries like the ones I was facing now.

Mrs. O yelled, "Come down quick before you miss it, again!"

Grabbing my backpack, I slid down the stair rail and jumped off before she caught me.

"Don't think I didn't see that, Rain Stephens. Come watch with me."

I flopped down on the couch next to her.

She punched a button on her cell and a hologram appeared. The guy didn't look over thirty. He sported shoulder-length, black curly hair, deep blue eyes, and dimples. He wore khaki pants and a fitted dark, denim short-sleeve shirt with a lime bowtie. He sat on top of his desk decorated with awards and spoke:

"Salutations on August 20, 2099. I'm Dean Woolfe of Cydrastearea-S709. Are you ready for something amazing that only happens once a year? I bet you are. If you're between the ages of fourteen and seventeen, then you're eligible to apply to become a Cydrastearean Cadet and travel to Cydrastearea-S709—Cydra for short—to join a special program to improve cognition and physical abilities.

Cydra is a magnificent planet between Zahadd and Vuumeon. It's full of natural beauty and incredible wonders. If you're selected and complete the program, then you'll be able to choose the university or specialty school of your choice back on Earth with a full ride and a generous monthly stipend until you complete your studies.

Your parents or guardians will also be handsomely compensated. A one-time payment will be deposited into their accounts, once you sign the contract. So, what are you waiting for? Apply today to the Cydra Cadet Program. It's easy—just complete the short application in your hologram direct message box. You'll be notified within 24 hours or less if you've been chosen and detailed instructions will be linked to you. Your school principal will also be contacted.

Before I close, take a look behind me at Cydra for yourself. This could be your new future!"

Humongous bay windows showcased turquoise, rose, and violet skies with thousands of stars beaming down. Burgundy, castle-shaped mountains outlined the wide landscape and colorful loopers, a two-headed hummingbird species, zipped back and forth. Cascading orange and plum palm trees blew in the wind. I'd heard about this planet and program from teachers and kids in my class. I'd even done some research about Cydra.

About five years ago, a satellite discovered Cydra, way outside our solar system and within a year, a classified group of astronauts landed there to study it. They found that the planet had some similarities to Earth, and humans could inhabit it with proper essentials. A multi-billionaire created this program, because he wanted to give youth exceptional opportunities.

"Mrs. O, I'm not sure about leaving Earth to go to some unknown crazy planet that could be infested with Xenomorphs, Predators, or worse, alien zombies."

She laughed and said, "Rain, there's no such thing. You've been streaming too many of those make-believe movies. Plus, this could be your ticket out of here. No more foster homes for you. You're always talking about what would happen if you had a chance to attend Spellman. If you get selected and complete the program, then there's a full ride with no strings, like Dean Woolfe said."

"It sounds really good, but nothing in this world comes without strings," I said. I think I knew that better than most kids my age, after being dropped into ten foster homes, since I was seven.

"You're right, but some strings are worth it, like this one. Just apply and see. Your chances are pretty slim, right?"

"Yeah... I guess," I said grabbing my lunch bag off the counter.

"You have nothing to lose."

Standing there, I thought about what Mrs. O had just rattled off. A place like that wouldn't want some poor, foster girl who had nothing to give back. I applied anyway.

Opening the front door, I slipped on my scuffed up, hot pink and black Jetters,—flying high-top, tennis shoes with butterfly-shaped motors attached to the back of them—helmet, goggles, and knee and elbow pads. I touched the buttons on the sides and hovered above the ground and into the gray sky towards school. Mrs. O told me stories on how the sky used to be bright blue years ago.

During lunch that day, I heard several students talking about how they applied to the Cydra Program. I ran into Rubee Goldstein in the bathroom. She would be voted the *Stuck-Up Bitch* of Class 2100 at Fern Valley High.

Looking down at my Jetters, she rolled her eyes and said, "Those are practically three seasons ago, Stephens. They're filthy. Surprised you made it here in one piece with those poking out wires."

She was right. I'd barely did. I had to stop at least three times to rewire. I almost crashed into a Supreme Telsa-ZX2 next to me. I'd somersaulted over it just in time. The driver honked at me and sped past while shouting out, "Stay out of the airlanes if you don't know how to operate your flight gear," as he zoomed away.

Rubee glanced over at me as her transparent, cosmetic plate floated up in the air. She tapped on a shade of plum with a wand and pointed towards her mouth, and it appeared on her perfect lips. "I know I'm a surefire to get in the program. My daddy knows Dean Woolfe, personally."

I was silent and turned away from her to dry my hands under the cherry, infrared lamp.

"Didn't you hear me, Stephens?" she barked still staring down at my shoes. "I'm wearing an early release pair, Moon Jetters 2101 signed by the Takibi Star Moon, an ultra-female gymnast/ice-skater/archer/make-up artist, who won several gold and silver medals in the 2084 Olympics. These are faster and smoother—very expensive and way out of your league."

Maybe my Jetters should've stayed in the trash heap when I found them a few months ago. I stared back at her and said, "Good for you, Rubee. I hope you don't get attacked in those pretty Moon Jetters, on the planet when you land there."

"Attacked… what the hell are you talking about?" she hissed, spraying saliva in my direction.

I ducked to my left.

"C'mon, you know every planet has its weird insects. Cydra has these crazy aggressive, venomous flying, red lizards with hairy bodies and six legs called drazosnappers. They're about the size of a squirrel with golden, whipping scorpion tails and protruding fangs. If one of them even scratches you with its tail or grazes you with one of its fangs, then your survival rate is less than three percent, if antivenom is not in reach."

"Whatever!"

"Hey, you can hologram me, if you make it, right?"

Rubee huffed and stomped out of the bathroom.

Her cosmetic plate remained floating in the air.

That evening when I returned home, Mrs. O, was taking out a huge pan of lasagna. The other kids—Joe, Mike, and Myrtle—were in the living room. Joe and Mike had despised me ever since I'd invaded their so-called home, but Myrtle, eleven and the youngest in the O foster family, had welcomed me.

Myrtle ran up to me and asked, "Are you leaving us, Rain? Mrs. O told us that you applied? I'm really going to miss you."

"I haven't heard anything yet, and I probably won't. Listen, Myrtle, I'm not getting in, so don't worry. Girls like me just don't." I started up the stairs.

Myrtle caught my hand and whispered, "Hey, maybe a girl like you just might." She smiled, hugged me around my waist, and joined the rest of the kids in the kitchen.

"Hurry back down, Rain. You know my lasagna seems to evaporate around here," Mrs. O said, as she untied her apron and smiled at me.

Taking a deep breath, I climbed the stairs to wash up.

I was about to go downstairs when a glowing, blue message image appeared on my ceiling. I hit the play button on my cell phone. "You have one hologram message from Dr. Woolfe."

My mouth dropped. I froze for a moment. Then, I ran out my room and yelled downstairs, "Mrs. O, please come quick!" I listened again to make sure I'd heard it correctly the first time.

Mrs. O dragged herself into my room out of breath, and the other kids were right behind her. Myrtle made her way over and stood next to me.

"What's wrong?" Mrs. O asked panting.

"I have a message from Dr. Woolfe," I said in a trembling tone.

"Oh, Rain, this is so exciting. Have you listened to it yet?" she asked.

"No, I wanted you all to be here when I did."

"Play it!" Mrs. O urged.

Before I could touch the button, Myrtle did it for me.

A full hologram of Dr. Woolfe appeared in the middle of my room. He stood there with both hands on his waist.

"Miss Rain Stephens, congratulations! You've been selected to become a Cydrastearean Cadet. Your flight will depart tomorrow morning from your local airport and then transfer you to a special transport with your travel companions. Your travel plans are attached to this message for you to download, including the contract.

Report to your check-in at 0700. Don't be late, unless you want your alternate to take your place. Congratulations again, Miss Stephens. You're about to embark on a new adventure that many can only dream about. I look forward to seeing you tomorrow night during the reception.

Please only bring three items—apart from your cell phone—that can fit in an 8x10 space. I'll discuss our communication protocol more at the reception. Return your signed contract to me this evening. Until we meet, Miss Stephens, I bid you your last night on Earth."

His hologram vanished and so did Mike and Joe. Myrtle grabbed my hand and said, "Rain, I don't want you to leave me, but you were chosen, so you gotta go. A girl like you made it in!"

"You really think I should go?"

She nodded, released my hand, and exited my room.

Mrs. O sat down on my bed.

"I guess this is it. It happened so fast," I said.

Standing up, she walked towards my open window and pointed towards the sky. "You're going to be way up there somewhere. Rain. You know other kids I've taken care of have applied, but were never chosen. You're the first." She turned around and hugged me. "Now pack your small bag, download your flight information, sign that contract, and send it back, immediately. We'll leave the house around 5:30 a.m. so you'll be there early. There's no way anyone else is taking your spot. Get some rest. Your life won't be the same after tonight."

On our way to the airport, I thought about how Mrs. O has taken care of me over the last year. She'd been the best foster mom I'd ever had. I knew I would miss her and Myrtle. She parked. Myrtle and Mrs. O stepped out of the car and hugged me. I didn't want to let either one of them go. I thought I could block my tears. I was wrong. We were all crying together. Mrs. O was digging through her purse to find tissue and handed Myrtle and me a few.

We embraced until Mrs. O whispered, "Rain, it's time for you to go. I'm going to miss having you around the house. I'll especially miss scolding you for sliding down the stair rail. You learn all you can on Cydra. Don't forget to holo-message me, if you're not too busy."

"I'll be messaging you both."

"Be careful out there," Mrs. O said.

I nodded.

As I started to walk away from them, Myrtle yelled out, "Check your bag when you get to Cydra! Love you!"

I waved and watched them get back in the car and drive away before I entered the airport. I checked in and boarded the crowded flight soon after. I wanted to know what Myrtle had added to my bag. It still felt the same, no lighter or heavier. I'd packed a picture of us at the beach from last summer, a faded vintage Brittany Spears T-shirt, and my lightning rod stud earrings. I pressed down and could hear paper crinkling.

After a few hours in the air, the plane landed at Chicago O'Hare International Airport II. I followed the instructions to head to Terminal CDY-S9, located in a deep end of the airport. Upon arrival, I noticed secure glass doors. I retrieved my paperwork from my pocket, and I glanced down at it. I found a code to enter into the keypad.

Seven other girls around my age were huddled up and talking. They were all dressed in mango and turquoise jumpsuits embossed with shiny letters, which spelled out Cydra Cadet 3, and assigned Roman numerals for each girl printed on the back. One girl looked up at me, but didn't say anything. A young lady on a levitating powerscooter came up to me with a glowing, green clipboard and pen in front of her.

"Greetings. My name is Miss Daphene York, and I'm the intake director. May I see your paperwork?" she requested.

I handed it over to her, and she scanned it with the pen.

"Thank you and welcome aboard, Miss Stephens. Please wait here."

She returned with a bag.

"You'll find your uniform inside. Change and join the other ladies. In the next thirty minutes, we'll complete a quick health scan on each of you, and then you all will be on your way to Cydra."

"What kind of health scan?" I questioned hugging my chest.

"Oh, it's nothing to be nervous about. Just a little finger prick for a blood sample and a walk through that scanner over there," she said, pointing over her shoulder.

After I changed into my comfy jumper, I noticed a shoe box at the bottom of the bag. I flipped off the lid and pushed back the red and white polka dot tissue paper. A shiny pair of silver and yellow Jetters rested. They looked like Rubee's, but sweeter—these were autographed by Wicked Crimson, my favorite and one of the coolest girl bands around. I kicked off my old ones and slipped them on.

Upon my return to the sitting area, I noticed that all the girls were standing in line waiting to be scanned. Triple, elliptical rings spun around each girl's entire body, as they stepped into the middle of the platform. When scanning was complete, we all ran our right index finger down a square glass on the side of the scanner's panel. Miss York tapped our fingers with a bandage pen that terminated the bleeding and a clear bandage wrapped around our fingers.

Only one girl was left to be scanned and when she gave a blood sample, loud sirens sounded off along with twirling, bright lights. We jumped, looking around. Miss York ushered the girl out quickly to a side door, where a guy in a suit and dark shades escorted her from the area.

"Is she okay? What happened?" I asked.

Miss York said, "She didn't pass the test—she'll become very ill within a year or less. Her replacement will arrive tomorrow and travel in her place to Cydra."

I wondered if I'd made the right decision to be part of this program after what I'd just witnessed. Could I still back out? If I did that, then Mrs. O wouldn't receive her compensation, and I really wanted her and Myrtle to be taken care of.

"Ladies, it's time to board. Now, if any of you are having second thoughts and wish to terminate your contract, this would be the time," she said and looked at each girl.

No one volunteered.

"Okay, please locate your assigned seats and follow the instructions from your captain. I hope each of you succeeds on Cydra and beyond. We'll *not* meet again. I bid you goodbye." She placed her scooter in reverse and faded out of sight.

We traveled down the spiral walkway and boarded translucent stairs. The aircraft we were boarding wasn't a rocket, but a Hyperboloid spaceship with rotating wings. The interior was all white with blacked-out windows. Each seat had Roman numerals that corresponded to the ones on our jumpsuits. A soprano voice spoke from the speakers.

"Good morning, ladies. My name is Captain Batwana. You'll find a magenta band secured on the arm of your chair. I'll need you to place it on your wrist and fasten your seatbelt in the next five minutes. Once you see green lasers shooting up and down the ceiling, you'll begin to feel sleepy."

I unsnapped the thick band and examined it in my hands.

Captain Batwana continued, "The band will release a dual medication into your bloodstream that will slow your heart rate and place each of you into a temporary sleep paralysis. This is necessary as you couldn't survive traveling from Earth to Cydra without it. Any questions?"

I didn't hear a chirp from any of the other girls, even though they sure were Chatty Cathies before we boarded.

"One more thing, ladies. Each band has been downloaded with your personal playlists and memories, which will accompany you during your rest," Captain Batwana said. "Alright, I'm about to begin the flight plan. I'll meet each of you once we land."

I pulled my seatbelt strap around my waist and was about to fasten it, when I felt multiple taps on the back of my headrest. I leaned over to my left. A freckled-faced girl with a midnight blue pixie haircut waved at me.

"Hi, I'm Shane," she whispered.

"Hey," I replied. "What do you think so far about all of this?"

"I think it's going to be exciting," Shane said.

The lasers danced on the ceiling.

"It's time. I'll see you on Cydra when we wake up," she said.

"Sure."

When I woke up, I recalled how I'd dreamt about when I first arrived at Mrs. O's home, and how she'd welcomed me in. I could even smell warm strawberry and lemon cookie drops from the kitchen. She never questioned what happened at my previous fosters. There was no judgement. This was the first time I felt safe in my life.

"Finally," a heartfelt ballad by Wicked Crimson, continued to play in my head. I knew we'd traveled for many hours. Yet, I felt as if I'd just been napping. All the other girls around me were still in their deep sleep. I peeked back and noticed Shane's seat was empty.

Footsteps approached. I watched a petite lady with a bald head wearing rainbow-colored goggles and matching boots make her way toward each girl to make sure she was up. I figured this had to be Captain Batwana. A badass Medusa tattoo decorated her muscular, upper arm.

"Are you feeling okay, Miss Stephens?" she asked me and stooped down, as she ran a thick, mahogany wand with buttons down my forehead and chest. She tapped a button on it—my vitals and heartrate readings all popped up in front of us with my name, weight, and birthdate underneath. "All clear. You're good to exit. Now, keep your band on, or you'll float away when you're outside. If your band malfunctions for some reason, then those special Jetters you have on will also prevent you from flying off to who knows where," Captain Batwana said with a grin.

"Thanks. Umm, where did the girl behind me go?" I asked.

"She woke up first. She's probably preparing for the reception tonight with Dr. Woolfe and the faculty."

"I almost forgot about that."

"That's a mandatory event, Miss Stephens—make sure you attend. You can exit how you entered, and an XC37 robot guide will be waiting to take you to your living quarters."

"Can I ask you a question?" I said as I stood up to collect my bag from the compartment above me.

"Of course."

"Is there anything I need to be concerned about?" I asked taking a few deep breaths.

"Not to my knowledge. In fact, since I've been transporting cadets from Earth to Cydra, no one has ever requested to return to Earth."

That seemed strange, that no one had wanted to return back to take advantage of the offered scholarships and opportunities. Were things so good here that they never wanted to leave?

"Enjoy your reception tonight and time on Cydra. I bid you nothing, but good fortunes here, Miss Stephens." She bowed and stepped away from me.

A slender, bronze robot, which reminded me of an ancient, standing fan I'd found in Mrs. O's attic last spring, guided me as I exited off the ship. "Follow me, please," it said in a choppy, metallic voice.

Pausing for over a minute to look back at the ship, I exited onto Cydra. I gazed in awe at its multiple moons and iridescent skyline that seemed to glisten. I'd never seen anything like this before. The ground was full of lush white sand with lilac crystals. A looper landed on my shoulder for a moment and dashed away, leaving shiny flakes circling around my face.

The robot demanded, "Please follow," as it made clunky sounds strolling down the pathway.

It waved its metal hand over a keypad and the building doors opened. The hallways were massive. Camera drones flew up and down, high above me. We walked for several minutes before we arrived at my room.

"This is your new home, Cydra Dorm #3. Your attire for the evening is in your closet. The start time is 1730 hours. I bid you goodnight," the robot said and rolled away.

Once I entered my room, the door slid closed. I heard water running. I inspected the room—no windows. I found a stiff A-line dress with the same colors and assigned Roman numerals as the jumpsuits, hanging in my closet with strappy, almond heels.

There were two twin beds, closets, chairs, and glass desks, plus, doors to separate bathrooms on each side of the room. When I touched the glass desk with my hand, personal memories of Earth flashed all over it. I could even rearrange them. I thought about a concert I attended last Halloween, and those memories popped up.

I backed up and sat on the bed thinking how I wasn't on Earth anymore, but on Cydra with all this awesome technology around me, waiting to be explored. Glancing down at my bag, I remembered Myrtle's gift. I unzipped it, and dug it out.

If you're reading this, then you're on Cydra. I bet that place is truly something. I'm sure it's not polluted and overpopulated like Earth. I knew you would be selected. They need someone brave and strong like you, Rain. Don't worry about me and Mrs. O. We'll be fine. Just do your best and do what's right, like you've always told me. I hope we see each other after your training is complete. Take care. Love always, your little sis, Myrtle

P.S. I cannot wait to hear about everything. You can't leave anything out!

Tears ran down my cheeks as I folded her letter up and placed it back inside my bag. I wiped them away. I looked at the floating digital clock. It was getting close to the time for the reception. I took a quick shower and dried off. As I zipped up the back of my dress, the other bathroom door opened.

"Hey, it's you, again," I said. "I didn't think I would see you this soon."

"Anything is possible on Cydra, Rain," she said, tightening the towel around her chest.

"Shane, right?" I asked as I placed my feet into the heels.

"You got it. Shoot, I better hurry," she said.

Handing her dress to her, I said, "You'll make it."

"Thanks, roomie."

"Welcome."

Shane slid her dress on and zipped up just in time before the door slid open, and a XC37 entered to escort us down to the reception area.

It was packed. Twinkling white lights hung down like swinging, jungle vines and starlight from the open ceiling made it look like a magical prom night. Shane and I found our seats. As robots served dinner, I looked all around the room in search of Rubee, but she wasn't here.

Shane nudged me.

"Are you okay?" she asked.

"Yes, I just thought a classmate of mine would be here," I said, squinting my eyes.

"She just wasn't Cydra material, but we are!" she said and laughed.

"Guess so… Hey, why are the only males in the room faculty?" I asked, staring down at the plate of shrimp scampi that had a red slimy sauce drenched all over it.

With her mouth full as she chewed, Shane said, "Boys distract… Isn't this good?"

I was about to respond back, but Dr. Woolfe began his speech:

"Welcome to the future and more. Each of you were hand selected to be part of our unique program on Cydra. Your school curriculums will consist of intense art, reading, writing, math, science, flight training, martial arts, horticulture, yoga and meditation, and special weapon training, which will be taught by the brilliant faculty behind me. A very strict diet will be followed for all your meals, especially ritual vitamin shakes in the mornings. These shakes are mandatory to your training and time here. Daily digital readings by your assigned XC37 will notify me, if you've skipped any. Skipping more than three may mean immediate expulsion from Cydra, including recall of the remaining monetary gift given to your guardian with repayment expectations. Once you complete your studies here, you'll be given the choice to return back to Earth to pursue your dream college or special studies, paid in full, or you may remain on Cydra, as long as you wish. One more thing, no hologram communications, until the end of your program. Enjoy your evening and sleep well. Your training begins early in the morning. I bid each of you much success here."

"Is he insane? No hologram communications! I don't remember him mentioning anything about that before," I said, raising my voice.

"That part is in the contract," Shane said in a calm tone.

"Well, I just don't recall it. I promised Mrs. O and Myrtle that I would holo them."

Looking up at me, she asked, "Your family back home?"

"Yes," I said as I moved the shrimp around with my utensil.

"You can write letters."

Glancing down at my plate, I said, "Just not the same as seeing someone." I twirled some of the pasta onto my fork, sniffed it, and placed in my mouth. "Shane, if those shakes taste anything like this fishy crap in my mouth, then I may just get kicked out of here."

"You won't. I'm going to help you get through all of it, even the no holo communications, and you're going to do the same for me, roomie. Eat up. We have a big day ahead of us tomorrow."

I thought about what Shane had said that night and convinced myself to do what I needed to do for four semesters and one summer. I read Myrtle's letter each night after classes to inspire me to keep going.

The days and weeks flew by—we were nearing winter and our second semester. The education that I was receiving on Cydra was mind blowing. I was learning complicated acrobatic, flight moves in my Jetters, growing strange plants, practicing Wing Chu and Hapkido, and reading banned books from a hundred years ago. My friendship with Shane blossomed.

I craved more. I wanted to know who the other girls were from Cydra Dorms #1, #2, and #4. I wondered how they were doing. However, that was forbidden. You were only allowed to engage with students from your own dorm house. Too many crazy *rules* and *secrets* existed here… I couldn't wait to return to Earth and see my family, and pursue my dreams.

After winter finals, Shane, a group of girls from our dorm, and I decided to go on an evening hike. The temperature was 89 degrees. We came across a crystal, tequila ocean and sat on huge rocks on top of Cydra Nine Peak to watch flying dolphins jump over two hundred feet in the air and dive back down. A few flew towards us and allowed us to pet them. They had large, purple eyes and made cooing echoes. Their glistening black and white bodies reminded me of an Appaloosa horse's coat pattern.

One of the girls wandered off from our group. After fifteen minutes, we heard her yell out, "Hey guys, I found a cool cave. Come check it out!"

I'd started getting off the warm rock when Shane grabbed my arm and whispered, "Stay."

Jerking my arm away from her, I said in a stern tone, "It sounds interesting. This is the first time in months we've been outside our prison walls without stalker robots or teachers watching our every move. We've earned this. You should try to have a little fun for once." I left her sitting alone.

Before I reached the cave, I heard piercing screams. All of the girls ran out as a swarm of drazosnappers flew out behind them. Their coarse hairs fired out and shot throughout the air, targeting the girls' bodies until they collapsed.

The drazosnappers pounced on them and started draining them. I stood still, trembling all over. Although I'd read about them, I discounted them being real. Shane came up behind me and softly spoke in my ear, "Move slow and be quiet... they sense rapid movement and loud noises. Follow me."

As we were just about to make it inside the perimeter, I stepped on a branch. A loud crunch echoed in the wind and a drazosnapper found us. Before Shane could push the force shield over our fortress, it punctured my thigh with its tail and fangs. I screamed out and tears zipped down my cheeks. It felt as if thousands of Texas fire ants and multiple jellyfish stung me all at once. The front half of its body swung back and forth, while the other half banged up against the shield until it ceased.

Shane dragged me to the closest infirmary, located in Cydra Dorm #4—a dorm that was off limits to all underclassmen cadets. I dropped down onto the medical table. My breathing quickened and my heart began to race. No staff were present. She flung cabinets, refrigerator doors, and drawers open to search for the antivenom. Medical supplies and medications cluttered the floor. My vision became blurry. I saw her stab two long needles in my thigh and chest. They stung for over a minute.

"Sorry, I had to do that before the toxin reached your heart. You're going to be okay," she said.

I closed my eyes and woke up a few hours later. I felt better, but had to pee.

"Shane, thank you for your quick actions. I should've listened to you and avoided the cave excursion."

"Glad you're okay." She squeezed my hand.

"Where's the bathroom?" I pleaded.

"Down the hall to the left."

"Thanks." I looked down and ran my hand over my bruised and swollen leg.

My orientation must've been off, after I went to the bathroom. I entered a different room instead. It was an oversized, cold, and full of miniature, glass aquariums with pale tadpole and octopus-looking creatures with spikes outlining their flailing tentacles, as they floated. I heard footsteps behind me, and I turned around.

"What in the hell are all these, Shane?"

"You weren't supposed to find out like this, Rain," she said with her head lowered. "I couldn't let you die because you've been my friend."

"Shane, you didn't answer me, what are these things?"

"Embryos... Cydrastearean embryos."

"For what?"

She looked away and mumbled, "You and the other girls... humans. Your date to have your Cydrastearean embryo implant is scheduled during the summer before your senior year. That's the magic year when a human body is ready for the delicate, medical procedure."

"Hold on. Are you telling me that I'm going to be a surrogate for one of those slimy, octo-tad little monsters?"

Clearing her throat, she said, "Cydrastearean embryo is the correct term, an alien being."

I walked around her and stared at the glass cases and began processing everything.

"Now, it all makes sense. That's why Rubee wasn't selected. Only *rejects*, like me, fosters or homeless girls are picked. I always wondered why most of the girls in our dorm came from foster homes. We can easily be erased. Just dangling a prize in front of us is all it takes. Then comes the isolation, forcing us to keep our mouths shut, feeding us those awful meals and shakes to prep our bodies, and lastly impregnating us. Boys would never be selected for Cydra—they're wombless."

"You summed it up well," Shane said.

"This program is a freakin' *roundup* of forgotten girls. Hottie, Dr. Woolfe, and his pack knew who they wanted all along. Guess what, I'm not keeping my mouth shut. This is all *ending* tonight! I'm killing every last one of those embryos. So, don't get in my way, or I'll kill you too," I said as a stream of sweat ran down my neck and back. My heart started racing.

"Rain, please stop! You don't understand everything. Cydrastearean females can't carry to full-term anymore. The planet's water poisoned the female's wombs, and genetic defects began to emerge. Before the poison impacted the protected queens, they were able to produce thousands of eggs."

"I don't care about Cydra history!" I screamed out and turned away from her.

"Just hear me out... In vitro fertilization procedures were conducted. Later, Cydra scientists replicated Cydrastearean eggs in labs. We've been doing this for the last ten years, ever since we discovered that young human girls are our last and best hope to host our embryos to survive. Due to the violent births by our species, the fatality rate of humans is inevitable."

Facing her, I replied, "Wait, you're a Cydrastearean? You look like me."

"Yes, we can *shapeshift* into any living thing. I'm sorry you feel how you do. I wish there was another way, but I'm afraid there's not." She frowned.

"Wow! You could've told me—you had so many chances to, but you didn't. You and your kind are heartless and so selfish. Girls only serve as incubators and then they die, after giving birth to your creepy spawn. The option to return to Earth was always a lie, right?"

"The way you feel about Cydrasteareans now would've been the same if I had told you earlier. I had to keep my secret. I was assigned to you before we boarded the ship. I sensed something special about you, Rain, and I wanted to be a friend to you for as long as I could. Yes, the specialized education and scholarships were only bait, but guardians are truly rewarded, when the contract is signed and again upon death of their cadet, due to unforeseen circumstances."

Rolling my eyes, I replied, "I can't believe all of this you're telling me. You and your friendship have both been fake, since we first met. You don't understand friendship at all!" I roared.

"No, that's not true." Tears streamed down her face.

"Oh, yes it is! You know everything you just told me is wrong, Shane!"

Dr. Woolfe busted through the doors and shouted, "You two shouldn't be in here!" Shane, I'm so disappointed in you, sister."

My eyes blinked and widened. "He's your brother?"

She nodded.

Caressing his perfect, bronze chin, he said, "Shane, you know that we're going to have to murder her before she talks."

Shane stared deep into my eyes and then looked over at him. She sideswept him with her left leg. He fell backwards. She turned around and focused down the hallway. A blue syringe zoomed in a wavy pattern through the air. It landed inside of her open hand. She flicked the top off and punctured the side of his neck without a blink.

"Wow, I didn't expect you to do that. So, you're telekinetic too? What did you give him? He looks dead."

"I injected him with Prolunvan-517. He's in a short-term coma and will awake tomorrow night. He'll be okay. Listen, switch Jetters with me. We're nearly the same size. I have extreme flame throwers in the back."

Slipping out of mine and into hers, I asked, "Are you serious?"

"Just press this button," she said as she yanked off a hidden auburn, oblong-shaped necklace from around her neck. "Touch it. It won't hurt you."

I was reluctant to do so, but I did. A warm, orange light illuminated my entire hand.

"All of your information has been captured. You'll have access to all of my financial affairs and other things." She smiled. "It also has a mini flash drive inside. You'll be able to download everything we've been doing here. Find Captain Batwana. She'll help you and transport you back to Earth, once she views this footage. Don't ever allow anyone to take this from you."

"Come with me, Shane!"

"No, Zamaun, my brother, won't stop—someone has to end this. Rain, you're right about everything you said about my kind. Cydrasteareans have been thoughtless—we've caused so much death to humans for way too long. I'm sorry. Now, go!" Her eyes began to tear up. She pushed me away with a slight wave of her hand.

Sliding almost twenty feet from her, I said in a rigid tone, "I'm going to stop this! No other girl deserves to go through this deception to find out she's only being trafficked. We have a right to control our own bodies."

"Yes, and you will now."

"Shane, I was wrong, you are a good friend. Thank you." I gathered up bottles of sangria~isopropyl from the other room and returned to douse all the aquariums. I pushed the button on Shane's Jetters to light them up, and I flew out of the infirmary to find Captain Batwana.

Now, I had a new mission—maybe this is why I was chosen for Cydra—and I was departing earlier than expected with no plans to ever return. ♜

LOVESOME

By Katya de Becerra

FROM A YOUNG AGE ARCADIA learned—and she learned it the hard way—that when it came to magic, nothing was ever free, not even a taste. Everything had a cost, a sacrifice, but the magic's wielder did not get to choose what to give away in payment. Magic took what it took.

But even knowing she was risking everything—her home, her life—when wielding her magic to help people, Arcadia couldn't stop herself from doing this work, just like a swallow couldn't stop its wings from beating. It was simply her nature.

Arcadia was thirteen when she first understood her magic's true cost.

One evening, Innah, her best friend at the time, came over to help Arcadia run lines for the school play with Arcadia in the lead. After several months of rehearsals, the prospect of finally going on stage was both tantalizing and terrifying. As the girls drank tea and gossiped about their classmates, Innah opened up about her heartache. Amid her parents' separation, her home life was upended, a chaotic and bitter sadness. Without fully understanding what she was doing, Arcadia enchanted Innah's tea, transforming it into a sadness-relieving potion. The act was instinctual, a pure intent. When Innah drank the tea, her eyes lit up and her lips stretched into a content smile.

Arcadia knew then that this was her calling. She was to mend the aches of the heart, to calm the weary souls. And because she hadn't immediately experienced the reverse effect of her actions, Arcadia thought such magic, the helpful kind, required no payment.

The following day, as Arcadia stood on stage, sweating in embarrassment, dozens of spectators staring at her in pity, she knew the reason she was suddenly incapable of speech was not nerves. As the cost of soothing Innah's breaking heart, Arcadia was rendered voiceless.

Her voice returned after a few days, when Innah's heartache started to come back. Arcadia's second lesson revealed that impermanence was the nature of magic. The binds of enchanted spells weakened. The knots of the spell loosened.

And yet, over the years to come, Arcadia continued to work her magic, giving away parts of herself, for a time, as a cost. Fifteen years had passed since Arcadia's first foray into magic, and she'd found her footing now. She lived on the outskirts of the kingdom of Hadyah, where she ran an apothecary she'd inherited after her mother passed. While the apothecary kept a roof over Arcadia's head and bread in her pantry, it was under the cover of darkness that Arcadia crafted her love potions. That's what she called them anyway, love potions, because that's what her mother called them and her mother before her. But Arcadia's love potions were not the type to trick someone into a relationship. No, her potions soothed or gave courage, they let suppressed feelings roam free, and they helped the broken-hearted to move on.

There soon came the day when Arcadia's skills were put to the real test. A cloaked visitor came to the apothecary, asking Arcadia for an impossible thing. When Arcadia's witch nature flared up in response, she was left with no choice but to wield her magic.

#   #   #

That day in the apothecary went by in a blink. Dozens of scripts for remedies were filled, and, as the sun began its descent, the steady flow of customers' faces had turned into a blur. The shop's wares were always more popular in the winter when the bone-chilling weather weakened the body which would otherwise withstand the illness in the summer time.

Today was particularly busy. The kingdom was about to endure a week-long festival celebrating the one-year anniversary of Torrin the First ascending the throne. Torrin's probationary year was coming to an end, and soon his reign would be absolute. The festival mandated most shops and public buildings closed, as everyone was expected to join in the festivities, whether they felt like celebrating or not. Torrin's ruling style over the past year alternated between trying to buy his subjects' love with free-flowing wine and fireworks and intimidating them. It was not uncommon for Torrin's critics to disappear into the night, never to be seen again. Some were believed poisoned and left to die in a ditch, others sent to rot away in the dungeons. Neighbors were encouraged to keep an eye on each other and report any dissent and anti-royal sentiment, no matter how small, to the King's secret police. In this atmosphere of suspicion and fear, while the upcoming festivities promised fun and games, they could as easily turn violent, plunging the country into darkness. Even Arcadia, who lived and worked far away from the capital, felt the pressure growing, and could see the unease in her customers' haunted eyes.

By the time the mechanical clock above the apothecary's shelves struck five and the last of the lingering crowd cleared out, Arcadia could barely feel her feet. Her focus was waning, and her insides curled in discomfort at the very idea of having to join in the celebrations of her country's feared ruler. But she'd be in trouble if the patrolling Royal Guard saw her in the shop after hours. *Sigh.*

Going through her end-of-day motions in an accelerated tempo, Arcadia opened the registry book and made a note of which ingredients and mixtures were running low. Ginger root, dried zeephoria, the romash extract. She'd place the refill orders after the week of forced festivities was over and the kingdom was back to its regular rhythm. Regardless of the political situation, Arcadia's allegiance was to her customers. She had to keep the apothecary running to help those in need. That's what her late mom would have wanted her to do.

The melodious ringing of the doorbell announced an after-hours customer.

At first Arcadia thought she'd imagined the sound, but the ice-cold blast from the street said otherwise. It was too early for the night-time patrol, and she wasn't expecting any supplicants tonight—that's what Arcadia called those seeking her magical offerings, to distinguish them from the apothecary's visitors, though at times the line between the two wasn't that well defined. Normally, however, the supplicants wouldn't use the shop's front door, instead favoring the shadowed alley in the back.

Didn't I lock the front door? Arcadia wondered. Something had been off with her lately. She was forgetful, and there was this nagging, odd feeling she couldn't quite pin down nor shake off. In fact, most of her last year had been a blur. She needed to be more careful, to use her magic less and care about her own wellbeing more. *Why not start now?*

"We're closed!" she said from behind the stand that separated her from the apothecary's customers.

Someone cleared their throat but said nothing.

Arcadia didn't look up. Making an eye contact was often enough for her magical skills to come to life, building a bond between her and the supplicant. Once that bond was in place, Arcadia had no choice but to help, to do all in her power to fulfill the asker's request.

"Would you perhaps make an exception?" said a velvety smooth voice.

A whole-body shiver went through Arcadia. *That voice.* Did she know this person? Or was it just its unusual timbre that had her react this way, as if she was speeding toward the edge of a cliff on a spooked horse?

Despite her better judgement, she looked up. The magic within her snapped to attention, its tendrils spreading out of Arcadia's solar plexus. *Damn it!*

She could still suppress it, prevent this bond from being made. If only she could stop herself from gawking at the visitor.

The woman standing before Arcadia was most unusual looking. She was close to Arcadia in age, but that's where their similarities ended. If Arcadia was petite and curvy, the visitor was tall, slender, and painfully straight-spined, her shoulders pushed back in a posture which spoke of many years of conditioning in some finishing school where the daughters of the wealthy had the noble manners drilled in to them with whatever means necessary. Arcadia herself has avoided such a fate on the account of being born into a merchant family, her time deemed better spent in the apothecary shop with her mother, learning about plants and medicines and their correct formulations.

And, of course, there was her family's magical side, but Arcadia's education in potion magic was clandestine and difficult to define on the account of not being bound by specific schedules or lesson plans.

What could possibly bring a noble woman to Arcadia's shop? It was unlikely this stern beauty was here to procure some medicinal brew. The rich had servants to do that, and besides, they wouldn't patronize some lowly apothecary in the industrial part of town, so far away from the glamour of the capital.

The woman was here for magic. Arcadia could almost sense her intent, radiating off her in waves.

"How can I help you, my lady?" Arcadia asked, fingers frozen over the registry book.

The woman eyed Arcadia, a measured look, and approached, cold air from the street trailing after her. Her fur-trimmed cloak was of the finest silken thread. It shimmered black, contrasted by its bright red lining. Her blue-black hair, dusted with brittle snow, was parted in the middle and pulled back into a tight twist that surely had to hurt. Her face, stunning but cruel, was deprived of a smile or even a smirk.

"Do you know who I am?" the woman asked, a trace of something like impatience briefly lighting her green eyes, a pale ghost of emotion.

Arcadia braved a longer look, ignoring the spikes of magic igniting in her blood. The stranger's voice definitely provoked some faint recognition, but did Arcadia know this woman? Had they met before?

"The lady seems familiar, but I cannot place her," said Arcadia, hiding her rising anxiety behind the proper speech.

The woman's lips stretched into a tight smile, but the change of expression didn't last, soon reverting to its severe state. "You needn't call me lady. Ravelia will suffice. Or just Lia."

Arcadia's face grew warm. Of course! From her velvety speech to her pale green eyes, Lia bore a striking similarity to Torrin the First. The blue-black hair, the tall stature. This was the tyrant king's only heir.

"Lia," Arcadia said, the name distant yet deliciously familiar on her tongue. "What can I do for you, Your Highness?"

"Well, funny you ask, Arcadia," said the royal heir. "I was hoping you'd make me a potion. And please, none of this 'Your Highness' nonsense. Everyone's equal under Father's rule, wouldn't you agree?"

Potion. Arcadia grew very cold inside and her magic flared painfully. "Your Highness... *Lia*, you've come to the right place." She nodded at the full shelves. "What ails you? Is it the winter cough? The head cold?"

"Oh, I thought I was being clear," Lia said. "I require a *magical* potion. A love potion, to be precise. Aren't you a potion witch? I hope I have the right address." Lia's words were perfectly polite, but Arcadia couldn't help hearing some mysterious subtext in the royal heir's speech.

Resistance would be futile, Arcadia knew. If anything, it might irritate

Lia to the point where she could order Arcadia's arrest, or worse, execute her on the spot. Arcadia had no doubt King Torrin's daughter had this kind of power. But… some unexplained sensation within her chest told her Lia wouldn't do that. Still, Arcadia had no interest in testing the heir's patience.

"What kind of love potion do you require?" Arcadia asked. "To renew your hopes? To free your spirit of unrequited desires? To soothe your broken heart?" *Did Torrin's daughter even have a heart that could break?* Arcadia wondered. This specimen standing before her was winter personified, cold and indifferent. Why then did Arcadia have this fire coming to life inside of her, ignited by Lia's presence?

A tiny facial muscle twinged on Lia's face. Her delicate lips pressed into a sad line. "My heart may indeed be in need of mending, but alas the potion I am after is not for me. It is for Father."

Arcadia nearly choked on her rapid inhale. Lia's father, the tyrant who had somehow tricked the Royal Council into voting him into power, was volatile, relishing his absolute power over his subjects. It was a miracle that no public executions were scheduled during the upcoming festivities. Torrin the First loved to remind the kingdom what he could do.

"Surely, our benevolent King will not subject himself to lowly potion magic?" Arcadia said, while her insides twisted with discomfort. She was beginning to see Lia's arrival to her doorstep for what it was: an ill omen. Everything about this woman, from her black cloak to her raven wing hair and blood-red lips, was a bad premonition.

"I'll be the judge of that," Lia said, then added, softer, as if sensing Arcadia's inner turmoil. "The potion is my gift to the King, it is meant to be a surprise which I'll present to him by the end of the week to celebrate the first anniversary of his rule."

Arcadia's blood jumped at the words, her magic reacting to Lia's intent. Much to her horror, Arcadia felt their magical bond starting to build, eager to fulfill Lia's unusual request. If Arcadia denied this urge, if she were to break this bond before it could fully take hold, she'd pay for it dearly, likely with her health. But wouldn't the alternative be so much worse? Denying the royal heir would surely have deadly consequences for Arcadia.

"And what would our dear King, let he live forever, wish to gain from drinking the potion?" Arcadia asked, resigning to her fate.

"The unconditional love of his subjects, of course," said Lia. The snow in her hair and on her shoulders had melted, the effect leaving her somehow more corporeal and less like some being from a cruel fairy-tale.

Perhaps Acadia didn't hear it right, though Lia's words were clear enough. Still, Arcadia asked, to be sure, "Torrin the First, the ruler of the realm, our kind and eternal Father, wishes to be... *loved* by his people?"

Lia nodded.

In a series of deafening claps, the first of the fireworks shattered the silence of the apothecary. Arcadia didn't even notice that the night had fallen, and the festivities begun. This week was meant to warm the reluctant, suspicious, fearful public to their King. But could it really be that Torrin the First wanted his subjects to love him for real and not because free wine and the fear of the dungeons made them?

A potion that would make a country love its tyrannical ruler—was such a thing truly possible? Arcadia's witch blood, which had ignited into action by Lia's request, seemed to think so. Arcadia had no choice now but to consent.

"I don't even know if such a potion is possible," Arcadia admitted. "I've never attempted it before."

"I have no doubt that if anyone can accomplish it, it's you. Will you come with me, Arcadia? I'd like to smuggle you into the Palace before first light. You can get started on the potion right way, with the entirety of the Palace's resources at your disposal. But I must ask you to keep a low profile and remain in the quarters I've had prepared for you."

"All my ingredients are here. I brew my potions in the back room…," Arcadia protested, but the heir's unwavering gaze cooled her protest.

"I need you in the palace," Lia said. "It has everything you could possibly need—and more."

"I don't really have a choice, do I?" Arcadia asked.

With a closed-mouthed smile, Lia beckoned the potion witch to follow her.

This woman will be the death of me, thought Arcadia as she reached for her coat.

As a discreet black carriage carried Arcadia and the royal heir away from the kingdom's outskirts and into its glittering center, the view outside changed. Gone were the simple, wooden houses of the working classes as well as the sturdier edifices of the merchants, replaced by the white-stone mansions and minor palaces.

The Awakening Avenue. The Resistance Square. The Revolution Palace. Every single place here was meant to commemorate the kingdom's turbulent past. And as the carriage went deeper into the capital's heart, the decadent luxury of Hadiya was contrasted by the grey efficiency of its surveillance cameras, while the sepia photographs of the disappeared citizens graced the building walls, peeking from behind the gold-plated statues.

#   #   #

Lia led Arcadia inside the Revolution Palace via one of its many hidden passages, keeping them away from the unwanted attention of the guards.

The moment Arcadia stepped on the palace's grounds, magic within her surged and rioted. *Like called to like*, an old saying went. Arcadia knew then that the rumors surrounding Torrin's sudden rise to power must've been true. Some dark and powerful magic was used to grant the tyrant king the power he craved. The bitter-burnt scent of this magic still lingered in the palace. Could Lia smell it, too? If she did, she didn't show it. But the deeper into the palace they went, the stronger the scent became, reaching its pinnacle in the quarters Lia called the Laboratory.

"Who worked here before?" Arcadia asked. She did her best to hide how the smell of this place affected her, threatening to turn her legs into jelly.

"Why does it matter?" Lia studied Arcadia in an unsettling way that made her cold and warm at once. When Lia looked at her like that, as if Arcadia was the most peculiar thing in this whole world, instead of the fear Arcadia knew she should feel, she felt... elated. She couldn't make sense of these feelings.

"Perhaps there are things I can learn from your previous potion master," said Arcadia.

Lia snorted, barely containing a laugh, not the unkind type. "I have no doubt you already know everything they knew."

"I seriously doubt it," Arcadia said, under her nose. Whoever dwelled in this Laboratory before her, had an incredible amount of power. Compared to the magic that still lingered in every corner and every crevice of this space, Arcadia's potion work seemed a child's play.

"You should get started," Lia said, already heading out. She hesitated by the door, looking like she wanted to say something else, her beautiful, cold face briefly lighting up with hope or expectation—Arcadia couldn't say.

But whatever it was, Lia must've changed her mind. Her shimmering black cloak swirled behind her as she exited the Laboratory.

Arcadia was left alone in the kingdom's biggest repository of magical ingredients with an impossible riddle to solve.

How do you make a hated tyrant loved by his people?

\#   \#   \#

Day after day, Arcadia's magic flared and ebbed, pulling at her senses like the moon pulled relentlessly upon the sea. Never before had it taken Arcadia this long to produce a potion. But then again, never before had the task before her been this complex. Lia said her father wanted to be loved by all of his subjects, but that meant Arcadia's potion would have to be powerful enough to affect the country's entire population all at once.

How could that be done?

A potion was typically meant for the supplicant himself, not requested on another's behalf. But Lia was adamant that Arcadia was the right, and only, person for the task, and that if anyone could accomplish such an unusual task, it was her. And though at times Lia's stare made Arcadia wonder what cruelties hid behind the black-haired beauty's implacable face, she also found she wanted to please the tyrant's daughter, to see her smile for real, if only for a brief moment.

Considering the potion itself could be a simple heart-opener—a brew that made its subject more mellow and less jaded, hence, in theory, making the crowds more predisposed to like their hated leader—the manner of delivery and distribution of such magic to then influence the people of Hadyah evaded Arcadia completely. She considered enchanting the clouds, so that her potion could be delivered as rain to the entirety of the tyrant's territories over the course of a single afternoon. But whenever she'd reached for the skies with her power, the clouds scattered, turning into fluff, immaterial, evasive…

Arcadia experimented with air itself. But the wind was not her friend, diluting whatever magic she'd managed to weave into the atmosphere within seconds.

Same went for pollen and dust. All Arcadia achieved with her experimentations was to give herself severe hay fever, her allergies making her time in the Laboratory even more restless.

It didn't help that this place, the Revolution Palace, and the Laboratory more specifically, made her so ill at ease, a permanent sensation of déjà vu stuck in her throat. Every shadow in the periphery seemed to move whenever Arcadia looked the other way.

Lia, her cloak trailing behind her in the air like a terrible bird of prey, paid Arcadia a visit twice each day, asking for a progress report. As the week went on, the pinnacle of the celebrations fast approaching, Lia's already dark predisposition has gotten darker, gloomier, leaving Arcadia feeling even more entrapped and helpless.

To make matters worse, in those rare hours she'd managed to catch some sleep, Arcadia was dreaming of Lia. In these dreams, the tyrant's beautiful, cold daughter was reaching for Arcadia's face, fingers gentle, her lips burning hot when they touched Arcadia's mouth.

#   #   #

"Come with me," Lia said when she showed up in the Laboratory on the morning of the celebrations' penultimate day.

Arcadia, who was slumped behind her work table, eyes red-rimmed and bloodshot, sat up straight. Her dreams of Lia have gotten so intense and frequent that a part of Arcadia wasn't completely certain anymore what was true and what was not, whether those dreams were dreams at all.

Uneasy but intrigued, Arcadia followed her dangerous supplicant into the dungeons. As they descended into the bowels of the royal oubliette, Arcadia felt a vague sense of recognition.

"I've been here before," Arcadia whispered, as a powerful wave of nausea swept through her. All those inappropriate dreams of Lia had returned tenfold, haunting her, only now those images were sharper, darker, and interspersed with flashbacks of this terrible, soul-crushing place. Arcadia remembered the grey walls, the rusted handcuffs, the chains. When Torrin the First came to power, he reopened the royal dungeons. The kingdom had electricity and mechanical tools, so the dungeons were the opposite of progress. But they were a symbol of Hadyah's darker history, a reminder of what protests against the ever-rising taxes and criticisms of the king would bring. Torrin wanted to be known as the Reformer King but the people were calling him the King of Disappearances, the King of Torture.

"I've been here before," Arcadia repeated.

"Yes," said Lia. "Do you remember why?" She looked at Arcadia expectantly, her dark eyes burning with... hope?

Provoked by the cadence of Lia's voice, another onslaught of memories came upon Arcadia, the struggle leaving her dizzy, swaying on her knees.

"The healer said it's better if your memories returned on their own. But we're nearly out of time, Cady," said Lia.

Cady.

No one had ever called Arcadia that, not anymore. Ever since her mother passed away, Arcadia hadn't shared her beloved pet name with anyone.

"How do you know to call me that?" Arcadia asked this enigmatic woman before her.

In the weak light of the dungeons, Lia's features were foreign and familiar at once. Her lips, bright red and perfect, were stretching into a tentative smile, more of a smirk really. And it was seeing this curve of Lia's mouth that was the final drop, the push Arcadia needed to remember.

The return of her memories, an entire year's worth of them, was swift and reality-altering. The leftover magic in the palace surged once more, flooding Arcadia's consciousness, filling the hole in her chest she didn't realize until now was scooped out, and making her whole again.

"It was me. I've done it, haven't I?" Arcadia whispered, as the last of the terrible memories came back, memories that were temporarily taken away in payment after her potion swayed the historical vote and installed Torrin the First on the throne. "He held me in these dungeons until I agreed to do it..."

"You were, and still are, the only one in this whole damn country with that kind of power," said Lia. "Afterwards, Father allowed for you to be taken back to your little shop. He thought the loss of your memories was permanent. After the first few months of keeping an eye on you, I was starting to worry that it was truly the case. But when I came to you a week ago, I saw something in your eyes, recognition. Do you remember yourself now, Cady? Do you understand what needs to be done?"

Arcadia nodded, moving slowly as the last of her recovered memories settled down. She remembered all of it now, not just her time in the dungeons followed by the days spent in the Laboratory, but also her nights in Lia's bed, their kisses and their whispered plotting. Lia knew her father's rise to power was unavoidable. But she played a long game and her patience was bottomless. It lay coiled in the lair of her devious mind like an enduring snake.

"When you asked me for a potion so that your father could be loved by his people..." Arcadia said, as the words of their pact from one year ago came rushing into her mind. Theirs was an agreement made in the secrecy of silk bedsheets.

"The only loved tyrant," said Lia.

"Is a dead tyrant," Arcadia completed her lover's sentence.

"Do you understand now what needs to be done, Cady?" Lia asked again.

In response, Arcadia's magic came alive.

#   #   #

Crafting a poison is a hundred times easier than formulating a love potion. Emotions are complex, wide-ranging, often unpredictable. Death is simple, absolute. And once Arcadia's memories were back, once she knew what she had done in the past and what she needed to do now, her hands flew with purpose, her heart beating in a determined, measured way.

When the last day of the festivities arrived and Torrin the First climbed the podium to address his subjects, his heir Ravelia brought him the ceremonial chalice of the covenant. Drinking from it would bind Torrin to Hadyah, his transformation from the King Elect to the King Proper complete.

Torrin watched his heir taste the drink first, which Lia did without breaking eye contact with her father. Torrin didn't see the thin film of the antidote coating Lia's lips, but he did see an odd emotion flickering in her eyes, an emotion he mistook for fear. It was only after he emptied the chalice, the untraceable poison making its way down his throat, that Torrin saw his daughter's expression change from what he thought was fear to triumph.

#   #   #

The king was dead.

Taken in the night by a sudden illness.

An artery in his brain's burst, said one healer. His heart gave out, said another. None of the poison experts could detect any trace of a single chemical known to bring death, because none of them knew magic and the damage it could do.

The Royal Council held an emergency meeting, casting a unanimous vote. A new monarch was chosen. The one who's been waiting in the shadow of the late king for far too long.

No one noticed the odd scent permeating the Council's meeting rooms nor the bitter aftertaste of the tea that was served to the members during the vote.

In the fledgling light of the coronation day, Arcadia stirred awake in the empty bed, Lia's pillow still warm next to her.

Sliding out of bed, Arcadia found her naked lover standing by the large mirror in the adjoining dressing room. Lia's hands held the dead king's crown. She raised it over her head then lowered it 'til it sat snug, a perfect fit. In the open closet to her right hung a pristine white pant suit shot through with golden thread. Lia's attire for the coronation.

Too absorbed with her own reflection, Lia couldn't see Arcadia watching her from the bedroom. The way Lia's eyes shone in the mirror made Arcadia's hands turn slick with adrenaline.

With her blue-black hair loose from its usual tight bind, Lia looked so much like her father, the resemblance even more striking when she put that crown on her head. A self-crowning queen, her eyes were distant and cold.

Arcadia felt a deep unease forming in her chest.

Arcadia braced for it, for that magical kick in the gut, the sensation of loss, or pain—an inevitable cost of her recent magic. But it didn't come. Arcadia's unease intensified. Perhaps the cost this time wasn't personal. After all it affected the entire kingdom.

What have I done, Arcadia thought, watching Lia. *What has she made me do?* ♜

WHEN DREAMING ENDS

By M.J. Addy

"TELL ME ABOUT THEM."

"About what?" I asked with as much innocence in my voice as I could muster. I knew the answer, but I wasn't ready to admit it yet. Not to myself. Definitely not aloud.

"Your dreams," the therapist replied patiently. "Tell me about your dreams."

I hesitated. I didn't know why I was even seeing a therapist. It wasn't something that was part of my normal routine. Taking a deep breath, I finally said, "If dreams could kill, my life would be easier."

"What happened?"

"I… I woke up in darkness," I said as I began to describe what I didn't see.

I struggled to open my eyes, but I could hear something dripping as it hit the pavement. Gasoline. It had to be gasoline. The sharp stench always gave me an instant piercing headache. My mind flashed back to the sound of breaking glass and the scrape of metal against the rough pavement. I was driving. No, wait. I was on the passenger side, but whose car was it? I couldn't see it in the dream, but somehow, I knew it was blue. A sudden heat washed over me in waves, daring to come closer with each passing moment. Was the car on fire? Who was driving? Where were they? My thoughts blanked trying to cling to anything I could remember, but everything was just out of reach. Everything came back into sharp focus at the sound of a familiar voice shouting nearby. I couldn't make out the words. Was it because of the distance or the ringing in my head that wouldn't go away?

"Help! I'm stuck," I screamed, desperate to have my words reach anyone that could hear me, but my voice strained before any sound came out.

Something wet slid across my eyes and down my cheek. I reached up to wipe it away. Correction. I tried to reach up, but no matter how much I willed myself to move, I couldn't. Blood. The tang of blood gathered on the tip of my tongue as it coated my face. A heavy weight settled over me as I realized I still couldn't open my eyes. Panic settled in as my heart raced, a steady pounding in my ears while my breathing shortened into smaller and smaller breaths leaving me gasping for air. Then it all stopped.

"Go back to sleep," I thought in a lousy attempt to order myself to go back to sleep as though it were that simple.

"And then...?" The therapist prompted for more. Part of me wondered if this was really therapy or more investigative journalism.

"Going back to sleep is never really an option. At least, it's never that simple."

"Why is that?"

"This time? Too much adrenaline. It just felt so real."

"And you don't get out of bed because...?"

"As soon as I open my eyes to find out what time it is, it's infinitely harder to sleep. Whenever I give up and do check the time, sometimes I luck out and it's 6AM. Other times, it's 3AM or worse, just barely past midnight. If it's early enough, sometimes I luck out and can catch a second nap before I jolt awake again."

"And have you taken any medication to help you sleep?"

"I've tried all the methods to get a full night's worth of uninterrupted sleep short of doctors and prescriptions. Nothing's helped so far. I usually let my mind wander, wait for it to finally tire itself out after reliving my life again and again."

"I see. Tell me about that. What do you usually think about?"

"Oh, I don't know. Nothing extravagant. I guess my mind likes to replay all my past memories like a greatest hits collection. A front row seat at my very own personal theater and I get to play film critic." I debated on how deep down the rabbit hole I should go.

I still wondered if analyzing these bits of my life was therapeutic or aggravating. There was something incredibly familiar about my dream, but I couldn't remember why. Whose voice was it that I had heard? I felt like I should know, but my mind was drawing a blank. It didn't help that I was distracted by the dull ache I felt along the side of my nose, radiating from an old injury I got when I was a kid.

"And when in your life do the memories start?" the therapist asked.

"Uh, I guess I started to become more aware of things in middle school. That summer before middle school."

That summer, it was discovered my sister and I both needed braces. Well, my sister needed braces. Apparently, I needed a whole satellite installation that would pick up radio signals from Mars. To a ten-year-old before the evolution of cellphones, tablets, and other devices, a normal wait at the dentist's office felt like an eternity. I wasn't allowed to play with the actual toys, as they were filled with germs according to my mother, so my only form of entertainment was flipping through the magazines on the table in front of me. The Highlights magazines, all of them old editions, were mother approved as they were viewed as educational entertainment. I guess the educational value outweighed any germ concerns. I sat curled up in the office chair, flipping through the pages, listlessly searching for something I hadn't already seen in the magazines from last month to catch my eye and occupy my brain to make time move faster.

My sister was called in early as hers was the easier of the two procedures. She was older, in high school, and was what most kids in her grade would consider generally attractive. She was also right at that age where she felt the need to ensure nothing hindered that fact. My mother paid extra for her ceramic braces that made the brackets barely noticeable and tooth reshaping to ensure everything was evenly matched and photo ready. Every time the door opened, and the next name called, I perked up, hoping to just get the day over with, but when I looked at the clock, only another five minutes had gone by. It felt longer than that. Maybe staring at the same Highlights puzzle for the third time wasn't speeding things along as much as I thought.

My attention shifted to the large aquarium tank that sat between me and the next set of unoccupied chairs. I watched as the colorful fish chased each other between various pieces of greenery and around rocky caves. Part of me wished I could trade places with the fish. Even if they were confined to a four-foot-wide aquarium, they still seemed blissfully unaware of the larger world around them—a world free of the boring routines of dental procedures. My daydream of imagining life at the bottom of the ocean wasn't broken until a face suddenly appeared on the other side of the glass, staring back at me.

I blinked. The features were opposite mine. Rounded eyes of crystal blue versus my muddy, brown eyes. Sunflower tinged with pink curls against pale skin opposite my flat black hair cut into a bowl shape. The face smiled at me, and I smiled back. They made a face and I made one back. I don't remember how long we played like this back and forth until I was suddenly yanked out of my reverie. My mother had pulled me by the collar toward her, trying to get my attention.

"Stop that," she whispered with a seething tone in my ear.

"What? I'm not doing anything," I countered with uncertainty, louder than my mother liked. I looked back at the kid whose attention was now captured by their own mother as they tried to avoid eye-contact with us but were clearly eavesdropping.

"You don't act like that in public. You don't talk to those kinds of people."

"Why?" I had the audacity to ask.

"Don't argue with me. I said no. Now sit straight."

There was a small shake of my shirt that caused me to sway before I sat straight up again and longed for my name to finally be called. It wasn't until I was in high school that it finally clicked what set my mother off. The other mother had allowed her child to dye their hair pink while she sported tattoos of her own. These things, according to my mother, were marks of bad people. The list also included smoking, lip gloss, and fingernails that were allowed to grow too long for her liking. In my youth, I couldn't pinpoint exactly where this strict mentality came from. I guessed it was her heavily religious upbringing or the cultural dissonance from moving to a foreign country. I wished it was that simple.

Finally, the door opened once again, and as my sister came out, I went into the area beyond. Unlike my sister, I was still in that awkward pre-teen phase that was now guaranteed to last until well into my teenage years. Strapped with a set of upper and lower metal braces, I also had rubber bands connecting from the upper front of my teeth to the lower back to force my jaw forward, which was meant to correct an overbite. The worst of it was this thing called a rapid palate expander cemented to the roof of my mouth. I lovingly referred to it as my own personal dental torture device. Naturally, my mom was less concerned about any sort of photogenic appearance for me as there was no disguising all this metal. Instead, she asked if my dentist could install another rubber band diagonally across the front of my teeth so she could see from a distance to make sure I was wearing them. She did not want to waste her money. Thankfully the dentist said no.

That summer, instead of real food, I spent a lot of time drinking soup. The rapid palate expander cut my mouth and tongue frequently. Everything I tasted had a faint metallic taste, but that wasn't the worst of it. The expander had a key that fit into a small hole on the device that, when turned, would slowly push my upper jaw apart so it would be widened over time, allowing enough space for my teeth to come in naturally. At least, that was the plan according to the dentist.

"It hurts," I finally told my mother in protest over having the device turned another time. "You're supposed to stop if it hurts."

"Don't lie to me. You just want to get out of doing it," she told me. "You'll spend the rest of your life wearing that if you don't get it over with now. Open up so we can get this done."

I laid down on the couch and opened my jaw wide so she could see the thing attached to the roof of my mouth. My head tilted back, I stared at the much smaller aquarium tank we kept at home. It wasn't as large as the palace-like one at the dentist's office. There were some fake plants at the bottom and a little plastic diver which was more likely to entertain us than the two goldfish that lived within.

It was enough of a distraction for a few weeks, but eventually it wasn't enough to keep my brain occupied. Argument after argument began and ended the same way every night. Every night, I'd do anything to numb myself from the persistent pain in my jaw and the uncomfortable feeling the braces left behind. I snuck extra pain medication whenever I could, desperate to find a new form of relief.

The evening my mother ran late from work, my sister was left in charge of turning the key. Hopped up on pain medication, I tuned out as my sister cranked the gear on the palate expander. There was a snap and pain flooded my face. My eyes welled up with tears instantly as a sharp stinging filled my senses. To this day, I don't know what happened, if my sister turned it too much or if the consistent pain was a warning sign.

"How did this happen?" I remember the doctor asking my mother while hovering near my bed, chart in hand.

"Oh, her sister got angry at her because she wasn't listening and overturned it to teach her a lesson," my mother supplied readily.

I didn't remember it being like that. I thought it was an accident. I don't remember my sister being so vindictive that she would do something so intentional. My eyes searched the hospital room looking for confirmation from my sister, but she wasn't there. We'd rushed to the emergency room, but I couldn't remember much about the trip itself.

"I see. Well, we're going to have to remove the palate expander," the doctor said. "I'm afraid it's been putting too much pressure on the roof of her mouth. It split the upper jaw and broke her nose. We're going to keep her here for observation overnight, and you should talk to the dentist in the morning."

"Does it have to be removed?" my mom asked. "It was expensive to put in."

"Yes," the doctor said patiently. "She needs time to recover before attempting this procedure again."

"See? I was right," I said as I looked at my mother. She nodded in agreement, unable to counter the point. At least, that's how I imagined the conversation went. I'd replayed this scene in my head so many times. Sometimes, my imagination left it with an 'I told you so' moment. Sometimes, I went further, believing my mother would apologize for not listening to me.

Neither one truly happened. I was in too much pain to say a word to anyone.

Vindication felt hollow. The device being removed meant I wouldn't have to deal with it for the moment, but it'd take longer for my teeth to be straightened out when it was replaced again. The bandage on my broken nose still made me feel trapped in my own skin. After leaving the hospital, I became my mother's baby who needed constant protection. While my sister was allowed to go outside and see her friends, I don't think I spent a single day outside my mother's presence. She said it was for my own safety, and my child brain at the time accepted it as simply that. As an adult, I often revisited that night in my memory and wondered if I could have done anything differently. But, no matter how many times I reimagined that scene, I knew that ultimately, what actually happened directly led me to Avery.

#   #   #

Was that what I was dreaming about before? I could hear yelling in my dream. I thought it was random, but was it an argument or someone calling out to me? I had blocked out thoughts of Avery for a long time, especially after Avery died.

I asked my sister to help me get dressed. It was the first day of middle school for me, and she'd always had the sense of fashion that I lacked. I attributed her popularity to that. Her looks. Her A-type personality. Her ability to attend all the parties with the "right people." See and be seen. That was how it went, right? I knew she'd started crafting the persona in middle school. She practically said as much to me when she started. Despite the mouth full of braces and the crookedness in my broken nose, I was just as determined to reinvent myself.

"What are you wearing?" my mother asked. While my sister rode the bus to school, my mother insisted on driving me.

I knew this tone and already I didn't want to answer. However, I also knew that wasn't an option. "Lip gloss," I finally replied, my voice tiny. Sometimes, I imagined what she would have said if I had told her it was Chapstick, but no matter how many times I re-envisioned the conversation, it ultimately led to the same question.

"Who gave that to you?"

"Kamilah," I said. My sister wore it all the time. I didn't see the problem.

"Wipe it off. Whores wear makeup," my mother told me bluntly.

I wasn't sure what she was implying about my sister. At the time, I didn't even know what the word meant. Confused, I wiped it off anyway but wondered why my mother never said anything like that to my sister.

"And go change clothes. It's too cold out to be wearing shorts."

I'd forgotten my mother had a rule about the weather. Anything below 85°F meant that it was pants weather. I never understood it as I always found it to be too hot to wear jeans, but arguing with my mother was asking for trouble. Pants, a light sweater, and a jacket later, we finally made it up to the school. As soon as I got in the door, I was already removing my jacket, shoving it into the locker with my backpack and rolling up my sleeves.

"Aren't you hot wearing all that?" a voice asked me. "It's 78 degrees outside."

"Yeah," I replied, not looking up as I figured out which books I needed for my first class. "But I have to wear it anyway."

"Why?"

"It's a long story."

"I've got some time."

Looking up, I shut the door to my locker to find a girl leaning against the one next to mine. Wow. Red. That was my gut reaction. She had the most vivid red hair that I'd ever seen in my life. Instantly, I was drawn to her. I wanted to say something. Anything. All I could do was smile awkwardly instead.

"Uh, well. Maybe it's not that long of a story. My mother makes me."

"Makes you? You mean your mother dresses you still? Aren't you a bit old for that?"

I wished I'd said something—anything—else at that moment. This was how rumors got started and spread across the school, but in this instance they'd be correct. So much for reinventing myself into a new person.

"It's… her thing," I stammered, rubbing the dent in my nose. It'd become a habit over the summer. "Easier to go along with it than not."

"Ah," she said, seemingly dropping the issue. "What happened to your nose?"

"Oh this? I um, broke it over the summer. It looks dumb. It's still healing."

"I like it. It gives your face character. I'm Avery, by the way."

I'm not sure how someone becomes another person's best friend, if there's a mutual agreement between two people for it, but that was when I realized Avery was someone I wanted in my life. Between classes and lunch, we were two peas in a pod as Avery helped me realize things about myself that I'd have never known without her. We talked about so many things, and she never told anyone that my mother still had strict rules about virtually everything. Avery made me realize that school popularity was an artificial world, one that was full of people pretending to fit in. Maybe that was my sister's real secret. She was far better at fitting into the norm than I was.

My mother hated Avery. She was coldly polite at parties whenever Avery would appear, but after everyone left, Mother would always comment about how my best friend wasn't a good person. "I don't see why you like that girl," my mother would always say. "She is too big to wear that kind of outfit. She should exercise more. You need to stay skinny. Boys don't like curves."

"Avery doesn't care what boys think and neither do I," I said aloud and immediately regretted it.

"That's her attitude rubbing off on you. You will never find a man if you think like that. Look at me. I have eleven men interested in going out with me."

To this day, no matter how many times I relived that conversation, I couldn't think of a response. I think I said "good" or maybe it was "yay," maybe even "congrats," but all of those played sarcastically in my head. While I still couldn't fathom what she wanted me to say, I definitely knew what she did not want me to say. Then she got in the parting shot while I retreated to my room.

"You don't want to wind up alone for the rest of your life," she said. I didn't know how to process that either.

#   #   #

Months came and went, but it was spring break of eighth grade when everything changed. My sister dropped me off at home before heading to her friend's house. I found my mother sitting at the dining room table, apparently waiting for me to arrive.

"Come here," she said bluntly. I knew by that tone that no matter what happened, it wasn't going to end well.

"What?" I replied as though that would hurry things along. My weight shifted as I repositioned my backpack, but my feet didn't move.

"Come here and sit down."

With an inward sigh, I sat down on the far end of the table, my backpack at my feet.

"What is this?" she asked as she held up a book. I recognized it immediately. She had my journal. Realizing she must have searched my room, my heart sank.

"My journal," I said as plainly as I could, but even in my own mind it sounded defensive.

"You want to tell me what's in it?"

"Just writing," I said numbly. There were tons of entries since my English teacher encouraged me to write more throughout middle school. I couldn't pinpoint anything in particular.

She snorted at me. Flipping deep into the entries told me roughly how far into it she'd read. It looked like she had read the entire thing. Wonderful. Whatever set her off must have been a recent entry.

"'Avery and I went to the creek today,'" my mother began.

As soon as I heard those words, I started to piece together what her issue was, and in that moment, I wished I was anywhere else but there.

The creek was one of my favorite childhood spots. Through the backyard gate, beyond the hedges, a small creek ran past my house through the neighborhood. Avery lived on the other side and often we'd meet at the creek to hang out and talk about all kinds of things. As my mother's dating life increased, she cared less about who I hung out with or how much time

I spent outside the house, even if her opinion about Avery never wavered.

Three days ago, we sat talking, watching the sunset on the horizon about life and what next year would be like. Everyone said high school was the best years of their life and that everything changed in high school. The conversation was so trivial, I don't remember as much of it as I wished I could. Sometimes, I'd make up a conversation in my head when I thought about it. Other times, I'd just remember basking in the warmth of the fading sun and how it reflected against the water in the creek beneath our feet.

"I like you," Avery told me. It was the one thing I could remember vividly. My heart soared when I heard those words. There was a different weight to them than there normally was.

"I like you too," I said back, admittedly stunned.

"I mean... I like... like you."

"I think I like... like you too."

It was at that moment that Avery leaned toward me, and my world view shifted as we shared our first real kiss together. The fond memory came crashing down around me as I felt something hard hit my cheek. My mother had thrown my journal at me to get my attention as my mind had wandered off.

"You kissed a girl," she screeched. "Are you a gay?"

English was not her first language and the misplaced article caught me off-guard, almost making me smile. I'd grown up around so many of my mother's immigrant friends that I'd become interested in languages and the nuances of how non-native speakers translated between them to blend sentence structures. My smile must have been more visible on my face than I thought as my mother didn't like what she perceived to be a smirk. I guess she thought that I was happy to be cheeky.

"It's not a gay," I corrected. "It's just gay."

Apparently, that was a mistake too.

"Do you think you're so smart?" she said as she slammed her hand on the table. "Answer me. Are you a gay or not?"

"No," I said as a reflex. I hadn't sorted out any sort of identity at that point. I really didn't know how to respond.

"I told you that girl was a bad influence. She's trying to turn you into a gay. You will not see her again."

"I'm fourteen now," I reminded her. "You don't get to control who I talk to."

That was strike three. Sometimes, I wished I hadn't said it and maybe things would have turned out differently. As idealistic as my teenage brain was, I soon realized that my mother could, in fact, control more of my life than I thought. She'd just broken up with her most recent boyfriend and I became her hobby once again.

For the last couple months of my eighth-grade year, my life was on lockdown. My mother called everyone she could think of, including the school, to separate Avery and me. It didn't entirely work as we were in different classes with different lunch periods by that point, but her complaining made the administrators move Avery's locker from next to mine to an entirely different area of the school. We still managed to drop notes in each other's lockers when we could. It wasn't the same, but we hoped that high school would bring us more freedom as events became a distant memory.

Three weeks before the end of school, my mother told us we were moving. My sister was accepted to college in another state, and she decided it'd be a good idea for us to move with her so we'd all stay together as a family. At least, that was the story my mom told everyone. I knew that this was related to Avery in one last attempt to sever all connections as permanently as she could. Avery hadn't been at school for the last few weeks either and I couldn't help but wonder if that was also somehow the work of my mother.

My suspicions were confirmed when my sister handed me an envelope. "Don't tell mom," she whispered before hurrying off to her room to finish packing for our big move.

I recognized the handwriting immediately. It was from Avery. Avery's older brother was in the same grade as my sister and must have gotten a message out that way. Tearing it open, I read the contents quickly. It said this would likely be the last time she'd get a chance to say anything to me for awhile. Her parents were sending her away to a camp to deal with "mentally troubled youths" like her. My mom had called her parents and being equally

318

steadfast in their viewpoints, they'd come down on Avery in their own way. My heart sank. Avery had no idea where she was going but promised that as soon as she figured out a way to send me contact information, she would.

#   #   #

I never heard from Avery again and my sister had left for college. Three years later my sister called and told me what happened. She said that Avery's funeral was well-attended by my former classmates. I'm not sure if that helped, knowing others could be there while I was thousands of miles away. Some people said it was senseless. They couldn't understand how Avery could be so selfish and not consider how it would affect those she left behind. I wasn't one of those people. She must have felt it was her only option.

I was alone again with only my mother for company. I swore off the pain medication after my trip to the ER so many years ago out of fear of my mother's wrath, but now I searched for anything to fill the void left behind, but what could I do that wouldn't be turned against me? I hadn't touched aspirin since the ER trip. I didn't dare take up journaling again, knowing my room would be searched. My mother, sensing my depression, decided it was a good idea for me to go to therapy. I agreed. I expected to be alone with a trained psychologist. Instead, I found myself sitting across from a youth minister she'd made contact with through work. And, of course, Mom sat in the chair next to me.

"Your mother tells me you've been having trouble at school and at home," he began gently. "She says you have a history of violence and drug abuse. We're here to help you with that."

"Excuse me?"

"You don't think you have a problem?"

"The last time I took any kind of medication was when I was in the ER. My mother doesn't even keep aspirin in the house."

"And why were you taking those kinds of drugs?"

"Because I just had braces and some kind of bracket cemented to my mouth and every day after that my jaw hurt? Especially when my sister broke my nose from turning the bracket too much."

"Do you see how she talks? She shouldn't be talking like that," my mother interjected.

"Yes. Your mother told me you and your sister got into a fight. She said you yelled at her and threw a flowerpot at her, which made your sister take revenge on you by breaking your nose."

"None of that happened!"

"She's a liar and a drug abuser," my mother insisted. "And she doesn't listen anymore. She needs to listen to me. I'm her mother."

I did my best to not roll my eyes, but at seventeen, I had to admit that my self-control on that front was still greatly lacking. My mother, catching the look, gestured toward me as though to make a point.

"See that? So much disrespect. She had the wrong friends in middle school. She needs good friends now."

"Ma'am," he said, becoming a bit more formal than I expected. "Perhaps you need to let go and let your daughter be her own person."

I almost laughed at that point because there seemed to be a dawning realization on the minister's face. Pulling out a piece of paper, he proceeded to draw her a literal chart showing how over time, parents needed to let go of control and become more of a guide. I watched her face redden before she finally picked up her purse and marched us out of there.

It's odd, but I still attribute that moment to my first real taste of independence. I don't know why my mother decided to listen to the minister, but I was grateful she did. I strongly suspected my sister's influence from afar. For my graduation, my sister gave me her old car. It was this deep blue that I loved, and it meant I could get a real job. Of course, what I didn't realize was that old cars had old issues. Stranded on the side of the road on my way to work, I stared under the hood of my car, trying to figure out what was wrong with it. That was how I met Remi.

"Hey, you're the new girl at work, aren't you?"

"Uh, yeah, I guess. Remi, right?"

"Yeah," he answered as his eyes drifted from me to my car. "You look like you need a ride."

"I do," I said sheepishly.

"Man, that sucks. Well, you don't look crazy, so I'm sure someone will come along and give you one."

"Hey!"

"I'm kidding. Hop in," he said with a laugh as he waved at me to get in his car.

It was as easy as that. Remi had this effortless charm about him that I couldn't resist. Everything was a whirlwind as we went from friendship to dating in a matter of a couple months. Every shift we worked together, every evening we spent in each other's company. I hadn't dated often or all that well. Everything after Avery felt like I was walking through a haze, but somehow Remi cleared away the fog and made things seem bright again. Three months later, we were practically living with each other when Remi made the proposal that I ought to finally just stay the night with him. I finally took the chance and had Remi come with me to my mother's house so I could pack a bag.

My mother didn't like him when she first saw him. It was that same cold politeness that she'd shown to Avery. As I went to my room to gather up more of my things, she stopped in the hallway, watching with a narrowed look.

"Where are you going?" she asked.

"Out with friends," I replied.

"And that boy?"

"Yes, he'll be there too."

"I don't want you being friends with him."

"Because…?" I asked skeptically. At nineteen years old, I had to admit that I was growing tired of my mother deciding who I ought to be friends with. I certainly wasn't about to tell her about my relationship with him.

"He's not good company," she said in a manner that sounded far too familiar.

"What now?" I asked tiredly.

"Why don't you listen to your mother? Tattoos and strange eyes means he's not a good person. You should only be with good people."

"You don't even know him," I countered. "He has heterochromia. So what?"

"It's the mark of an evil eye," she said with absolute conviction that must have come from her own beliefs. "I forbid you to see him."

"I am literally an adult. You don't get to decide that anymore," I said before I moved past her, bag in hand, and ignored the rest of the yelling as she followed Remi and I out the door.

"Sorry about that," I told Remi as I handed him the keys to my car. I was shaking far too much to be driving. We rode in silence for a long while before he finally reached over and took my hand in his. I think it was that evening that I finally laid out all the random stories about my mother that I could think of, trying to make sense of it all. They were all odd, but mostly harmless in the end. She had strong beliefs, but what parent didn't have strong beliefs about their child? By the end, we'd decided that we'd officially move in together, and I'd finally be free from the stress of dealing with her.

Of course, it wasn't that simple. The following evening after our shift at work, we'd gone out to the parking lot, and my car was gone. In a panic, while we tried to sort out what had happened, I finally broke down and called my mother to let her know we were going to file a police report.

"No report is needed," she told me, much to my confusion.

"What do you mean?"

"I took the car."

"You can't do that! My sister gave me that car," I protested.

"Who do you think pays for her car? Me. I'm not dumb. I see you with that boy more than you think."

"You're saying you've been spying on me and you purposefully stranded me at work without telling me and made me think someone stole the car?" I asked with an increasing mix of emotions. Confusion, anger and disbelief all fought for which one would win out that evening.

"You're an adult," she repeated the words back at me that I'd told her the night before. "You can decide if you want a car or a boyfriend."

There was a level of smugness in her voice when she said it as though she had me trapped in a corner. I had trouble believing she'd be so petty, but the evidence was laid out before me. Hanging up the phone, I wasn't even sure if I told her goodbye as I mentally played through the options in my mind. No matter what path I took, the outcome always remained the same. I wasn't going to let her take Remi out of my life the way she took Avery from me.

"We'll get through this," Remi said as he put an arm around me. "We have other options."

#   #   #

I don't think I talked to my mother again for well over two years after that. I had fully intended to never speak to her again until a different sort of obligation appeared. I stared at the two pink lines that told me my life was going to change permanently. Breaking the news to Remi, I burst into tears. Maybe it was hormones or just the overwhelming pressure that a child brought, but I couldn't help myself. The only thing that kept me grounded was the way he didn't say anything as he held me in his arms. There was no commentary needed.

"You should call your sister," he finally offered.

I froze, swearing my heart skipped a beat. "I'm not sure about that," I said between hiccupped breaths as I regained my composure.

"It's only right," he urged. "Someone in your family should know."

With a deep sigh, I finally picked up the phone and dialed her number.

Each passing ring was longer than the last as my brain mentally cheered them on, hoping for an end to them with no answer.

"Hello," my sister's voice finally responded. It had been years since we spoke regularly. She was too busy living her life.

"Hey, sis. I uh... need to tell you something."

"You okay?"

"Yeah, sure, depending on whether or not you're ready to be an aunt?"

"What?" came the excited response. "I have like a million questions."

It was a good night. We talked about Remi, our relationship, and potential baby names. I told her that I was nervous and excited. I wasn't sure if I was ready to be a wife and I knew I wasn't ready to be a mother. Months flew by as college plans turned into nursery plans. Doctor's visits became the norm as we planned our whole lives together.

"I should tell you about a situation," the ob-gyn said to us.

Immediately, my mind raced to a million possibilities, all of them imagined something was wrong with the baby.

"What is it?" Remi asked as he held my hand, already anticipating my unspoken response.

"Your mother called our office," he said. "She said that she was concerned about your health and wanted to know the details of your pregnancy."

"I uh... what?" was all I could say.

"We didn't give her the information but thought you should be

326

informed," the doctor said calmly.

"How did she even know?" I said, but it was more a question for Remi than for the doctor. We exchanged a look that said we both already knew how my mother could have possibly found out about the baby. Kamilah. It was the simplest option. My sister must have told my mother.

"We should talk about your hospital stay," he transitioned the conversation away from the increasingly uncomfortable subject. "Since your due date is only a couple weeks away, we want you to be as prepared as possible."

It was a courtesy. We'd already been packed for ages. First child nerves, I suppose. As soon as I could after we left the doctor's office, I called my mother. I can't think of how long it'd been since we last spoke, but as soon as I heard the shrill voice, my blood pressure rose. No matter how often I reimagined the conversation, I still couldn't recall all the details.

We yelled and screamed. My mother denied ever saying anything like that to the doctor, stating he was making it up to make her look bad. She insisted that he was out to get her. Everyone wanted to make her look bad to keep her from me. I think that's when I lost it.

"I've put a block on you for the hospital. You're not allowed to see me or the baby," I finally told her. "You wanted me to make a choice? I choose my family. You're to stay away from me. From us. Forever."

I think she was still screaming when I hung up the phone, but I tuned it out by then. There were so many things to look forward to that I had lost any desire to look back.

Remi held my hand and pulled me into a tight hug. "Let's go get dinner," he said. That's the last thing I really remember him saying. Why couldn't I remember anything after that? I tried to think of any tiny detail from the next day but all I could draw was a blank.

"If you can't remember, try a smaller detail. Like perhaps a taste or a smell," my therapist said, interrupting my thoughts again.

"We went to dinner… and I tasted… blood. My head hurts… Oh, I see an accident. There was a car. It was trying to race us on the road, I think. It… it swerved at us."

"Security to the 3rd floor. Repeat. Security to the 3rd floor." I didn't recognize the voice or why it sounded staticky, like a drive-thru window box.

"What?"

"Who do you think you're talking to?" My therapist nudged me gently. "Look at me."

I finally lifted my head to look at my therapist. Instinctively, I felt like I already knew what to expect, but there was nothing quite like confronting myself. I saw the reflection of myself in my therapist surrounded by an empty darkness. I heard pounding again. Was it my heart? No, I couldn't feel that. Why couldn't I feel my own heart race? The dull thud echoed in my ears. Between each thud I could hear a familiar voice shouting my name. It sounded like someone was pounding against a wall, yelling to get my attention.

"I want him removed," came another voice I recognized. The shrill, demanding tone that curdled my blood. What was she doing here? "He's a stalker that kidnapped my daughter and caused this accident when I tried to rescue her."

The accident? More pieces started coming back to me as full consciousness flooded back to me like an ocean's wave washing over me. I recognized the car that ran us off the road. It wasn't just any blue car; it was my blue car.

"She's a liar," I called out and realized I was speaking only to the emptiness that surrounded me as my voice echoed inside my head. The ghost of my therapist faded from my mind as I tried to make sense of my world. I had to be lying down in a hospital bed. I couldn't feel anything past my neck. I couldn't get my eyes to open.

"You can't do this," I heard Remi's voice yell. He was okay. He swerved to get away from the car before it hit us, and the car spun out. The tree hit my side of the car, setting off the airbags. "That's my child!"

I tried to move, to sit up in desperation to set the record straight but realized I couldn't open my eyes. I wasn't sure if I imagined it, but I thought I felt a hand reach out, gently holding mine. Instinct made me want to recoil, knowing the proximity of my mother's voice next to my side. If I could have clawed my way out of my own body, I would have in that moment.

"Sir, you need to come with us," another voice said as I heard a shuffling of feet and then a struggle. The heart rate monitor beeping increased, matching my inner turmoil as I struggled along, straining to hear anything that told me the outcome. The sounds muffled as the door clicked shut, cutting off any additional sounds that would have carried into the room.

"The doctors say you may not wake again, but I know you can hear me. We'll always be together. Just the three of us as it should be," came the voice of my mother. I felt her breath on my ear as she whispered to me. I felt her fingers stroking my forehead like she had when I was a child. "I'll care for my granddaughter just like I did with you." ♜

MAIDEL

By Beth Kander

MY MOTHER'S DRESS WAS SUFFOCATING me. The yellowed lace crawled all the way up my neck, clinging to the thin skin of my arms and covering every inch of my flesh. A woman's body was something to keep covered and hidden away, and this dress was up to the task. The stiff fabric's scratch was intensified by the bland heat of August in Hungary, sweat and starch combining to make me break out in angry red hives no one could see. But more than any of the physical misery, what I hated most about the accursed dress was the way my mother looked when she handed it to me.

The half-smile tugging at her thick lips was smug, conveying her belief that all her prayers had at long last been answered. By wearing this wedding dress, I was finally living up to her expectations after eighteen long years of subverting them. That night, when the Sabbath ended and *havdallah* separated the sacred from the mundane, my own willful life would end when my father gave me in marriage to Velvel Lazar.

Velvel was twenty-two, four years older than I, but he looked at least thirty. He was smart and from a good family, for which I should have been grateful, as my mother reminded me daily. *A man like that, a scholar and a provider all in one, choosing you for a bride! How could a girl like you even hope for such luck, Miriam? It's a blessing!*

It did not feel like a blessing. Velvel had his eye on me since I was thirteen, perhaps even earlier than that. He would steal glances as he hurried past my home, on his way to the yeshiva where he studied with the other boys in our village. His eyes were hungry in a way that frightened me, even before I knew I would be served up to him on a platter.

I did not hunger for Velvel. He turned my stomach. I did not want him, nor any of the things that came with him, things I was supposed to crave. I did not want this dress, this marriage, this life. I did not want children, God forbid. Standing on the precipice of married life, I was horrified by the landscape stretching out before me. Decades and decades of washing linens and kneading challah and slaughtering chickens and being pulled into bed by someone I reviled. Trapped in a life where the drudgery was interrupted only by unwanted attention, his dry hands on my rigid body—the thought of it was more than I could bear.

This domestic dread was something that had been building within me my entire life, witnessing my mother's daily toil. She would not describe her existence as miserable, but I could not recall a time she appeared to experience anything akin to joy. I suppose a happy life was never a goal for her. Productive and reproductive; steady, prescribed, devout; and above all, communally-approved—in my mother's eyes that was *a sheyn laben*, a beautiful life.

A clap of thunder sent my hand flying to my lace-encased chest. While sunset was still an hour away, a storm had settled over our village and ushered in an early darkness. Intermittent thunder and lightning kept startling the landscape. The foreboding weather matched my mood, and an unrelenting corner of hope within me wondered if perhaps the storm would pick up speed, rumble through the shtetl, bringing heavy rains and delaying the damned nuptials.

Another loud crack rattled through me. But this rap was not thunder; it was a knock at my bedroom door. Probably my mother, I thought, heaving a weary sigh. She had been relentlessly altering the dress, wanting it to fit me perfectly, something it stubbornly refused to do. Despite all of my mother's efforts, taking in here, letting out there, hemming and re-hemming, the dress hung awkwardly on my slim frame, too tight in the shoulders, too loose everywhere else.

But no, it could not be my mother coming here to tug at the seams of the dress; it was still *shabbos*. Mother would not be able to hem or adjust or do anything else. Any work, including tailoring, was forbidden on the Sabbath. I wondered what other torture my mother was going to inflict on me while she was forbidden from actual labor. Perhaps a lecture about childbirth and wifely duties, or maybe a stern reminder for me to eat a little something.

I opened the door, and exhaled sharply. It was not my mother standing in the doorway.

It was Velvel.

He smiled wolfishly, small mouth turning upwards beneath his scraggly dark beard. His hat and the pinched shoulders of his dark coat were damp, evidence of the storm outside and his willingness to march right through it. This was not a man whose wedding would be delayed by a few drops of rain. A fresh clap of thunder slammed through the sky outside, and my lupine suitor did not flinch. His greyish eyes moved from my face down the length of my body, lingering on my breasts before traveling lower down. Without any shame, he took his time returning his gaze to my face.

"My bride-to-be," he said, his breath smelling of stewed meat and onions.

"You should not be here," I told him, taking a step backward. "It is bad luck for you to see the bride before the wedding."

He chuckled, waving my meaningless words away with his spindly fingers.

"That's a *goyishe* notion, Miriam," he chided. I hated the sound of my name in his carnivorous mouth. "Jewish men, we know to check first. Ever since Jacob was given Rachel instead of Leah. Don't want to wind up with the wrong bride, now do we?"

I gave a tight smile, knowing I was expected to do so. I was all too familiar with the story of Rachel and Leah. They were sisters. Jacob, our forefather, fell in love with the beautiful Rachel. But the girls' father, Laban, drove a hard bargain—if Jacob wanted Rachel's hand in marriage, he would first have to tend to Laban's flock as an unpaid shepherd for seven long years. Jacob agreed, and toiled for seven years. When his obligation was at last fulfilled, the wedding was celebrated. Jacob took his veiled bride back to his tent, they spent the night together—and in the morning, to his shock and horror, he discovered that the woman in his bed was not Rachel, but her elder sister Leah. The ugly sister. Laban explained that according to tribal custom, the oldest daughter should be married first—and then made Jacob work for him for another seven years to earn his beloved Rachel's hand.

We were told that this was why the Jewish wedding ceremony had come to include the groom lifting the veil, to verify that he was being presented with the right bride. God forbid the groom be cheated in this transaction, given an ugly girl instead of a beautiful one. But the wronged groom was never what interested me about the story. What I always wondered about was what Leah thought about the whole thing.

Leah, the "ugly sister." What was her role in this deception—willing participant, innocent victim, something else entirely? Was she warned before being sent to the bridal tent, or was she merely a pawn in her father's cruel maneuverings? She was the elder sister, and yet unmarried. She was not only unmarried when Jacob first fell in love with her sister Rachel; she remained unmarried for the seven years Jacob first labored in order to win her younger sister's hand.

Why did she not find another husband in that time? Could it be she was uninterested in men? Or was she truly so breathtakingly ugly that no one would have her unless deception and a thick veil tricked them into taking her? I wished for such ugliness.

"You look quite beautiful," Velvel said, licking his lips, thin tongue snaking out beneath brambling beard. His eyes were alight with lust, his thin fingers flexing in anticipation. A wave of nausea rolled through me as I dreaded what he desired. His pleasure will be my pain.

"Thank you," I said, looking down, not out of modesty but to hide my disgust. My fear.

He leaned in closer to me. Too close.

"I cannot resist you," he whispered, the stench of him and his lurid words curdling my stomach. "I will take you as a man takes his woman. No one will hear us over the sound of the storm…"

I wanted to scream, to shriek louder than the thunder, the rain, louder than anything. Where was my mother? My father? After so many years of guarding my purity, why had they allowed this man into our home, to visit me unaccompanied? It was *a shonde*!

"We are not yet wed," I whispered through gritted teeth.

"What is a few hours?" Velvel asked with a ravenous grin.

Before I knew what was happening, he began shouldering his way into my room. I stood frozen, which served me well. I was never a small woman, thank God. I was thin but broad-shouldered and strong, and exactly as tall as Velvel Lazar. If I did not move, he could not get into the room. Not without knocking me down. Still, in his lunge forward he made brief contact with me; a touch our society forbad before marriage. I shuddered but held my ground.

"*Ikh bin a froy fun Got,*" I told him.

I am a woman of God.

Somehow I thought the words would give me strength, but they felt hollow falling from my powerless mouth. I willed myself not to cry, jutting my chin as high as I could, claiming every inch of height, every bit of space I could take up.

"Are you?" Velvel purred.

"We are not yet married," I said. "My parents are in the next room, and—"

He took a step back, lifting his hands; the gesture and his upturned lips suggested amusement, but his eyes snapped fury. He glanced over his shoulder, finally acknowledging that other household members might be nearby. Might take offense at his lack of propriety.

"We will be married soon enough," he said, his voice soft and dangerous. "And then, *froy fun Got* or not, you will certainly be *my* woman."

He left. I shut the door behind him and collapsed against it, trembling so hard that I feared I would rattle the walls of my family's small home. I would do anything, anything, anything to never have to touch him, to never have to see him again, to escape this life and go literally anywhere else. Anything.

"*Ikh volt ton epes*," I whispered, over and over again: *I would do anything*.

Ikh volt ton epes.

Ikh volt ton epes.

Ikh volt ton epes.

"Anything?"

Gasping, I scrambled to my feet, scraping at the door and nearly tripping over the swaths of lace constricting my movement. For a half-moment I was certain it was Velvel, back to take what he wanted. But instead, standing impossibly in the middle of my closet-like room, was a woman.

She stood as if suspended from a string, back straight, feet barely touching the dull wood floor. She was my height, my build, but looked nothing like me. Her hair was as thin as mine was thick. Her eyes were light, an icy cold blue. Her face was sharply angled, high cheekbones and a long nose. Just before a scream could find its way out of my throat, she held aloft

338

an elegant finger and made a little clucking sound, *anh anh anh.*

"Your parents will not hear you if you cry out. And even if they did, would they come for you? Have they ever saved or sheltered you from what you most fear most, little Mireleh? Have they ever helped you move closer to the things you truly want?"

"Who are you?" I managed to ask, my voice a ravaged whisper. "How did you get inside—?"

"I only go where I am invited," she said, and her smile was both repellant and seductive. She radiated confidence and control, right down to her flawlessly aligned sharp white teeth, lined up like rows of small regimented soldiers. "Look at you, such a *shayna punam,* such a *shayna maidel.* Oh, yes, I think you need me, Miriam."

"What do you want?" I asked, not certain I wanted to know her answer.

"'What do you want?'" she repeated, and her mockery of me sounded shockingly like my own voice. "Ah, Miriam, I do like the questions that you ask. *Who are you? How did you get here? What do you want?* Those are truly important questions. Truly haunting inquiries, the big mysteries we're all trying to solve."

She cocked her head, and in a flash of lightning I saw her pale blue eyes studying me. The room was dim between lightning strikes, obscuring the details of my mysterious visitor. But then another electric flash of light briefly illuminated us, and to my horror, I could see right through this strange

339

woman. She was transparent, wavering, my pine bed flush against the wall behind her plainly viewed through her insubstantial self.

"*Sheyd*," I whispered, heart twisting in my chest.

Demon.

She smiled, seen.

"I have a name, you know," she murmurs. "Sheyd is only what I am, not who I am, Miriam. I am called Hael. A pleasure to make your acquaintance, sweet one."

"Evil spirit—" I began, knowing I should attempt to cast her out, but unsure of how to do so. She interrupted my outburst with a whispery laugh, grating and guttural.

"Evil spirit, indeed," she said, lifting a translucent eyebrow. "*Evil* is such a difficult thing to define. One person's *evil* is another person's righteousness. Their *right*. Do you not think that what your husband wants to do with you is evil?"

"He is not my husband—"

"But he will be," Hael said smoothly. "And he wants to do things to you that you find evil, yet he sees his actions as right. Merited. Good. Do you think what he will do to you is good, Miriam? When that wolf takes you as his bitch, when he slides his furry manhood between your thighs—"

"*Sha*," I said sharply, sickened. "Quiet."

That whispery laugh again.

"*Libling*," she murmured. Hearing the starkly beautiful demon call me *darling* made my stomach clench, then flutter. "I can assure you that while I am a sheyd, I am no more evil than your own darkest thoughts. And I can promise you beyond the shadow of a doubt that in Velvel Lazar's heart, there are recesses far colder and more hardened than the most wicked of *sheydim*. I have known men like him, *libling*. History is full of them. Wolves hungry to ravage all manner of prey."

I shivered, feeling in my bones the truth of her words. My parents were swayed by Velvel's intellect, by his family name, by his money. They believed they were doing something good, marrying me off to him. But I could see the darkness within him, and it terrified me.

"Why are you here?" I asked again, and this time I wanted to know.

"Ah, good, returning to better questions," the sheyd said, silently clapping her luminous hands. "I am here to offer you a deal."

"A deal?"

Hael smiled with all those perfect pearly teeth.

"You said you would do anything," she said.

My own words returned to me.

Ikh volt ton epes.

"Yes," I said.

"As you can see," Hael said, holding her arms aloft as another bolt of lightning lit up the sky and revealed her transparency, "I am not quite... here, am I? Not fully realized. Not like you, with your lovely flesh and bones. You see, *libling,* I need to inhabit a body in order to walk the earth, to have my fun. It seems you do not care for where yours is headed. So if you would prefer to be relieved of it, I will gladly take it on."

"You want… my body?"

"Exactly," she said, thunder outside banging against the sky, lending dramatic exclamation to her words. "Do not worry, *libling.* I will guard it well."

"So I… would I… where would I…?"

I tried to form a coherent thought, but found my mind was as insubstantial as the demon's form. My flimsy stuttering elicited another breathy burst of laughter from the sheyd, who looked at me with something akin to pity.

"As I am now, so you would be," Hael said. Seeing my confused expression, she went on to explain. "We would not share the space of your body. You would be a spirit, free to roam and wander until you were ready to inhabit this world again."

A cold terror trickled like ice through my veins. She wanted my body. She would cast me out of it, make me into whatever she was: a haunt. A sheyd.

She went on. "No one would see you, no one could claim you. You would be without a body, yes, but you would also be free of all obligations this body carries with it. No more marriage to endure, no children to bear. You would be free."

I closed my eyes and saw Velvel looming in my doorway, and suddenly her proposal went from terrifying to tempting. More than tempting. Tantalizing. Seductive. An offer I could not refuse, depending on the caveats.

"So… I could have my body back at some point," I said slowly.

"At some point, you will be able to slip back into skin, if that is what you truly want," the sheyd said, with an offhand shrug that seemed to indicate that I might well decide never to seek flesh again.

"And in the meantime…?"

"In the meantime, no one will see you. No one will bother you or ask anything of you. You will be able to see everything, to experience a thousand moments you might never otherwise witness. You will be able to travel. To fly through the air by the light of the stars. To slide into dreams and whisper ideas into the ears of those you deem worthy."

Her words sent a strange tingle through me. Such a novel notion, traveling unbound and unburdened. Thinking or feeling whatever I like, without needing to hide my thoughts or apologize for my voice or offer up my body. Being able to let my gaze linger on the people I wanted to see and to move swiftly away from the people that repulsed me. Being able to choose where I went, what I did. Being able to be *me,* whoever that might truly be.

Hael watched me intently, as if every thought crashing through my mind was something she could see.

"All you will be missing is a body," she reminded me, her tone urging without demanding. "And be honest, dear one… will you miss it, knowing

343

its fate? In your world, a woman's body is her greatest liability, for it is never truly hers. Would you rather be free, or would you rather inhabit your body while your husband—"

"No," I said, firm and fast. That was the reminder I needed. If I stayed in this body, at sunset I would have to yield it to Velvel Lazar, to let his stale rotted breath dampen my skin. "I do not want to be burdened with this body when Velvel comes to possess it. But… when I return to myself… my body… when you vacate it, and I get it back… he will still be my husband, won't he?"

Her tiny army of translucent teeth glinted at me from the darkness, and she gave a small shimmering shrug.

"Bad things happen to husbands sometimes," she said.

I trembled, unable to pretend there was no element of evil to the deal we were about to strike. I wanted to ask more about what she might do to Velvel, but found I could not form that question. At least, I could not ask what she would do to him. To my shock I found I was able to form words when I made them, instead, about myself.

"I might return… a widow?" I asked.

"You might," she said, in a tone that meant *you will*.

I nodded, exhaled, and made my decision.

"How do we do it?" I asked.

The sheyd smiled.

"Take off your dress."

I shed the thing like an unwanted skin, letting it fall the floor with a lace-muted thud. I stood before the demon in my underclothes, waiting. Ready. She glided toward me, wrapped her arms around me, an embrace so much gentler than I expected. Her limbs entangled with mine, and I shuddered at the forbidden and surprising pleasure of this encounter.

I closed my eyes and surrendered myself to this exchange, the sensation of becoming one before we would split and separate. Tangled together, then melting into one another. For a few moments it was impossible to discern my flesh from her shadowy presence. But then there was a rending. She pulled away from me, her body beginning to take more definite form, as mine seemed to blink in and out of existence.

I held up my hand, a flickering shadow in the dark, five fingers all unformed. It was strange, even after so many years of feeling unseen, to slip into actual invisibility. In the end, I was not certain if it was a blessing or a curse to finally disappear.

Was this really what I wanted? Was there another option, another way, another path to a life where joy might be possible? Cold dread threaded itself through my fading veins as I realized that I had just entrusted my fate to a demon.

"Wait," I said, as I felt myself diminishing and saw the sheyd solidifying. "How will I know when to come back? When to reclaim my body?"

"You will know," Hael promised. She stretched, reveling in the feeling of her new body. *My* body. She slid her hands down her hips, onto her thighs, delighting in all her newfound flesh. *My* flesh. "You will be ready when you are prepared to claim your body as your own. When you are strong enough to take it. You will feel an aching want in your weightless bones and know that you are ready now to protect yourself. To be yourself. To do what must be done in order to seize the life you want."

"I will feel all that?" I asked, my voice barely a whisper, my throat dissipating.

"Yes, eventually," the sheyd said, almost gently. She drew the last remnants of me toward her, her newly-full lips so close to my evaporating ones that her words felt like a poisoned kiss. I was fading, fading so fast I only just barely heard her final words to me. "Did I forget to mention? These lessons take time, you see… it took me years and years. The life you reclaim, and the body you return to, will not be the one you stepped out of. Did I not mention that, Miriam? Ah, so sorry, *libling*. I knew I was forgetting something."

And then she was gone, and so was I. ♜

⊰ CONTRIBUTORS ⊱

P. J. (Tricia) Hoover wanted to be a Jedi, but when that didn't work out, she became an electrical engineer instead. After a fifteen-year bout designing computer chips for a living, P. J. started creating worlds of her own. She's the award-winning author of *The Hidden Code*, a Da Vinci Code-style young adult adventure with a kick-butt heroine, and *Tut: The Story of My Immortal Life*, featuring a fourteen-year-old King Tut who's stuck in middle school. When not writing, P. J. spends time practicing kung fu, fixing things around the house, and solving Rubik's cubes. For more information about P. J. (Tricia) Hoover, please visit her website www.pjhoover.com.

Instagram and Twitter: @pj_hoover

Facebook: facebook.com/AuthorPJHoover

Product designer by day, writer by night, and a Jedi on the weekends, **M.J. Addy's** interests are as widely varied as her imagination. Born in the middle of nowhere Kansas, M.J. was the first child born in the U.S. to a family of immigrants, giving her a unique perspective on growing up Filipino in a landlocked state. Presently located near Austin, Texas, she blends her Asian American upbringing with tales involving thrilling mysteries and fantasy adventures. Find her debut work in the Castle of Horrors: Femme Fatale Anthology.

Jessica Lee Anderson is the author of over fifty books for young readers, and she's also published fiction and nonfiction in a variety of magazines and anthologies. Jessica graduated from Hollins University with a Master of Arts in Children's Literature, and she's enjoyed teaching as well as editing. She lives near Austin, Texas with her husband and daughter, and she loves spending time outdoors. Her fear of snakes turned into a fascination after encountering many different types of snakes on hiking trails. Visit www.jessicaleeanderson.com for more information.

Miracle Austin is a Texan Gal who works in the medical social work arena by day and in the writer's world at night and weekends as a YA/NA author. Miracle loves horror, Marvel/DC, 80s music, Stranger Things, and daydreaming!

Instagram and Twitter: @MiracleAustin7

Facebook: Miracle Austin Author

Website: miracleaustin.com

Miracle's books: Boundless & Doll Trilogy

Katya de Becerra is the author of *What the Woods Keep,* which The Bulletin described as "a thoughtful and compelling horror fantasy", and *Oasis*, which earned a starred review from Booklist. Katya has a PhD in Cultural Anthropology from the University of Melbourne and works at the Swinburne University of Technology. Katya's short fiction and poetry appeared in The Antonym, Dark Edifice Literary Magazine, Dot Dot Dash, and Ygdrasil Journal of the Poetic Arts. She is a contributor to the Sherlock Holmes anthology, *The Only One in the World* with Clan Destine Press, and has several short stories included in various forthcoming anthologies. Katya's non-writing hobbies include watching horror movies, making lists, giving advice, and daydreaming.

Christina Berry (christinaberry.com) is an award-winning author of character-driven feminist romance, horror, and sci-fi. Her debut novel, Up for Air, won "Sexiest Consent" in the 2021 Good Sex Awards and is the 2021 Independent Press Award Romance Winner. A citizen of the Cherokee Nation, Christina is originally from Oklahoma, and currently resides in Austin, Texas with her husband and two robot cats.

Joy Preble is the author of a medium-long list of young adult novels. She is fond of clever conversation and clever cocktails, teaches writing at Writespace Houston and is also a bookseller at one of Houston's grand indie bookstores. You can visit her at joypreble.com or follow her on Twitter or IG @Joy Preble

Shelli Cornelison lives in Austin, Texas and can confirm it is not a dry heat. Her short fiction for adults has appeared in *Smokelong Quarterly, The Forge Literary Magazine, The First Line,* and *The Saturday Evening Post,* among others. She also writes for children of all ages. In a former professional life, she worked with numbers. She prefers words. You can find her on Twitter as @Shelltex and at shellicornelison.net.

S. de Freitas started making up stories as a kid, writing puppet shows to perform for neighbors. When she was old enough to drive, she graduated to writing real stories for newspapers and magazines. Now she combines those two skills to write made up stories that might or might not be inspired by real ones.

Carmen Gray is a Native Texan and had her first story (science fiction) published in Children's Digest at age 10. As an adult, she's had several short stories (horror) published both online and in anthologies. Carmen enjoys crafting fiction, employing elements of the supernatural and magical realism. Her Mexican-American heritage and the Spanish language is often reflected in the characters of her stories. You can see her reading an excerpt from *The Smoke's Gotta Go Somewhere,* (fall 2019 edition of Road Kill: Texas Horror by Texas Writers) here: youtube.com/watch?v=g6ZuJG4DI7A

Poetry Blog: walkersonthejourney.com/

Author Page: amazon.com/Carmen-Gray/e/B001JOXDZK

Jess Hagemann has an MFA from the Jack Kerouac School of Disembodied Poetics. Her work has previously appeared in *PANK Magazine*, *Kweli Journal*, and the *Southwest Review*, and her debut novel *Headcheese* won an IPPY Award in Horror. For more, see jessicahagemann.com

Britta Jensen's debut novel, *Eloia Born*, won the 2019 Writer's League of Texas YA Discovery Prize and was long-listed for the Exeter Novel Prize. Reviewers are calling the book "both a dystopian narrative and a quest story; consider it a spiritual successor to Lois Lowry's *The Giver* and M. Night Shyamalan's *The Village*." The sequel, *Hirana's War* released October 1, 2020. Her stories explore themes of persevering through disability, parental separation and the intersection of various cultures on new worlds. Her novella, *Ghosts of Yokosuka* released this year. She earned a BA in Acting Performance from Fordham University, an MA in Teaching of English Literature from Columbia University and is an alumni of the Faber Academy. Friends often refer to her as a polyglot—which is a product of living twenty-two years overseas in Japan, South Korea, and Germany before settling in Austin, Texas. She enjoys mentoring writers and editing books with The Writing Consultancy and Yellowbird Editors and teaches freshman composition at St. Edwards University. Learn more about her work at britta-jensen.com or @brittajensenwrites on IG.

Bernadette "Berni" Johnson began her career as an author at age 6 when she crayoned a book about her mom that received a rave review from its lone reader. She keeps herself in pens, paper, and other writing paraphernalia with an IT job, and spends her free time writing both fiction and nonfiction, voraciously consuming TV and movies (mostly horror), reading random stuff, mindlessly surfing the Internet, and doing the bidding of her terrier. You can read Berni's blog, find links to her writing, or join her mailing list at bernijohnson.com, read some of her short stories for free at vocal.media/authors/bernadette-johnson, and check out her social media ramblings on Twitter (@Bernij), Instagram (/infocomgirl), and FaceBook (/BerniJohnsonWriter).

Beth Kander is an author and playwright with tangled roots in the Midwest and Deep South. The granddaughter of immigrants, she is interested in the intersection of new ideas and identities with old stories, secrets, and legends. Follow her on Twitter (@ByBethKander), Instagram (@bethkander), or visit bethkander.com.

S. N. Rodriguez is a writer in Austin, Texas whose work explores themes regarding nature, culture, and motherhood. She is a Writers' League of Texas 2021 Fellow. @nicole4thoughts

Madeline Smoot has never personally met a ghost, and she's hoping to keep it that way. Instead, she prefers to spend her time writing about them and other paranormal subjects from her home in Austin, Texas. When not chronicling the adventures of Poe and Milton, she also writes adventures for teens under the pen name Lori Bond. For more of her books, you can find Madeline online at madelinesmoot.com.

If you liked *The Castle of Horror Anthology Volume 6*, you might also enjoy reading the following titles available on Amazon from Castle Bridge Media:

Austinites By In Churl Yo

THE CASTLE OF HORROR ANTHOLOGY SERIES
Castle Of Horror Anthology Volume 1
Castle of Horror Anthology Volume 2: Holiday Horrors
Castle of Horror Anthology Volume 3: Scary Summer Stories
Castle of Horror Anthology Volume 4: Women Running From Houses
Castle of Horror Anthology Volume 5: Thinly Veiled: The 70s
Edited By Jason Henderson

Castle of Horror Podcast Book of Great Horror:
Our Favorites, Top Tens, and Bizarre Pleasures
Edited By Jason Henderson

FuturePast Sci-Fi Anthology
Edited by In Churl Yo

Isonation By In Churl Yo

THE PATH
Book 1: The Blue-Spangled Blue By David Bowles
Book 2: The Deepest Green By David Bowles

Surf Mystic: Night of the Book Man By Peyton Douglas

Nightwalkers: Gothic Horror Movies By Bruce Lanier Wright

Please remember to leave us your reviews on Amazon and Goodreads!

CASTLE BRIDGE MEDIA
DENVER, COLORADO, USA

THANK YOU FOR SUPPORTING INDEPENDENT PUBLISHERS AND AUTHORS!

castlebridgemedia.com